To Marty –
Follow your
dreams –
Donna Bevans

WHATEVER IT TAKES

DONNA BEVANS

authorHOUSE®

AuthorHouse™
1663 Liberty Drive
Bloomington, IN 47403
www.authorhouse.com
Phone: 1-800-839-8640

This book is a work of fiction. People, places, events, and situations are the product of the author's imagination. Any resemblance to actual persons, living or dead, or historical events, is purely coincidental.

Published by AuthorHouse 1/5/2012

ISBN: 978-1-4259-9598-0 (sc)
ISBN: 978-1-4678-1319-8 (e)

Library of Congress Control Number: 2007901047

This book is printed on acid-free paper.

ACKNOWLEDGEMENTS

To all my friends and family who kept asking, "How's the book coming", here it is! For those of you, to numerous to mention, who have encouraged me, "thank you".

To my former and present patients who will go unnamed, your hard work in therapy has been an inspiration to me. The patients in this book are fictional but their case histories are drawn from many of your experiences.

To my colleague and friend Sherry Helton, MFT, your expertise in the field of drugs and alcohol helped to make the characters Cash and Squirrel come alive. To Andrew Tyler Sun of the Jeffrey Michaels Salon, thank you for your help with the character, Marcus.

Many members of the writing community have played a part in the writing of this book, a giant "thank you" to you all. Shirl Thomas, whose workshops sometimes brought tears to my eyes but who taught me to tighten, tighten, tighten; The Palm Springs Writer's Guild and the Tuesday critique group, you kept me going when I wanted to give up; The Laguna Woods Village critique group, the first people to read the manuscript from beginning to end, you all hung in there with me to meet my deadline. To Mary Jane Roberts, instructor at Saddleback College Emeritus Program afternoon creative writing class, without you, the wonderful program, and my many classmates, this book would never have happened.

To Matthew Stewart, your water color of one of my favorite places in Laguna Beach brings alive the setting for this book. I have watched your artistic talents develop over the years. Thank you for allowing me to use this painting for the cover of my book.

This book was conceived in Ixtapa, Mexico, as my husband, Bill Easterbrooks, and I watched the sunset from the beach. From that time on Bill has been my first line editor, critic, and cheering section. Without his support this book may never have been completed or may have simply collected dust hidden away in a drawer. He has tolerated take out dinners, laundry pilling up, and late nights on the computer during the writing of this book. Bill, I thank you for believing in me, you are the love of my life.

CHAPTER ONE

Elizabeth didn't see the black Mustang parked by the curb less than a block from her house. She didn't see the man slumped down behind the steering wheel wearing a baseball cap, and she didn't hear the car engine idling.

What Elizabeth saw was the neighbor across the street picking up his morning paper, Mrs. Jacobs, two houses down waiting patiently, plastic bag in hand, for her poodle to do her morning business, and the jogger coming toward her, sweaty from his run. The joggers nodded to each other, neither one wanting to break their pace to say a word. She heard the slapping of his feet and hers against the pavement, the birds singing their morning songs, and the cry of a baby impatient to be fed.

The man in the Mustang watched the tall slender redhead jogging away from him. You are so predictable, he thought.

Elizabeth concentrated on her running. She didn't want to think about the nightmares that had awakened her early this morning. The blurred memory of unrecognizable faces chasing her, grabbing her, and pinning her down. The nightmare that seemed more like a memory than a dream; the nightmare that reoccurred so often that even when it woke her, she knew how it would end.

She tried to concentrate on her breathing, letting the fresh morning smells of sweet alyssum growing nearby and newly watered grass permeate her nostrils. She ran, waiting for the release of tension that came from pushing her body to perform at optimum speed. She ran to forget. But the sound of a telephone ringing in one of the houses distracted her.

Ringing and ringing like her phone does when she doesn't want to answer it. When she knows it's *him*, the man who's been calling her for the last three weeks. The voice that seems strangely familiar, the voice she can't identify.

The dialogue in her head started again. *I should hang up when he calls. What does he want? I should call the police. What if it's one of my patients? If I talk to him maybe I can figure out who he is.* She could just imagine what Tim Henderson, her colleague and officemate, would say if she told him about the calls. "Call the police. You can't save everyone you know!"

The ringing of the phone had broken the mood for her run and Elizabeth headed back home. *Damn him, even when he's not calling he's in my head.*

3 Hours Later

The private line in Elizabeth's office rang. She hesitated before answering it. The caller ID showed "unavailable number." She knew it was him. She knew he would keep calling until he spoke to her. Taking a deep breath, she picked up the phone.

"This is Dr...." but before she could finish, he interrupted.

"Hey, Dr. Bitch, trouble sleeping? I saw the light on last night."

Oh, God, now he's watching my house!

"Enjoy your run?"

Elizabeth didn't rattle easily. But she was rattled. *First phone calls, now he's stalking me. I should hang up. I should just hang up!* But she didn't.

"Talk to me, Elizabeth," the caller demanded.

She wanted to scream, "Who are you, why are you doing this to me?" but she simply replied flatly, "What do you want?"

"You know what I want."

He panted into the phone, laughed, and then added, "Tell your mother I send my love. So long, bitch." Heavy breathing, laughter, and then, a dial tone.

Her heart began pounding and she could feel her stomach knotting up. *I've got to figure out who this is.* The tension kept building. Using her skills as a psychologist, she tried to calm herself. *Forget what he said. Breathe and relax. Focus on your breathing.*

She walked to the window of her corner office and looked out over the city of Long Beach; she loved the view of the mountains to the east and the Pacific Ocean to the west. Her office had always been a place where she could feel free from the stress of her busy life. Now her space has been violated by menacing phone calls. *Relax. I have to relax. Breathe, breathe. Damn him.*

She thought the first call had been just a random obscene call, but they had continued, and the caller knew far more about her than any stranger could possibly know. Thinking that it must be one of her patients, she had decided not to notify the police. Maybe it was a bad decision. Maybe she could figure out who he was. Maybe she could help this man. *How could a patient know so much about me? Why does he keep mentioning my mother?*

Anyone who knew Elizabeth well would know that she had not been close to her mother in years, to either of her parents for that matter. They lived in Spain, visited once or twice a year, talked on the phone, did all the socially expected things, but they were never close. As a teenager, Elizabeth would visit her friends and watch their parents. Watch how they included the children in their activities, watch how the parents interacted with each other; it was always loving and friendly, but not like her parents. When Elizabeth's parents were together it seemed like no one else existed. At parties she would see them dancing and looking into each others eyes as if they were the only couple in the room. Her parents gave her everything she needed, and more, but she often felt like she was an intruder, not a member of the family. Her parents had each other, and they didn't need anyone else.

Elizabeth had seen the same look of love between her grandparents, but with them she had never felt excluded. She dreamed of the day when she would fall in love and a man would look at her with love in his eyes and it would be just the two of them, together forever. But her marriage had lasted less than a year, and her husband had been more interested in his work than in her. Now, she dated only occasionally, and tried not to think about what was missing from her life.

Wanting to protect her privacy, she hadn't let anyone know about the calls, not even Tim Henderson. When she and Tim finished their internships, they decided to share office space. She'd hounded her real estate agent for months looking for the perfect location. When she'd seen this suite of offices with the magnificent view she told her real estate agent price was no object, she had to have it. Tim agreed that it was perfect for their practice, and they have shared the space ever since. Elizabeth knew Tim cared about her, probably even loved her, but as much as she liked and respected him as a friend and colleague, she didn't love him.

On the desk, a gold and glass antique clock she had purchased in France chimed the hour; her first patient would be waiting. Looking at her schedule, she was grateful for the busy day ahead. She forced herself to push down her fear and anxiety. Trying to ignore the knots in her stomach, she couldn't keep from asking herself what this man would do next. *I have to find out who he is. I have to find out why he is calling me. But most of all, I need to know why the frightening nightmares that I had as a teenager have returned.*

CHAPTER TWO

After a morning of patients Elizabeth drove to the university for the first class of the fall semester. But on the drive, she couldn't shake the uneasy feeling that someone was watching her.

Now, she looked around at more than fifty students crowded into the classroom. Eager faces looked back at her; the older woman in the front row, paper and pen ready to take notes; the young man in shorts with sun-bleached hair looking like he may have left his surfboard outside; the black woman with tiny braids down to her shoulders, leaning against the wall. It seemed like so long ago that she herself had been a student sitting in just such a class anxious to begin seeing patients. As she did each semester, she wondered who would be left at the end of the term.

"Good afternoon, I'm Dr. Elizabeth Wing and this is Psychology 408, Practicum in Clinical Psychology."

Tall and slender, she stood with apparent confidence in front of the class. Dressed professionally in a feminine, yet very businesslike, cream-colored pantsuit, she was a definite contrast to many of the teachers in the psychology department. Most of them dressed like leftovers from the hippie generation.

Despite her look of confidence, fear and anxiety plagued Elizabeth. Shortly after she had returned from her summer vacation, the terrifying nightmares had started disturbing her sleep. She had experienced night terrors as a teenager after visiting her grandparents, and now for no apparent reason they were back.

To an outsider, Elizabeth Wing looked like she had it all; attractive, financially secure, intelligent, a teaching position at the university, and a successful career as a psychologist. She wasn't in a relationship, but aside from that, what more could she want?

But peace of mind evaded her. Struggling to stay focused she continued.

"This class is designed for seniors with a psychology, sociology, or pre-med major," she continued, trying to shake the anxiety of the morning caller. "If you are a graduate student see me later. If you're in this class for an elective, or an easy A, you don't belong here."

A few students left the room. *Round one, she thought.* She knew from past experience more would leave before she'd finished speaking.

"There are four classes that are prerequisites for this practicum course. You must have completed three of them and be taking the fourth concurrently. There are no exceptions."

Five or six students grumbled, picked up their belongings, and left. *Round two.*

"During the first half of the semester, you will observe and critique patient intakes and counseling sessions at the University Community Clinic. In the second half, you will be doing the intakes and counseling, and your fellow students will be observing and critiquing you. If you're not prepared to work your ass off, you can leave now." Seeing their look of surprise at her choice of language she added, "If you find my language offensive, get used to it, your patients will use worse." A little taste of what to expect was good for them.

A few more students left the classroom. *Round three.* The black woman leaning against the wall hurried to a vacated seat. Surfer boy still sat on the floor, not bothering to scramble for a chair. There were still too many students who wanted the class.

"Believe me when I tell you that as a therapist, your worst nightmare will walk into your office and expect you to make things better." *I've had my share of unpredictable patients.* "If you intend to become a social worker, you will be expected to go into the homes of your clients. Some of these homes will be so filthy that you won't want to sit down, but you will. At other times you will be in personal danger."

A young woman with long dark hair and a short mini-skirt left the room. A baby-faced young man stood up, picked up his backpack, and mumbled, "I'm out of here." *Round four.*

"As you can see, there aren't enough seats. If history repeats itself, of the thirty students who will be accepted into the class, a third of you will not be here at the end of the semester." In this class, they would need to face their own personal demons; students often found this more challenging than the course work. *Do the personal demons ever end?*

She knew the students called her the *Ice Queen* because she wouldn't break the rules, or even bend them. To them, she appeared unemotional. They too would learn to keep their emotions in check if they wanted to become good therapists.

At the beginning of every semester, Dr. Peter Brewer, the department chair, received complaints about her strict policies regarding class enrollment and completion of prerequisites before taking her class. Her classes were tough, and that's the way she intended to keep them. Her reward: At the end of the semester when the students filled out their evaluations, her scores were always the highest in the department. Peter Brewer hated that. Peter Brewer hated everything about her.

As she thought again about the phone calls she'd been receiving, she wondered if he would stoop to that level to frighten her. Ever since they joined the staff together five years ago, he had been jealous of her successful private practice and her teaching abilities. She was a threat to him. If she had wanted the department chair, she could have had it. She knew it and he knew it. But she wanted to have time for her volunteer work at the rape center along with her private practice and had declined the invitation to apply for the position. She wouldn't buckle under to his dictatorship. She refused to date him. She knew he'd give anything to have her out of the department and he would keep trying until he found a way.

Standing at the window of the hotel room, Cash watched Squirrel make contact with the dealer. Once or twice a week, Cash would rent a cheap hotel room in Los Angeles, always the same hotel, always the same room. He would invite Squirrel to join him. Squirrel wasn't really a friend; he was an acquaintance, someone who would do anything for a chance to get high. Together they indulged in the euphoric world of cocaine, the only thing they had in common. The rest of the week, Cash stayed clean. His family, his friends, even the people he worked with, didn't have a clue he still pursued his secret habit.

He was on the edge and he knew it, the craving for drugs encroaching more and more on his life. He wanted the magic powder but he couldn't risk making the buy. Another bust and all the money in the world wouldn't keep him out of jail. For a little coke, Squirrel took all the chances. Someone like him came in handy. When he heard the knock, he hurried to open the hotel room door. "Did you get it?" he asked as Squirrel darted inside.

"Yeah, and it's good blow," Squirrel replied.

Cash locked the door and grabbed the package out of Squirrel's hand. Hastily he opened the bindle to inspect it himself. The color would tell him the purity of the buy.

"Yeah, this is good," Cash confirmed.

Not wanting to take a chance on getting a tainted batch, he always bought his cocaine from the same contact. He wanted the purest form he could find. Wasting no time, he began his ritual. Carefully he spooned the white flakes onto a plate, applying enough pressure to crush them into powder. His craving grew as the ritual progressed. Razor blade in hand, when the desired consistency had been reached, he carefully scraped a small pile of powder onto a piece of mirror and divided it into lines. Cash took a crisp C-note out of his wallet and rolled it tight, snorted a line, and passed the mirror to Squirrel. The instant rush took hold but within minutes he craved another line. Passing the mirror back and forth, they reveled in the high.

The two men sat on the sagging couch sniffing the coke, listening to rock music blasting from the stereo, divulging secrets, and sharing the exhilaration brought on by the cocaine.

"Cash, what's your real name?" Squirrel asked.

"If I wanted people to know my name I'd use it."

"Right. So why do they call you Cash?"

"I always have money. Have you ever seen me without cash?"

"Oh. So they call you Cash because you've always got cash, I get it," Squirrel responded, jumping up and walking around the room.

"How about you? Why do they call you Squirrel?"

"'Cause I'm fast. The cops can't catch me. But if they do, I always find a way to squirm out of it, just like a squirrel."

Cash turned up the music until the sounds vibrated through the room. Holding back on another line, not wanting to become so strung out that he couldn't think, he brought up his favorite subject.

"I called her again today," Cash bragged, as he paced around the room. "The first time I called her she hung up. The bitch wouldn't even talk to me. She won't do that again. Now she listens to me. Sometimes she asks me questions like she's trying to figure out who I am but..."

"What do ya say to her?"

"Whatever comes into my head. Call her names, tell her I want to see her naked, that sort of thing."

"Do ya talk sex stuff to her?" Squirrel asked, getting more and more excited.

"Yeah, sometimes. She gets pissed off, but now, no matter how often I call, or what I say, she doesn't hang up," Cash boasted. "I'm in control!"

"Bitchin'."

Cash poured some bourbon into a glass and added a splash of water. He knew the alcohol would intensify his euphoric state. Ways to frighten, even terrify, Elizabeth Wing danced through Cash's mind as he continued consuming line after line late into the night.

CHAPTER THREE

It had been a hectic week. To Elizabeth's relief, Tim Henderson had agreed to be on call this weekend. He had been a good friend for a long time and she could always count on him to help when she needed a break. *What would I do without Tim?*

Elizabeth locked the file cabinets, placed a report she wanted to put the final touches on into her briefcase, turned off the lights, and pulled the door closed behind her. She tried the knob, assuring herself the office was secure, and headed for the elevator. Exiting on the first floor, she struggled with her purse and overflowing briefcase.

The security guard glanced up briefly from his newspaper. "Good night, Dr. Wing," he mumbled.

"Good night, Ned," she replied as she walked toward her car.

All this week she had noticed a black Mustang at the far end of the parking structure. She wondered if a new tenant had moved into the building. In the past she had always been the last one to leave. Monday she would find out who owns that car. No use fretting over the presence of a strange vehicle. As a volunteer at the local rape center, Elizabeth had given many talks to college classes and women's groups on rape prevention. Always be aware of your surroundings, wear shoes you can run in, carry your keys in your hand, not in your purse, lock the doors of your car as soon as you get in, and use the buddy system. *Well, I follow most of my own advice.* She started her car, pulled out of the building, and headed home. At the last minute, she decided to pick up something at the grocery store and made a sharp turn into the Ralph's parking lot.

As she got out of her car, she saw a black Mustang go by the entrance. *That can't be the same car. I'm getting paranoid.*

Once home, Elizabeth forgot about the car, the papers waiting in her bag, and the busy week that had finally come to an end. She kicked off her shoes, poured herself a glass of cabernet sauvignon, and sank wearily into her favorite easy chair. She took a sip of wine and rested her head against the back of the chair. In the background, the piano music of Richard Clayderman played "Somewhere." She could feel the tension of the day leaving her body as the music and the wine blended together, the sharp edges of reality softening and then melting away.

Elizabeth woke with a start to the shrill ring of the phone.

"Hello," she answered sleepily.

"Hi, Elizabeth. Are you asleep already?"

"Tim, no. Just dozing in a chair. Don't tell me one of my patients is having a crisis this early in the weekend."

"No, but I picked up a disturbing call from your machine. It was a man's voice, muffled like he was holding something over the speaker. He said he had a message for 'the bitch.' Then he said something like, 'You think you're pretty damn smart, don't you? Just you wait.' I'm concerned, Liz. Do you know who this might be?"

"No. I didn't mention it before, but I've been getting calls like this for a while."

"For God's sake Elizabeth, why didn't you say something?"

"I can handle it, Tim."

"Have you called the police?"

"No, I don't want the police questioning my patients. I figured whoever it is would get bored if I didn't respond. Instead, they've escalated."

"Well, be careful. If you need anything this weekend, give me a call."

"Thanks, but I really don't need you to protect me."

"Liz, if this nut calls you at home, call the police."

She hung up the phone and felt a shiver run through her body. *When is this going to stop?* She drank the rest of her wine and headed for her bedroom. *Forget dinner, I just want to sleep.* She hoped the terrifying dreams she had been having the last few nights wouldn't recur again tonight.

Friday night and time to party. Cash was late getting to the hotel but Squirrel would wait. Squirrel always waited if he could get some coke. Besides, Squirrel liked to hear the latest in his game with Elizabeth.

"Listen," Cash said after they had done a few lines. "Don't bring some skank up here from the bar. I can't take a chance of anyone recognizing me."

"The chick I brought up here last week didn't look twice at you. She was too busy giving me a blow job so she could get some coke." Squirrel jumped up and started pacing around the room.

"Hey, moron, just listen to me!"

"Asshole, just 'cause you got a college education doesn't make you smarter than me." Squirrel looked out the hotel room window then pulled the drapes closed.

"Just don't do it again. If I get busted I have more to lose than you do." Cash's paranoia was becoming more intense.

"Okay, I hear ya. Did you call that broad this week?" Squirrel asked, changing the subject and reaching for the mirror holding the cocaine.

"Don't call her a broad!"

Squirrel responded with a sarcastic, "Well, excuse me."

"Yeah, I called her. And listen to what else I did," Cash bragged. "I rented a car and I've been following her all week. Those car rental people are so dumb. They couldn't even tell the picture on the license wasn't me. Serves them right to get stiffed for the bill."

"Where'd she go?" Squirrel asked as he bounced in his seat waiting for his turn to snort another line.

"Her office, the university, that clinic where she works, the gym. The same routine, nothing exciting," Cash replied, rubbing his nose and passing the coke back to Squirrel.

"Didn't she see you?"

"Not until tonight. I parked at her office all week. I followed her everywhere she went and she didn't even see me, until tonight."

"What happened when she saw you?"

"Nothing. I drove on by. She couldn't see me inside the car," Cash bragged.

"So what are you going to do next?" Squirrel asked, pacing around the room again.

"I don't know. The phone calls aren't enough." Cash snorted another line and rubbed his nose again with the back of his hand. "They don't scare her anymore. *If she knows I'm watching everywhere she goes, that will get to her. I'll make her afraid of me.*"

"I bet my phone calls could scare her. Can I do it? Ya know, call her and say stuff to her," Squirrel asked, anxiety building in his voice.

"No, I don't think that's a good idea."

"Come on, Cash. You know I can be scary."

"I don't know," Cash answered tentatively. Then thinking more about it, he wondered, *what harm could it do? Maybe a strange voice, different words, would spook her.*

"Okay. But you've got to cover the mouthpiece with a cloth or something, and disguise your voice. And you've got to tell me everything you say and if she says anything to you, okay?"

"Yeah, yeah," Squirrel agreed.

"And you've got to call her a bitch. I always call her a bitch. Then, at the end, you've got to tell her to call her mother. Something like, 'If this really scares you, you can always call your mother.' You got that?"

"Okay, okay. I've got it," Squirrel said.

Cash scribbled Elizabeth's office number on a scrap of paper and passed it to Squirrel, then went back to telling him what he had done.

"After I followed her tonight, I called her. The machine picked up the call. I hate it when that happens. Usually I just hang up, but tonight I left a message. When her secretary picks up the messages, Elizabeth will have to explain me."

"Bitchin'," Squirrel replied, snorting another line.

Cash poured himself a glass of bourbon and sat staring off into space. *How can I frighten Elizabeth more? If my phone calls don't do it, I'll leave her another kind of message.* Draining the last of his drink, he suddenly jumped up from the couch.

"I've got it," he shouted. "I know how to get to her!"

Elizabeth walked into the office on Monday morning and placed the revised reports on Joanne's desk. The look on her secretary's face told her something was terribly wrong.

"What is it, Joanne?"

"Dr. Wing, your voice mail is filled with obscene phone calls. Some man saying terrible things about you."

"Don't worry about it, Joanne. Just erase them…no, put in a new tape. I'll listen to that one and see if I can recognize the voice."

"Do you think it's one of our patients?"

"I really don't know."

Elizabeth wanted to downplay the incident. Joanne appeared visibly shaken by the phone messages and she needed her to be calm when the patients arrived.

"There's a large envelope on your desk. It's marked personal. I found it on my desk when I unlocked the office this morning."

"Thank you, Joanne."

Elizabeth went into her office and closed the door. She walked to the window and looked out, trying to clear her mind. The Santa Ana winds had blown the marine layer out to sea, and Catalina Island was visible in the distance. She turned back to her desk and stared at the envelope. Intuitively, she knew that whatever the envelope contained, it was not good news. A cold chill ran through her. *Maybe I'm being silly, but I don't want to open this by my self.* In fact, she debated whether or not to open it at all but she knew she had to. Not wanting to upset Joanne further, she called Tim and told him about the phone messages and the envelope.

"I'll be there in ten minutes. Elizabeth, you've got to call the police."

She knew he was right. This had gone on long enough. Who knows what this person might do next?

When Tim arrived, he went immediately into Elizabeth's office.

"Is that it?" Tim asked, as he sat down across from her.

Elizabeth nodded.

"Do you want me to open it?"

"No, I'll do it."

Tim sat with Elizabeth as she slid the silver letter opener along the sealed edge of the envelope and dumped the contents onto her desk. Photographs spread out in front of them. Photographs of Elizabeth. Elizabeth jogging in the park on Saturday morning, Elizabeth planting flowers in her yard on Saturday afternoon, and washing her car on Sunday. But the last picture surprised her most of all. It had been taken of her working out inside her health club, a club that boasted an elite membership. The color drained from Elizabeth's face and a look of terror filled her eyes. *How could he get in there?* Tim stared at the stack of pictures in front of them and then at Elizabeth.

"Liz, what is this?"

"This guy watched me all weekend."

Hands shaking, Elizabeth picked up the phone and called the police.

"They're sending a detective over," she said as she hung up the phone.

"I'm going to clear my schedule. I want to be with you when you talk to the police," Tim said, as he walked out of her office and headed down the hall.

Alone, Elizabeth sat and stared at the pictures. *Who would do this?* She started going over everyone she knew in her mind. Past patients, angry patients, students who may have been unhappy with their grades, but she couldn't think of anyone who had been angry enough, or unstable enough, to do this. She had done this before but maybe she'd missed someone. *Colleagues, friends, relatives…who could it be?*

CHAPTER FOUR

Detective Frank Gualdoni spent the weekend as usual—at the office finishing up paperwork. Two years ago, his wife gave him an ultimatum: spend more time with me and the kids or we're leaving. But Frank worked, and went to night school, worked, and studied, and worked. So his ex-wife packed up their two kids and moved to Taos, New Mexico. It was no place he wanted to live, but she liked the fresh air and the mountains, not California smog. Now, with nothing else to do on the weekends, he worked, and studied, and worked even more. He hated not being able to see his kids, but in New Mexico, his ex wouldn't need to work with the money he paid her for child support and alimony.

Sitting at his desk, drinking coffee left over from the night shift, he wondered what his next assignment would be.

"Hey, Gualdoni. You look terrible, you been here all night?" Lieutenant Brooks asked as he walked past Frank's desk. *Couldn't this guy ever just say "Good Morning"?* When Brooks transferred in a year ago, Frank thought he would get used to the guy. It never happened. He just disliked him more.

Gualdoni could feel his jaw tighten but he didn't respond. The only thing that kept him from telling Brooks just what he thought of him was his retirement package, filled out and sitting in his bottom drawer. One month away, on October first, after twenty years on the force, he would hand his retirement request to Brooks. Ninety days later, he would be a free man. How sweet it would be.

Frank pulled the crumpled college catalogue out of his drawer and looked at it. Just one more class and he'd have the bachelor's degree he'd been working on for seven years. He thought back to when he joined the force, just a twenty-one-year-old kid who'd always wanted to be a cop. During his years on the force, he'd seen more horror than any man should. He'd been underpaid, shot in the line of duty, and lost his wife and kids, all because he loved his job. Yet over the years, his dream changed. Justice wasn't always served when the cops caught the bad guys. The real challenge played out in the courtroom, proving their guilt beyond a shadow of a doubt to the judge and jurors. As a lawyer with the DA's office, he could make that happen. Just one more semester, then, law school.

"Gualdoni, I hope you've got a clean shirt," Lieutenant Brooks remarked as he tossed the paperwork for Frank's next assignment across his desk. "This one's made for you. Some shrink's being harassed." He smirked at Frank and walked back into his office.

Frank didn't like the lieutenant's humor. In the locker room, he glanced in the mirror and had to admit he looked a bit scruffy. He shaved, splashed on some cologne, and put on a clean shirt. A few minutes later, he headed for his car. *A shrink's office, just my luck.* Gualdoni relished a challenge and this sounded too routine for his liking.

"Dr. Wing, Detective Frank Gualdoni is here to see you," Joanne announced as she showed the tall, good-looking man into the doctor's private office.

Detective Gualdoni looked intently at the attractive, and very poised, young woman who stood to greet him. *Nice. Damn nice.* He wasn't sure if the pantsuit was an effort on her part to look professional or to hide her sexy body, but he liked what he saw. As she walked across the room, her clear blue eyes met his, and when she shook his hand with a firm handshake he felt an unmistakable attraction. His only contact with mental health professionals of any kind had been during his divorce. He and his wife had spent less than an hour with a mediator from the court deciding child custody issues, and the frumpy social worker had not impressed him in the least. This woman impressed him. She did not act like the typical victim he so often interviewed, whining and sniveling about their bad luck. She was all business. He just might like this assignment.

"Please sit down, Detective. I've asked my colleague, Dr. Tim Henderson, to join us."

Gualdoni sat on the couch eying his surroundings. *Expensive. She must be good at what she does. Paintings, plush carpet, fancy furniture, it all spells money. This will definitely not be a typical case.*

Tim Henderson walked confidently into the room, his sleeves rolled up, his shirt unbuttoned at the neck with his tie loosened. He looked at Elizabeth without saying a word and took a seat in the chair across from Frank. The hair on the back of Gualdoni's neck bristled. He didn't like the way the man sauntered across the floor. He didn't like the way he plopped down in the chair. And he especially didn't like the way he looked at Elizabeth Wing as if he owned her. *What is my gut trying to tell me?* The men eyed each other like two bucks pawing the dirt before starting to battle over a doe. Did his professional instincts detect something, or could these feelings be something else? Something personal. *Personal? Never. I never get personally involved in cases.*

Gualdoni cleared his throat. "Well, tell me what happened. Why did you call the police?" he asked, taking out his notebook and pen.

Gualdoni took copious notes as Elizabeth enumerated in great detail the many phone calls she had received on both her private and business lines at the office. She told him about the black Mustang she had noticed for the last week when she left work at night, and finally, she showed him the pictures taken of her during the past weekend.

"Dr. Wing, do you have any idea who might be doing this?"

"No, detective, I don't."

Gualdoni turned to Dr. Henderson. "How about you; do you have any clues as to who would do this?"

"Not a one."

Gualdoni watched Henderson suspiciously.

"What's your role here in the office?"

"Dr. Wing and I are colleagues. We've shared this suite for five years," Henderson answered curtly.

Gualdoni didn't like his arrogant attitude. Was it his imagination or wasn't he getting much cooperation from Henderson?

"And is there a personal involvement?" Gualdoni asked. Needing to know what the vibes he felt coming from this man were all about.

"We've been friends for a long time," Henderson replied in a brisk tone.

Sounds like he'd like it to be more!

"Tim only found out about the calls Friday night. This morning I asked him to be with me when I opened this envelope," Elizabeth said as she pushed it toward the detective. "I had a feeling it might be something connected to the calls. Tim doesn't have any other information," Elizabeth said protectively, interrupting Gualdoni's questioning of Tim.

Picking up that there may be more to their relationship than he'd been told, Gualdoni backed off. "Well, with no obvious suspects we'll need to take a look at everyone. Give me a list of your patients, colleagues, students, friends, relatives, rejected lovers, anyone you can think of."

"That's just it. I can't think of anyone who would do this," Elizabeth replied.

"You're too close to it all. Get me the list, and I can check them out from an impartial point of view."

"I can't give you a list of my patients, that would be a breach of confidentiality, but I'll have the others for you tomorrow morning."

"I'll be discrete. But I need a complete list." Gualdoni stood up and headed for the door. Tim Henderson stood also and without saying a word, walked past him and left the office. Something bothered him about this man and his relationship to Elizabeth Wing. She seemed to trust him, but in cases like this, the perpetrator is often someone the victim knows.

"I'll start by checking out that Mustang. If it belongs to someone in the building it will be easy enough to find out. As soon as I get the list I'll start checking out possible suspects. I'll call and set up a time to meet with you again." He walked to the door, then turned back, "Don't worry. I'll find this guy."

Only Monday, and Cash craved more rails. It was easy enough to get, that wasn't the problem. His craving for the cocaine was the problem. But his craving for the high he felt when he talked to Elizabeth, followed her, tormented her; that was an even bigger problem.

He imagined how angry and frightened she must be. He imagined her looking over her shoulder to see if someone was following her. Was she scared enough to ask for help? He wanted her to be terrified. He knew, eventually, if things got bad enough, she would make that call to her parents.

Cash contacted Squirrel. He needed him to make the buy, but he needed to talk as well. Squirrel was the only one he could tell about Elizabeth. After snorting a few lines, the two men began to talk about their favorite subject, Elizabeth Wing. Squirrel told Cash how he repeatedly called Elizabeth's office all weekend leaving sexually explicit messages. Messages telling her all the things he wanted to do with her.

"I was busy, too," Cash gloated. "I followed her all weekend and took pictures of everything she did. I used two roles of film and she never even knew." He opened an envelope and dumped an array of photos on the table. "Look at these close-ups."

"God, she's beautiful," Squirrel said. "Look at her hair."

"This is the best part; I left copies at her office."

"Why'd ya do that?" Squirrel questioned as he paced around the room.

"So she'd know I was following her, stupid. She'll know I spent the whole weekend with her. I'll bet that will scare her."

"Bitchin'."

"I went to her office and gave the cleaning lady an envelope stuffed with photos and asked her to put them inside."

"What if she tells somebody you were there?"

"It won't matter," Cash explained. "I wore a black wig, a hat, and a mustache."

"How do you think of all these things?" Squirrel asked, pouring each of them a bourbon.

"They just come to me. Ways I can scare her, make her angry, they just pop into my mind. Someday she'll be sorry for the way she's treated me." Cash downed his drink, then snorted another line. Too strung out for conversation, he tossed Squirrel a picture of Elizabeth, her auburn hair hanging in loose curls over her shoulders.

CHAPTER FIVE

Elizabeth didn't like feeling afraid. She prided herself on being strong and in control of her emotions. Tim often told her to stop holding her emotions in, but she never wanted to reveal her true feelings to anyone, even herself. The turmoil of the obscene phone calls and the pictures taken without her knowledge left Elizabeth feeling emotions she had not felt in a long time. Emotions she did not want to feel. Constantly on guard, she found it difficult to concentrate on her patients.

She and Tim had gone through the files of former patients looking for anyone who might have reason to be angry at her or who might be unstable, paranoid, or vengeful. Only one possible patient, who had terminated therapy after he lost custody of his children and blamed it on Elizabeth's report, surfaced. It had been four years since the incident but Elizabeth put his name on a list of possible suspects for Detective Gualdoni to check out.

Before each current patient came in for their session, Elizabeth would reread their file. She carefully looked for clues that might relate to the phone calls, a mother issue, anger at women in general, anger directed toward her specifically, but she hated to think that any patient she was currently seeing would do this to her.

When Mary Ellen Barker came for her session, Elizabeth didn't need to worry. There was no husband or boyfriend in her life who could be making these calls. Elizabeth could concentrate on her patient's problems.

Elizabeth picked up Mary Ellen's file from the corner of the desk and studied it. About four months before, Mary Ellen had reacted hysterically at her stepfather's funeral, shaking uncontrollably and unable to stop crying. She hated him and couldn't understand her reactions. Weeks later, depressed and unable to concentrate, she sought help. Mary Ellen could recall fond memories of her childhood up until the age of ten, when her father had deserted the family. Missing were the years between ten and seventeen, the years she lived with her stepfather. At seventeen, Mary Ellen left home, but hidden in her subconscious were the missing years, and Elizabeth believed the answer to her depression would be found when she could recall those years. After six weeks of treatment, with very little improvement, Elizabeth suggested hypnosis in an attempt to recover the repressed memories.

The intercom buzzed and her secretary's voice announced that Mary Ellen had arrived. "Please send her in, Joanne," Elizabeth replied, putting the file on the table next to her chair. Turning on the tape recorder, Elizabeth opened the door and greeted her patient.

Mary Ellen looked awful. She wore no makeup. Her hair, tied back with an elastic band, needed a shampoo. Dark circles under her eyes, a telltale sign she hadn't been sleeping well, gave her face a hollow look. Despite all this, Elizabeth asked the usual question.

"How are you this week?"

"Not very well," Mary Ellen said, sinking into a chair across from Elizabeth. "I can't sleep. I still cry at the stupidest things. I have no desire to do anything and I missed two days of work this week."

"These are all signs of depression. We've talked before about medication. Would you like to reconsider that option?"

"No. I don't want to take drugs. I want to see if the hypnosis will help first. Are we going to use hypnosis again today, Dr. Wing?"

"Yes, we are. As I've told you before, you're an excellent subject and you're telling me a great deal. I think we're making progress."

Ever since graduate school, Elizabeth had been fascinated by hypnosis. She had taken every class offered at the university, attended seminars and workshops all over the country, and now held credentials from the American Society of Clinical Hypnosis and the Society for Clinical and Experimental Hypnosis. Over the years, Elizabeth has used her skills many times with outstanding success.

Mary Ellen sat back, leaned her head against the back of the chair, and closed her eyes. Elizabeth watched as she willingly followed the instructions.

"Take a deep cleansing breath and then continue breathing normally. As I count backwards you will relax. The years will slip away and you will be a child again. Twenty-seven...twenty-six...twenty-five...you are relaxed, more and more relaxed." The induction process was the same each time and Mary Ellen slipped easily into the hypnotic trance. Elizabeth continued to count, "...fifteen...fourteen...more and more relaxed...thirteen...twelve...Mary Ellen, are you ready?"

Mary Ellen raised the index finger of her right hand, the signal for an affirmative answer.

"How old are you?"

"I'm twelve," Mary Ellen answered in a childish voice.

"Can you tell me what's happening?"

Elizabeth watched her patient's eyes move rapidly beneath the closed lids, indicating she was in a deep trance. Her calm facial expressions changed. Her jaw tightened, and her head twitched as she started to speak.

"I'm pushing the dresser in front of my bedroom door. No way is that man coming into my room again. If Mama won't stop him, I will."

"What man, Mary Ellen?"

"Al. He rents the big room in the attic. It was my playroom, but Mama says we need the money because Daddy left us and ran off with some woman. He's tapping on my door. I can hear his heavy breathing."

"Do you know what he wants?"

Elizabeth listened as Mary Ellen repeated her conversation with Al.

"He says he's got something for me. He tells me to open my door. I tell him to go away. He says he's sorry if he scared me last night. Then he tells me again to open the door so he can give me a present." Mary Ellen pauses, as if remembering the scene.

"Do you open the door?" Elizabeth asks.

"I tell him to just leave the present by my door but he says one of the other kids might find it. I never get gifts anymore. Not since Daddy went away. I push the dresser away from the door, unlock the latch, and slowly open the door. Al is standing there with his hands behind his back. Which hand, he says. I point to his right hand and Al passes me a small box tied with a pink bow. I grab for the box but his rough hand catches my arm."

Elizabeth hears the fear in her patient's voice and watches as she gasps for air.

"He smells like beer and I yell at him to let me go." Mary Ellen's breathing is irregular and rapid.

"Mary Ellen, you're safe. Al's not here. Take a deep breath, and another, good girl."

Elizabeth watches Mary Ellen relax as she reassures her that she is safe. Her breathing becomes steady again.

"Tell me what's happening now, Mary Ellen."

"He lets go of my arm. Then he says not to make such a big deal out of things. I start to push my door closed but he holds it open with his foot and runs his fingers down the front of my blouse, playing with the buttons until he gets to my skirt, he puts his fingers into the waistband and tries to pull me closer to him. I push his hand away, pull back, and slam the door, lock it, and push my dresser against it. I can hear him laughing as he walks down the hall toward Mama's room."

Mary Ellen sits silently for a few moments. Elizabeth watches for facial expressions or body language that may indicate her patient is struggling with the memories. Seeing none, she continues.

"What's happening now, Mary Ellen?"

"I open the present. It's a pretty box. It's soft and feels like velvet. It's a pair of earrings. I don't want anything from *him*. I hate him. I hate him and I hate the way he looks at me, but I love the earrings."

Elizabeth glances at the clock on her desk. "Mary Ellen, it's time to come back to the present. Take a deep cleansing breath. When you wake up you will not remember anything you have told me. You will feel refreshed and relaxed. I will count backwards from five to one. When I reach one you will take another deep breath and open your eyes. You will feel rested and relaxed."

Elizabeth watches as Mary Ellen takes the first breath. "Five…four… three…two…one. You are rested and relaxed."

Mary Ellen takes another deep breath, her eyelids flutter, and she opens her eyes. She glances around the room, looking somewhat disoriented.

"How do you feel?" Elizabeth asks.

"I'm okay. Did it work?"

"You did very well. You told me some new things today."

"Do you know why I'm so depressed?"

"I'd still like more information. But yes, I do have a good idea why you're depressed. I think on Friday we may be ready to discuss some of what you've told me." Elizabeth put her arm around Mary Ellen's shoulder as she walked her to the door, "I'll see you on Friday, same time."

Elizabeth sat at her desk writing her notes on the session. She liked to schedule her patients a half-hour apart to give herself plenty of time. Mary Ellen was typical of many of Elizabeth's patients. Family-of-origin issues, stepfamily issues, and childhood abuse often surfaced after years of being repressed. Elizabeth was drawn to working with these patients. Maybe that was because she had many questions still unanswered from her own childhood. She knew what it felt like to have no memory of periods of time. Her professional training suggested that this often happens with victims of childhood abuse but she could not believe that she fell into this category.

Elizabeth pondered the new information that her patient had revealed. She was not surprised. Early in her training, she had discovered that many patients are not prepared to bring information from their subconscious to their conscious memory. Doing so could retraumatize the patient when forced to remember distressing events. Especially in cases like this one of repressed memories of molestation. Because of this, she made it a practice to always give her patients the posthypnotic suggestion that they would not remember what had been said under hypnosis. She always received permission from her patients to record the session before hypnosis began. This enabled the patient to listen to them at a later date if they so chose.

The buzz of the intercom interrupted her thoughts. "Dr. Wing, Mr. and Mrs. Cunningham are here."

Roger Cunningham, I don't like that man. I don't know what he's doing to his wife but I need to find out why she's so controlled. Could this man be the one harassing me? Elizabeth didn't like the feeling that she may be sitting across from someone who could do this to her.

"Thank you, Joanne. Show them in."

Joanne ushered Roger and Sandra Cunningham into the counseling office. A month ago, Mr. Cunningham had called to schedule the first appointment. He had led Elizabeth to believe the couple needed marital counseling but she was unprepared for the obvious mismatch. Roger Cunningham stood over six feet tall, a handsome blond, with the presence of a well-to-do-professional. He wore a tailor-made dark gray suit, obviously expensive, a lighter gray silk shirt with initials monogrammed on the cuffs, and a color-coordinated tie. Sandra, by comparison, wore no makeup or jewelry, except for a gold wedding band, and dressed in a plane white blouse, brown cotton slacks, and tennis shoes. Her outfit was not trendy or shabby chic, and it was obviously inexpensive. Elizabeth could see she was a beautiful woman and wondered why she was hidden beneath a plain exterior. With the right clothes, makeup, and hairstyle, Sandra would be gorgeous. Elizabeth was definitely curious to learn more about this couple.

Now, on the fourth session, little had changed. Roger Cunningham continued to arrive impeccably dressed while his wife remained dowdy. He had not allowed his wife to be seen alone even though he had repeatedly identified her as the patient. During the last session, Elizabeth sensed, from a look Sandra gave her, that there was much she wanted to say but was too afraid in front of her husband. This week as usual, Roger started talking, taking charge of the session before Elizabeth could begin asking questions.

"Doctor, I'm worried about my wife," Roger Cunningham announced. "She's depressed."

"What makes you think Sandra is depressed?" Elizabeth asked.

"She can't seem to do anything right and she explodes into hysterical outbursts."

"Sandra, do you think you're depressed?"

"How would she know?" Roger said sarcastically.

"Mr. Cunningham," Elizabeth said more forcefully than she had intended, "if you don't let Sandra speak for herself I can't help her."

Roger Cunningham looked surprised and Elizabeth surmised from the look that he wasn't used to people standing up to him, especially women.

"Sandra," Elizabeth said again, addressing her directly, "do you think you're depressed?"

"I don't think so," Sandra said in a soft voice.

"Of course you are," Roger boomed. "Why, you couldn't even explain to the principal at Roger Jr.'s school that he belongs in advanced classes."

"He's only eight years old," Sandra said with a little more confidence, "he's an average student. I don't think…"

"That's it, you don't think. You're stupid and you think *my son* is stupid. Well, he isn't. He's smart and he belongs in advanced classes."

"Is that why you think Sandra is depressed?" Elizabeth asked.

"Well, that's not the only reason," Roger stated. "This week Sandra was supposed to enroll our four-year-old daughter Patti in preschool. She couldn't even get that right."

"I enrolled Patti in the school that's two blocks from our house. She needs to attend school in our neighborhood where she can be with her friends."

As Elizabeth watched the interaction between this couple, it became apparent that Sandra was capable of defending her children from Roger's bullying tactics. It was also apparent that she didn't, or couldn't, do the same for herself.

Roger started in with a monologue on how his wife squandered money, wasted time, and was a disobedient wife; it continued for several minutes. Every time Elizabeth tried to ask Sandra a question, Roger answered without giving his wife an opportunity to respond. His final statement, "She's depressed and needs to be medicated," gave Elizabeth the opportunity to once again address his wife directly.

"Sandra, do you think medication would be of help to you?"

"I…don't…know, doctor," Sandra whispered.

By the end of the session, Elizabeth's frustration at the way this man controlled his wife gave her a clear understanding of why Sandra might be having hysterical outbursts. She also had the feeling that Roger Cunningham was trying to manipulate her. *Well, it wasn't going to work. He may be angry, he may even be the man harassing me, but I won't be able to help this woman if I can't talk to her alone.* Roger had spent most of the session berating his wife and Elizabeth intended to put a stop to it.

"Since this is not marital counseling as you led me to believe," Elizabeth said, looking directly at Roger, "I'm going to schedule the next appointment for Sandra alone."

"No, doctor. I think I should be present to make sure she follows your instructions."

"That won't be necessary, Mr. Cunningham. I'll see your wife alone."

Elizabeth noticed a slight smile on Sandra's face as she left the session, a confirmation of what she had suspected.

"We'll see," Roger Cunningham muttered as the couple left the office.

The next morning, Joanne informed Dr. Wing that an emergency patient had been added to her schedule for 8:00 a.m., a time usually reserved as prep time for the classes she taught at the university. Much to Elizabeth's surprise, Sandra Cunningham walked into her office. This morning she was smartly dressed, her hair was pinned up stylishly, and she wore makeup.

Sandra sat on the edge of the couch across from Elizabeth folding and unfolding a tissue in her hand.

"My husband doesn't know I'm here. For weeks I've been trying to arrange a time when I could leave the house without his knowledge. Late yesterday afternoon he told me he would be in San Diego on business today. He can't come home and check on me so I had to see you today. Thank you so much for fitting me in."

"There's no need for your husband to know anything about your visit," Elizabeth assured her.

With a sigh of relief, Sandra sat back on the couch.

"Sandra, I must ask, why the difference in your appearance today?"

"Roger keeps all my clothes locked in a closet. Whenever we go out, he picks what I will wear. If he sends me out to the children's school or on some errand, he decides what the appropriate outfit will be. I have no choice but to agree."

"And today...?"

"I have a friend. She is...helping me...plan for the future. I've been able to hide some clothes, makeup, copies of important documents, and even a small amount of money at her house. When I need to sneak out without my husband's knowledge, she brings me what I need and often drives me to my appointments. Roger treats me like his child, not his wife. Sometimes he hits me. At other times he punishes me by taking away TV time. He gives me extra chores like washing his car or yard work if he thinks I've done something he wouldn't approve of. He even checks the mileage on the car whenever he leaves it with me."

Sandra continued telling Elizabeth details of her marriage at a rapid pace. It was as if they had been bottled up for a long time and someone released the cork.

"Doctor," she continued, "if he knew about this friend or my visit here to see you today, he would kill me. Believe me, he would kill me."

Sandra then showed Elizabeth the bruises that covered her back, old bruises fading and turning yellow, newer bruises, still purple, fresh bruises, swollen and bright purple and red from last night after their session with Elizabeth. Roger had been so angry that Sandra had spoken up against him during the session that he had beaten her in the car before they even arrived home. Elizabeth believed this man was indeed capable of killing his wife.

"I need to take pictures of those bruises," Elizabeth said, trying to hold back tears as she realized what courage it took for Sandra to come to see her today.

"No. I can't let you do that. If Roger ever found out I don't know what he'd do."

"It's important. Have you ever called the police when he's hit you?"

"No. I've been too frightened. He says I'm crazy and he'll keep me from seeing the children if I tell anyone. No one but my friend has ever seen the bruises. He only hits me where they can't be seen. That's why he doesn't want me to see you alone."

"We can call the police now. They will come out and take a report."

"I can't. I know I should but I can't do it yet."

"Well, if you don't have documentation it's just your word against his."

"I know."

"Why did he bring you to therapy?"

"He wants proof that I'm mentally unstable. He needs something he can hold over me for control."

"Will he let you come to see me alone next week?"

"I doubt it. He wants everyone to think I'm crazy but he knows I'm not. Dr. Wing, I will find a way to see you again without him. I need your help."

"Then let me take the pictures. Roger won't find them, I promise."

With a nod, Sandra agreed. Elizabeth used her digital camera to take several pictures of the bruises on Sandra's back and stomach. She transferred them to her computer, then printed them out.

"Sandra, I need you to sign and date these pictures. If you ever need proof of Roger's abuse, now you've got it."

Sandra did as Elizabeth asked. Elizabeth then created a file under a fictitious name and placed it in the file cabinet drawer that held the files of former patients.

"They're safe here. You and I are the only ones who know the name they're filed under."

"Thank you, Dr. Wing."

"You said a friend is helping you plan for the future. Are you planning to leave Roger?"

"Yes. Just as soon as I have everything I need. I've been making copies of the children's birth certificates, Social Security cards, and even a couple of bank statements. I'm trying to save a little money, but Roger doesn't even let the children keep money in their piggy banks very long so, I don't have much saved."

"I'm worried about your safety, Sandra. Do you have an escape plan in case Roger gets totally out of control? Do you know about shelters for battered women?"

"Yes, my friend can come anytime I need her, and I called one of the shelters and they told me what papers I should try to get copies of. I'm on their waiting list."

"How long is the wait?"

"Usually only a few days but I can only leave when Roger is away on business. When he works in town, sometimes he shows up at the house unexpectedly. If he found me packing, I don't know what he'd do."

"Don't wait too long before you leave. You're strong and courageous, Sandra. I promise I will do whatever it takes to help you get away from this man."

After Sandra Cunningham left the office, Elizabeth wrote pages of notes documenting the bruises she had seen and everything she had been told. She knew that someday this information might be needed in court to help Sandra. As a therapist, she had heard many women describe the abuse they had received at the hands of the men who claimed to love them, but the years of calculated degradation and maltreatment Sandra had just revealed left Elizabeth fearing for her patient's safety, and maybe her own. Now she had even more reason to think Roger Cunningham might be the man harassing her.

Elizabeth had only seen her next patient a few times. His first visit had been the week she had returned from vacation. Reading over his file, she underlined words describing his affect and behavior during the sessions. Angry. Defensive. Hostile. Withholding. Paced during first session. Taps foot when answering questions. She tried to recall if the phone calls had started before or after Mark Stevens had become her patient. She couldn't remember. *How could he know so much about me in such a short time? He can't be the one.* Then she read the intake form. Referral: Court mandated. *Oh, God.*

The buzz of the intercom cut short her thoughts. "Dr. Wing, Mr. Stevens is here," Joanne announced.

Elizabeth turned on the tape recorder. She had no signed consent from this patient to record the sessions, but she turned it on anyway. Whether out of habit, because she taped so many of her patients, or a subconscious need to have his voice on tape didn't matter. It was on. Elizabeth stood and walked over to the door; she took a deep breath and tried to relax. *Just another patient, he's just another patient.*

"Come in, Mr. Stevens," she said, opening the door trying to smile.

Mark Stevens walked into the room and circled the chair he usually sat in and then sat down, much the way a dog walks in a circle before settling on a spot.

Before Elizabeth could say anything, he started talking.

"Well, she did it again. The bitch did it again."

The grating sound of the word "bitch" tore at Elizabeth. She had heard her patients use foul language much worse than that and accepted it as a way for them to express their feelings. But with some unknown person making harassing phone calls and calling her "bitch," that particular word had more meaning.

"What happened, Mark?" Elizabeth asked, trying to remain in control.

"We went to court, the divorce was supposed to final, and the bitch got it postponed again!"

"What does that mean exactly?"

"Until we get the property settled she gets to live in *my* house. I get to pay all the bills. But as long as we're still married I can't kick her out, the judge said so." Mark pounded his fist against the arm of the chair. "It's *my* house. I bought it with *my* money."

"Mark," Elizabeth said, trying not to aggravate him further. "You do understand California is a community property state?"

"Of course I do. My attorney explained all that. But I bought the house before I even met her. It's *mine*! What makes women think they can do whatever they want and get away with it?"

"The judge will sort it out," Elizabeth said, trying to calm him down.

"The judge, right, another woman trying to screw with me. She's the reason I'm here."

"The judge sent you to counseling?"

"She said I was angry. My wife ran off with another man. Of course I'm angry. I told Veronica off in court, so the lady judge said I had anger issues."

"But she didn't order anger management counseling?"

"I didn't hit my wife, I only yelled at her in court. Once Veronica gets out of my house and out of my life, I won't be angry."

"And that happens when the divorce is final?"

"Yeah. Once the divorce is final, I only gotta pay alimony for a year. Good thing we don't have kids or I'd be on the hook for child support."

"How long is the postponement?"

"Two weeks," Mark said, dejected.

"Okay, for two more weeks she gets to live in your house. I know it doesn't seem fair but have faith in the court system. You can keep it together for two more weeks."

Mark sat staring into space, his foot tapping on the floor, his hands tightening into fists and then relaxing again.

"Mark, have you been working on the stress management techniques we talked about?"

"Yeah, that breathing stuff. It works sometimes."

"How about exercise, are you going to the gym?"

"I was, but I stopped going." His foot started tapping again.

"Why?"

"Every time I went, Bruce was there," Mark said, his voice getting louder.

"Who's Bruce?" Elizabeth asked.

"He *was* my best friend, until he fucked my wife."

"The man your wife had an affair with was your best friend?"

"Do we have to talk about this?" Mark said, folding his arms across his chest as if daring her to help him.

"You're angry. I don't blame you. But your anger is what we need to talk about. You need to learn how you can express it in a way that won't get you in trouble."

"What I'm going to do is stay as far away from that cheating bitch as I can."

"And Bruce?" Elizabeth probed.

"If he doesn't stay out of my way I'm going to bash his face in."

"That will get you jail time. You're already labeled as having an anger problem. The next time something happens you won't get a second chance. Now let's work on the relaxation techniques we practiced last week."

During the rest of the session, Elizabeth helped Mark with the breathing exercises, progressive relaxation, and meditation. She discussed proper nutrition, limiting his use of caffeine and alcohol, and the possibility of him doing some journaling to ease the stress. Mark tried, but at best she considered him a challenge to work with. In the back of her mind, even though she tried to ignore it, she couldn't shake the idea that Mark may be the man who is calling her.

After two more patients, each running over in time, Elizabeth hurried out of the office, stopping briefly at her secretary's desk.

"Joanne, if Sandra Cunningham calls for an emergency appointment she is to be scheduled at whatever time she needs. Rearrange patients, cancel my lunch, call me out of a meeting, it doesn't matter. This woman is in danger. Be sure you never tell anyone when she has an appointment, especially her husband."

CHAPTER SIX

Detective Frank Gualdoni sat across from Elizabeth for the second time in as many days and tapped his pen against his notepad. She knew he must be frustrated by her apparent lack of cooperation, but she wouldn't reveal the names of her patients without their permission. To obtain their consent, she would need to explain why the police wanted the information, and she had no intention of disclosing information about her personal life to her patients.

"Dr. Wing, I must insist that you give me a list of your patients," Detective Gualdoni stated impatiently.

"I can't."

"You mean you won't. How can I do my job? How can I find out who's stalking you, if you won't cooperate?"

"My patients expect confidentiality. Dr. Henderson and I have gone through all of my former cases. We looked at every patient I've seen in the past five years. We couldn't find anyone who would have a reason to do this."

"What are you, some kind of saint? Do you mean to tell me that none of your patients ever got mad at you?"

"There was one man, he became extremely angry when he lost custody of his children because of my report, but that was four years ago."

"I want everything you've got on the man, and I mean everything. This is the only possibility you've given me so far. Are you sure there are no other patients?"

"Well, there is another possibility but if the police start investigating this man his wife will be in real danger."

"Why would his wife be in danger?" Detective Gualdoni asked.

"Because he's a batterer. This woman showed me bruises all over her back and stomach where this man hit her. This is one of the worst cases of domestic violence I've seen in a long time. If he thought she had told me about it she would be in real danger."

"Why doesn't she just leave?"

"It's not always that simple. Experience working with battered women has taught me that if a woman leaves before she's ready, she usually goes back to the abuser."

"And this woman's not ready?"

"I think she's ready emotionally but the logistics need to be worked out. She's on the waiting list for a shelter, that's a positive step, but when children are involved you need to make sure all your plans are set before you uproot them."

"Gee, my wife just up and left," Gualdoni said, more to himself than to Elizabeth. "How long before she'll be ready to leave?"

"It's hard to say but I think it will be soon."

"Good. Are there any other patients you haven't told me about?"

"There's one other. He's a fairly new patient, a court referral. He's angry at women, but I think the calls started before he came to see me."

"Are you sure?"

"I'm not positive."

"What about your personal life? The last time I was here you avoided any mention of boyfriends, ex-husbands, guys you wouldn't go out with. You've got to give me something."

Elizabeth sat quietly debating how much to tell Detective Gualdoni. *I don't want to talk about this. I can't imagine any of my friends doing this to me.* She had always made it a point to keep her personal life separate from her professional life.

With a sigh, she began to talk. "There have only been two men in my life," she said, not mentioning her first love, who still lived in Europe. "I met them both in graduate school but neither one is capable of this kind of behavior."

"You let me be the judge of that. Who are they?"

"Daniel, my ex-husband, and Tim." Elizabeth took off her glasses and moved from her desk to the easy chair across from the sofa where Detective Gualdoni was sitting. *God, I hate dragging this all up, Tim and Daniel can't be involved.*

"Tim. Do you mean the doctor who was here the other day?" Gualdoni questioned.

"Yes, Dr. Tim Henderson. Is this really necessary? Neither one of them would do this to me."

"If I'm going to eliminate them as suspects I need to know about the relationships."

"If you insist. During our last year of graduate school we formed a study group. We were in the same classes and spent a lot of time studying, going to the library, and relaxing together on weekends. At some point, both of them became interested in me. I liked Tim as a friend. Our goals were similar but he was just like everyone my grandparents introduced me to in California…blond, good looking, in the same economic bracket, and usually boring. Tim wasn't boring, just not for me. But I found Daniel fascinating. He was a brilliant student; he worked hard and played hard. I even found our cultural differences exciting."

"What do you mean, cultural differences?" Gualdoni asked.

"I grew up in Europe. I went to school with kids whose parents worked at various embassies. I experienced people from a wide range of cultural backgrounds. Daniel and his family were intriguing. His parents were professionals in China but gave up everything to bring Daniel to the United States. Here his father could only get low-level jobs and the family scraped by, but Daniel was at the top of his class and he earned a full scholarship to attend college. We had a whirlwind romance our last year in graduate school and eloped during the Christmas break."

"How did your family feel about the marriage?"

"They didn't meet Daniel and his family until after we were married. My grandparents were cordial to them but I knew they didn't understand why I married him. I think they thought he was socially inferior to me. With my parents, it was different. They understood that I didn't find it necessary to fit into the California lifestyle but they let me know they were disappointed that I had acted so impulsively."

"Disappointed?"

"Yes. I'm their only child. They were afraid I wouldn't finish graduate school. They had hoped I'd return to Spain and live near them, and I know they wanted to give me a big wedding."

"Did the fact that he was Chinese bother them?"

"If it did, they never mentioned it. I do know they were glad we didn't have children when the marriage didn't work."

"Okay," Gualdoni paused and then asked, "What happened with Henderson?"

Uneasy, Elizabeth uncrossed her legs, shifted position in her chair then crossed her legs again. "We all remained friends. Tim was the best man at our wedding."

"You mean he just stepped aside?"

"That's right. I think Tim knew we would never be more than friends. We all studied together as before, and when we graduated, Tim and I entered the same internship program. Daniel took a different path. He had taken a lot of experimental psych classes and was more interested in research. He accepted a job with a pharmaceutical company. It seems rats and monkeys were his thing, not people." Elizabeth paused; she didn't want to go over all this.

"And then?" Gualdoni asked.

"At first things went smoothly, but Daniel's research position was both time-consuming and at odds with my future goals. When the company offered him an opportunity to continue his research in South America, Daniel accepted without even consulting me. It meant we'd be separated for two years. Going on location with him wasn't an option since he'd be in the jungle most of the time and the company had rules about family accompanying employees. Daniel wanted that job more than he wanted our marriage. After much soul searching, we decided the marriage had been a mistake. An amicable divorce ended the marriage just before our first anniversary." Elizabeth sat back in her chair and sighed. She'd told the detective more than she'd intended to.

"I'm confused about one thing," Gualdoni remarked. "The marriage was a mistake. There were no children. But, you're still using this guy's name. Why?"

"I prefer it to my maiden name."

"So there's some family secret or something?"

Annoyed as she was, she had to give him credit. Detective Gualdoni knew how to uncover information.

"My grandfather was a very well-known attorney in the area and I didn't want to trade on his name to build my practice."

"And his name is…?"

"He died four years ago. No one knows I was related to him and that's the way it's going to stay."

"You're one stubborn lady." Gualdoni made a note to check out the name of Elizabeth's grandparents. "Your parents, where are they?"

"They still live in Spain and I certainly don't want them to know anything about this."

"Do you know where Daniel is?" Gualdoni asked.

"As far as I know, he's working for the same company and travels to their research labs throughout the world."

"That leaves us with Tim. What's the relationship now?"

"We set up a joint practice after we became licensed and have worked together for the past five years. He's my best friend. He stood by me during it all." Elizabeth wanted this to be over. *I hate talking about my personal life.*

"Any other family?"

"I told you, I'm an only child."

"You have no other relatives?"

"My father has one sister, Nancy. She and her husband Duncan have three children, Phillip, Tiffany, and Eric. We're not close and I only see them once or twice a year. Detective, my next patient will be here in ten minutes and I need to prepare. I'm not trying to be difficult but I've told you all I can."

"I'll call when I have some information. See ya later, Doc."

She cringed as he walked out the door. Detective Gualdoni both irritated and fascinated her. Elizabeth sat quietly, trying to stop thinking about the stalker and compose herself. Her patients weren't expecting a stressed-out therapist. The intercom buzzed and Joanne announced her next patient.

Janet Taylor entered the office wearing slacks and a long-sleeve blouse. Her hair hung loosely, covering part of her face, and she wore no makeup. At eighteen Janet was having a difficult time adjusting to college. It was obvious to Elizabeth that this had been a bad week for

Janet. At the end of an unproductive session Elizabeth felt like she was grasping at straws trying to find a way to reach her.

"Janet, I'd like to have your mother join us next week if that's all right with you."

"Yeah, it's all right. At least in here she listens to me."

After Janet left, Elizabeth couldn't help but think about her own adolescence. Despite family issues and the isolation she sometimes felt, her parents had always been there for her if she needed them. At times like these she knew she had been fortunate to grow up in a loving family.

Elizabeth had just finished writing in Janet's file when Joanne buzzed her that Mary Ellen had arrived for her second session that week.

"How was your week?" Elizabeth inquired as Mary Ellen walked into the office and sat down on the couch.

"I'm so sad during the day. I'm not sleeping well and I wake up in the middle of the night. I'm having strange dreams, but in the morning, I can't remember what they were."

"Keep a pencil and paper by your bed. When you wake up, write down anything you can remember, even if it seems disjointed or strange. When we put these dreams together with what you've told me during our hypnosis sessions, I think we'll have the answers we've been looking for." There was no man in Mary Ellen's life. It felt good to be giving 100% to her patient rather than wondering if they were somehow involved in the harassing phone calls.

"Dr. Wing, what's causing me to feel this way?"

"I have some ideas," Elizabeth said. She had planned on discussing the information from the last few hypnosis sessions but decided Mary Ellen might be too fragile to hear the facts. "I'd like to continue with hypnosis if that's all right with you."

"I want to find out what's wrong with me. If hypnosis is what it takes, then I'm ready."

Elizabeth began the usual induction process. "Close your eyes and take a deep cleansing breath. As I count backwards, the years will slip away. Twenty-seven...twenty-six...twenty-five...you are relaxed, more and more relaxed...seventeen...sixteen...fifteen...how old are you, Mary Ellen?"

"Fifteen."

"Tell me what's happening."

Mary Ellen's breathing became erratic and her facial expression changed to a look of anger. In a youthful voice, she described the scene she was reliving.

"I want Sue Ann to sit outside the bathroom door while I take a bath."

Mary Ellen sat in silence.

"Mary Ellen," Elizabeth prompted, "who is Sue Ann? Why do you want her to sit outside the bathroom door?"

"She's my little sister. We made a deal. I'll guard the door when she takes a bath and she'll do the same for me."

"But why?" Elizabeth asked again.

"Al. He took the locks off all the doors and he'll find a reason to come in if either one of us is in there alone."

Elizabeth could tell from the scene Mary Ellen described that she had gone to great lengths to protect not only herself, but also her younger sister from Al. It infuriated Elizabeth that a mother could ignore, even laugh at, her daughter's accusations that Al touched her or that he tried to watch her undress at night. Why would a mother do nothing when the locks were removed from the bathroom and bedroom doors?

Mary Ellen described moving Sue Ann's things into her bedroom.

"I told Mama, Sue Ann and me want to share a room. We want to be together now."

"Does your Mother know why you want to share a room?"

"I told her, but she doesn't believe me."

Mary Ellen sat quietly and Elizabeth watched while her facial expressions changed from anger to smiles.

"What's happening now, Mary Ellen?"

"Mama says we can share my room if we promise not to argue all the time. I tell her we won't."

Elizabeth could tell from what Mary Ellen said, that she thought being together would prevent Al from trying to come into their bedroom at night. On the third night, they forgot to push the dresser in front of the door. Sue Ann had fallen asleep as soon as she had climbed into bed but Mary Ellen studied for a while. Shortly after she put the light out, she thought she heard a noise. She listened for the sound of someone trying to open her door but heard nothing. She drifted off to sleep listening to her sister's rhythmic breathing.

Elizabeth watched Mary Ellen's expression turn to a look of fear. "What's happening, Mary Ellen?"

"Sue Ann's screaming and I don't know what to do. She's yelling 'Stop it! Go away!' I can hear Al's gruff voice whisper to her to be quite. Telling her he's not going to hurt her. Sue Ann screams again, 'Get him off me'!"

Elizabeth observed Mary Ellen's fear, but she could tell from her steady breathing that she could handle the memory.

"I turn on the light, grab my shoe, and fling it across the room and hit Al on the back and he scrambles off Sue Ann's bed. I'm scared but Al looks so funny standing there in his boxer shorts and socks that Sue Ann and I start to giggle. Al runs as I pick up my other shoe and yell at him to get out of our room. He stops just outside our door."

"You'll be sorry," he says looking directly at me. "If you'd be nice to me once in a while I wouldn't have to bother Sue Ann."

After a long pause, Elizabeth speaks softly to Mary Ellen. "What's happening now?"

She listens as Mary Ellen describes the memory of Al closing the door and how they could hear the floorboards creak as he walks down the long hall to their mother's room. Then, both girls jump out of bed and run to push the dresser in front of the door, vowing never to forget the dresser again. They know he'll be back. Not tonight, but one of these nights, he'll be back again. Sue Ann doesn't understand what Al wants and Mary Ellen doesn't want to tell her. But she promises to make sure Al will never hurt her.

That night the sisters slept in the same bed, the first of many nights that they slept together. At fifteen Mary Ellen knew exactly what Al wanted. But Sue Ann was only twelve. Mary Ellen was trying to protect her sister's innocence for a while longer.

Elizabeth glanced at the clock on her desk and realized that the time was up for this session. She instructed Mary Ellen to take a cleansing breath and brought her back to the present. She made sure to again give Mary Ellen the posthypnotic suggestion that she would not remember what she had revealed during the session.

"You did very well today. You've told me a great deal about Sue Ann and what it was like after Al married your mother. If you remember anything about this time in your life, write it down. It will be helpful when we talk again. I'll see you next week, Mary Ellen."

After Mary Ellen left, Elizabeth turned off the tape recorder and completed her progress notes. She wondered how long Mary Ellen had been able to protect her little sister from their stepfather.

Elizabeth never had an older sister or brother to protect her. She had always been independent and felt capable of taking care of herself, until now. She didn't like feeling vulnerable or needing someone to protect her. She didn't like being a victim, and that's just how she felt now that someone was stalking her.

Sitting at her desk, thoughts of who it could be filled her mind once again. Detective Gualdoni had asked her to think about who might want to hurt her. She couldn't stop thinking about it. She'd gone over and over her current and former patients, students, and reluctantly, her friends, without finding anyone with a reason to be angry or vindictive. Aside from her parents, her only family, an aunt and uncle and three cousins, were too self-centered to be interested in her life. Daniel, her ex-husband, had wanted the divorce and as far as she knew now lived in Mexico. She hadn't dated in months and there were no spurned lovers, except Tim. Dr. Tim Henderson. *He couldn't be the one making these obscene phone calls, following me, and leaving notes on my car. We've been friends and colleagues for years. Tim would never try to frighten me this way.*

Elizabeth saw two more patients after Mary Ellen and was exhausted by seven that evening when she could finally go home, and forget about her patients' problems for the night. Detective Gualdoni had insisted on new safety precautions. Now her routine included calling Ned, the security guard, and informing him that she was leaving her office. He would meet her at the elevator on the first floor and walk her to her car.

A new security system had been installed in her house, one that she could activate from any room, and the police had started doing drive-by checks of her home. While she did feel safer with the added precautions, she also felt like a prisoner.

At home, she couldn't help but think, *What next?* In her mind, she kept going over and over her patients, students, and friends, anyone who might be upset with her, but aside from two patients, Roger Cunningham and Mark Stevens, she dismissed everyone she thought of as incapable of harassing her this way. She had told Gualdoni about these patients, but if they weren't involved, what would the knowledge of the stalking do to their therapeutic relationship? As she lay in bed trying to fall asleep, the same thoughts kept going through her head. *What do I do now? Who is this person, and why is he so determined to disrupt my life?*

Cash had been trying to find Squirrel for almost two hours, calling everyone who might know where he was. Damn. He needed more drugs. Finally, in desperation he paged his dealer. By the time his page was returned, he was impatient to the point of agitation.

"Gimme a couple of grams," Cash told the dealer. "I'll pick it up myself."

He listened for directions to the meeting place. Then, even more agitated, he replied, "No. Not there." Cash paused and listened again.

"No. Not there either. It's not safe, too many undercover cops."

Another address was relayed to him and he started to object but was afraid his connection would tell him the sale was off.

"Okay. I'll meet you there. Thirty minutes. Make sure it's good stuff."

Annoyed that he had to make the buy himself, Cash hurried to the rental car. He didn't intend to use his own vehicle, that would be pushing his luck too far. He wanted to wear a hooded sweatshirt to conceal his identity, but the temperature was nearing 80 and he didn't want to look suspicious. Parking the car a block away from the meeting place, he tried to look casual as he dodged the kids on rollerblades and skateboards who used the street and sidewalk as a playground.

The connection leaned against a mailbox looking bored and biting his fingernails. Cash hesitated for a second. He didn't like making the buy himself, then he walked up to the mailbox. He dropped the envelope holding the money on the ground. A pimply faced kid rushed to pick it up, switching envelopes with one containing the drugs before passing it to Cash.

Completing the buy, Cash hurried back to the Mustang, paranoia building with every step. Once in the car he sat for a minute, looking around the street to see if anyone had followed him; then, he started the car and drove back to his hotel.

Alone, with only a dim light illuminating the table, Cash began his ritual. Carefully emptying the snow onto the mirror, he took a fresh razorblade from his wallet and began chopping the white powder even finer. He snorted the first line, enjoying the burning sensation and the anticipation of ecstasy. Then, in rapid succession, he snorted two more lines. The thoughts of Elizabeth flooded his mind, disjointed, irrational thoughts. Pictures of her running away from him, running toward him, laughing at him, crazy paranoid thoughts.

She called the police! That bitch called the police! The phone calls, following her, the pictures; they were all intended to scare her. He wanted to scare her. But he never suspected she would call the police. That wasn't something he ever imagined. He had to think. He'd been careful, hadn't he? He'd rented a car using a fake ID. What else? His drugged mind couldn't think clearly. Gloves. Yes, he'd worn gloves when he touched the pictures. Anything else? The calls. Pay phones, he'd always called from pay phones. Good. He'd been careful! The police couldn't trace anything back to him. He hoped Squirrel had been careful as well.

Another plan began to gel in his mind, one final way to get her to do what he wanted. This would work. It might be dangerous but it would work. Where was Squirrel when he needed him?

Another line. His nose burned, his hands shook, he was tweaked and he liked the feeling.

Chapter Seven

"Dr. Wing, Sandra Cunningham is here," Joanne announced.

Elizabeth struggled to maintain her composure for her last patient of the day. *Sessions with Sandra are always intense.* "Send her in, Joanne."

At Elizabeth's insistence, Roger Cunningham had begrudgingly allowed his wife to be seen alone, but he waited impatiently in the outer office. Joanne told her that he paced around the reception area and questioned her about the counseling session.

"How are things going, Sandra?" Elizabeth asked as Sandra sat down across from her.

"It's getting worse. Roger is suspicious of everything I do."

Sandra crossed her legs, and when she did, Elizabeth noticed bruises that had been hidden by her slacks while she was standing.

"Are those new bruises?"

"Yes. This week Roger came home unexpectedly and I was watching TV. He was furious and hit me with his belt."

"Before you leave, I want to take pictures of them," Elizabeth said.

Sandra nodded. "I don't know how much more of this I can stand. He's hitting me all the time. He questions every dime I spend for groceries and started questioning the children about what I do when he's not at home."

"Sandra, the way the abuse is escalating you need to get out of there." *If she doesn't leave soon this, man is going to kill her. I've got to find a way to get her out of there.*

"I know, but once I leave I can never go back. I've got to make sure I have everything I need. Not material things, but as much information as I can find about our finances."

Money. It always comes down to money. "What's happening with the shelter situation?"

"I'm on the waiting list. But a bigger problem is where I'll go after I leave the shelter. My mother isn't in a position to help me, and my sister lives in an apartment in Chicago with a roommate."

"You mentioned last week that you lived with your grandparents at one time. Is that an option for you now?" Elizabeth asked.

"No. My grandfather died a few years ago and Grandma is too old to have me and the kids live with her. Besides, Roger knows she lives outside of Portland, and I'm sure he could track me down."

"When did you live with them?" Elizabeth asked, remembering when she had lived with her grandparents as a child.

Sandra leaned back on the couch and sighed. "We moved there when I was twelve. That summer Mama took me and my three-year-old sister Lily to my grandparents' house on the lake. I thought we going for a visit and I was excited. We rode all day on the bus. I remember the smell of stale cigarette smoke and sweaty bodies but it didn't seem to bother Mama. She sat contentedly humming to herself. When Lily and I got tired of riding the bus she told us that when we got to the lake everything would smell sweet and clean."

"Had you ever been to your grandparents' before?" Elizabeth asked.

"No. My father would never let us go. He said they lived too far away. This time, Mama didn't ask. When Daddy when to work, she packed our bags and we just left. It was a long ride, and the bus was old, it rattled and bumped along the road. Late in the afternoon, the bus stopped at the end of a dirt road, and when we climbed off the bus Mama was smiling. Not the forced smile she gave Daddy, but a real smile that showed her teeth and made deep dimples in her cheeks."

"It sounds like your mother was happy to be going home."

"I think she must have felt free. My father was not a nice man. As we walked down the dirt road toward my grandparents' house, it seemed like Mama was dancing, not just walking. She showed us the house where her sister Emma and her family lived and told us we could play with our cousins later."

"How did you feel about going to see your grandparents?"

"At that point, I still thought we were there for a vacation. I was happy to be out of the city during the hot summer. It was all an exciting adventure. We lived in a dingy red brick apartment. In the country, the houses along the road were small and separated by groves of pine trees and scrub oak. We could hear birds singing. Everything was different than it had been back home."

"It sounds lovely," Elizabeth commented.

"Oh, it was. We walked around a curve in the road and I knew the house at the end was my grandparents'. Mama had talked about it so much, and it looked just the way she had described it." Sandra smiled as she reminisced. "The white shutters and trim sparkled in the afternoon sun, and gray weathered shingles covered the house. It looked comforting and homey, and it felt like I'd been there before. Mama started walking faster and Lily's short legs could hardly keep up with her."

"Did your mother grow up in this house?" Elizabeth asked, remembering the large estate that belonged to her grandparents and how she had loved to visit them.

"Yes, but she hadn't been home since before I was born. My grandparents would come and visit us in the city, but Daddy wouldn't let Mama go to visit them. My grandparents must have been watching for us because they came out into the yard and waved. When we reached the house, they hugged us all. Grandma smelled of lavender, just like the little satin heart she sent me to put in my underwear drawer. When Grandpa hugged me, his face scratched mine and he kept saying how much I'd grown."

"How long since you'd seen your grandparents?" Elizabeth asked.

"It must have been over a year. Daddy always got angry when they came to visit. We went inside and Grandma showed us to our room. It was off the kitchen and she told us that Grandpa built it so that Lily and I would have our own room. At the time, I thought that was strange. I still didn't know we were going to stay. She told us to put our clothes away and change into our swimsuits. She said there was time for a swim before dinner."

"Do you think your mother had planned to move back with your grandparents?"

"Yes, I'm sure she did, but I know she didn't expect it to end the way it did. After dinner that night, my grandparents went to a Grange meeting. Mama put Lily to bed and then she told me she wanted to talk with me. She called me Sandra. She only called me that if I was in trouble or if it was something very serious. I remember how nervous I felt when Mama took me out on the back porch with a glass of lemonade. We sat on the wooden steps and watched the sun slip behind the trees. She told me this was her favorite place in the whole world. The lake looked like a giant piece of glass as it reflected the sky and the trees. In the distance, at the other end of the lake, a sailboat sat almost motionless as the wind seemed to go to sleep with the sun. The sky turned shades of yellow and orange, pink and purple, and then it was night."

"It sounds like a beautiful place," Elizabeth commented more to herself than to Sandra, as her thoughts drifted to her own little house at the beach.

"It was. I could tell how happy Mama was to be back there. Then she got serious, almost sad, and she told me that Grandpa kept a loaded gun under his pillow. She told me I must never touch it and that I had to help her keep Lily from ever going into Grandpa's room. My childhood ended that day. Mama was telling me grownup things and giving me grownup responsibilities."

Elizabeth interrupted again. "That's a lot of responsibility for a twelve-year-old. Were you scared?"

"Not really. But I was surprised when she said weren't going back to the city, or to Daddy. There were tears in her eyes when she told me. It must have been a very hard decision for her. She told me she would explain it to me when I got older. She never had to, and now, here I am getting ready to try to explain the same thing to my children."

"You know that leaving Roger is the only thing you can do. His abuse of you is hurting the children too," Elizabeth said.

Sandra nodded and rested her head against the back of the couch and closed her eyes. Elizabeth watched as tears slid down Sandra's cheeks.

"Are you remembering something else?" Elizabeth asked.

"That night in bed I tried to figure out why we weren't going back home. It had been an exhausting day and I quickly drifted off to sleep listening to the gentle rhythm of my sister's breathing." There was a long pause. "I woke with a start, thinking I had heard a scream. I didn't move. I just listened. The chirping of the crickets was the only sound slipping into my bedroom. I can't be sure if I had really heard something or if it had been a dream. Then, muffled sounds of Mama's voice, high pitched and scared, drifted into my room. And then there was another voice. It was quiet at first. But the other voice got louder; it was Daddy's voice; a slurring, drunk voice that I had heard before. The voice he used to yell at Mama when he'd come home late and hit her. I heard Daddy say he wouldn't leave without us girls. He yelled at Mama that he would kill her if he had to, but he was taking his girls home."

Elizabeth felt a shiver go through her but she didn't interrupt. *Sandra was a victim of the cycle of violence going from one generation to the next. Would she be able to stop the cycle and prevent her daughter from being a victim as well?*

"I was scared and I knew Daddy always got mean when he was drunk. I crept quietly out of bed. Through the partly opened door I could see his back. I knew I could slip out the kitchen door without him seeing me, but I couldn't leave Lily behind. I shook her but she wouldn't wake up. I had to get away and I had to take Lily with me. I picked my little sister up in my arms and tiptoed through the kitchen and out onto the back porch. All the while, Daddy kept yelling at Mama. If Mama saw us, she never let on. I wished Grandpa were there. Wished he would get his gun and make Daddy go away. Silently I carried Lily down the steps and into the darkness. She was getting heavy, so I made her wake up. I told her we were playing a game of hide-and-seek and she needed to keep very quiet."

"Did you know where you were going?" Elizabeth asked.

"No. I just knew I had to hide so Daddy couldn't take us away. Lily started to cry. The pine needles hurt her bare feet. I could still hear Daddy shouting and then I heard a pop. It echoed in the night. And then…pop…pop. I grabbed Lily's hand and ran. She cried more but I kept pulling her through the darkness in the direction of lights that I hoped were Aunt Emma's house. There were noises all around us. I didn't know what kind of animals were in the woods or if Daddy was chasing us. I just ran, dragging Lily behind me. When Lily pulled away from my grasp I wanted to keep running, but I stopped and put my arms around her. Tears rolled down her little face and she put her arms around my neck, begging me to pick her up again. Dr. Wing, I'm never going to put my children through anything like that," Sandra announced emphatically.

"Sandra, you must have been terrified!"

"I was. I'd lost my way. I could see lights in two directions and I didn't know which one to run to. Lily and I sat down and I could feel my heart pounding in my chest. I leaned against the trunk of a pine tree, its rough bark dug into my back. Lily put her head in my lap, and I put my arms around her to keep her warm. I just sat there, not knowing what to do. After what seemed like a long time, I heard the sound of a car coming slowly toward us. Its lights piercing into the darkness scared me. I tried to hide from the glow through the trees but the headlights easily spotted our light-colored nightclothes. The car stopped and the driver opened the door and started walking toward us. The lights were in my eyes and I couldn't see who it was. Then I heard his voice call, 'Sandy, Sandy.' It was Grandpa. Grandpa had come home and found us."

"You must have been relieved to see that it was your grandfather. Did he take you back home?" Elizabeth asked.

"He asked me why we were outside. I told him what had happened. He picked up Lily in his arms and carried her back to the car. I walked beside him, and he kept telling me everything would be all right. He drove Grandma, Lily, and me to Aunt Emma's house and then he went to find Mama. It seemed like a long time before Grandpa called and told Grandma that Daddy was gone and Mama had been shot. Mama had tried to protect herself and us with Grandpa's gun but Daddy had taken it away from her. An ambulance took Mama to the hospital and the police came and wanted to know what I had seen."

Elizabeth looked at the clock on her desk and saw that Sandra's time was up. There were no other patients waiting and she let the session continue. "Sandra, was your mother seriously hurt?"

"Yes. She'd been shot in the stomach and there were a lot of complications. She almost didn't make it, and she had to stay in the hospital for a long time. My grandparents took care of Lily and me. Daddy had run away but the police found him, and after the trial, he went to prison. I saw him once in the courtroom, but I never saw him again. I don't even know if he's still alive. I lived with Mama, Lily, and my grandparents until I went to college. Mama never seemed the same after the shooting, physically or emotionally."

Sandra opened her eyes and sat up straight. "Dr. Wing, I vowed I would never marry a drunk, a man who would abuse me the way my father abused my mother. Now look at me."

"Times have changed, Sandra. You have many more resources than your mother had. You've already made plans to go to a shelter. They'll help you with a restraining order. I'm sure they will have other options for what you can do after you leave the shelter as well."

"I still hear my mother scream at night. I wake up and it's one of the children crying or a bird screeching, but in my dreams, it's my mother."

"We've talked about your escape plan; what about a divorce?" Elizabeth asked.

"I can't. My husband is just like my father. Oh, he's not a drunk; in fact, he doesn't drink at all. Maybe that's worse. But he would rather see me dead than allow me to divorce him and take his children away. I'm afraid to stay around long enough to get a divorce."

"What's taking so long?" Roger Cunningham's voice boomed from the outer office as he yelled at Joanne.

Elizabeth looked at the little gold clock on her desk. The session had lasted twenty minutes past the allotted hour. "Sandra, it sounds like Roger is getting impatient. I'll see you next week and we'll focus more on your options. Take care of yourself and call me if you need anything."

Elizabeth walked Sandra out to the waiting room, nodded to Roger, and went back into her office. *I wish I could tell her that everything's going to be okay but I don't trust that man. The sooner she gets away from him, the better. Thank God I don't have any more patients tonight.*

After Sandra left, Elizabeth realized she had forgotten to take pictures of the new bruises. She put her head down on her desk and sighed. She could feel herself becoming emotionally involved with Sandra Cunningham's dilemma. She needed to keep her professional viewpoint. She needed to stay detached. But most of all, if she was to be able to fight for her patients, she needed to put her own demons to rest, the demons that tormented her in nightmares each night.

"Dr. Wing," Joanne said, tapping on the partially closed door. "Do you want me to wait and walk out with you?"

"No. Dr. Henderson is still here and I want to speak with him. Thanks anyway."

After Joanne left, Elizabeth wrote the progress notes on Sandra's session, documenting the new bruises. *There has to be a better solution for these women.*

She thought about some of her patients who had escaped abusive relationships and others who had stayed with the abuser. She thought about patients who had gone through a divorce. She remembered how some stayed angry at their partners and others moved forward with their lives. *Why? What was the difference? Why could some women leave the abusive relationship and move on? That would make a good research project.*

Voices in the outer office indicated Tim's last patient was leaving. Elizabeth walked to her door and opened it.

"Tim," she said after the outer door closed. "Do you have a minute?"

"Sure. Come into my office while I put away a couple of files."

Elizabeth followed Tim down the hall into his portion of the suite. It always surprised her how different his office looked and felt. She had decorated her office in pastel blues accented with touches of mauve, using the color scheme of her favorite Monet painting, a copy of which hung on one wall. The soft colors and corner windows gave the room a light, airy feel. Tim had decorated his office in rich tones of dark blue with maroon accents. Elizabeth furnished her office in light oak with a country French style; Tim had picked a masculine mix of mahogany and leather.

Elizabeth sat in one of the leather chairs and watched Tim methodically put away files and tapes. "I'm not keeping you from a date, am I?" she asked.

"No. No dates tonight. What can I do for you, Liz?" Tim asked as he cleared his desk of pens, pencils, and pads.

Journals, reference books, and testing material were all neatly organized on his bookcases. She envied his organizational skills, thinking how every couple of weeks she would have Joanne come into her office and help her organize the array of materials that had somehow managed to end up in stacks around her desk.

"It's just these phone calls. They're getting to me. And today I had a couple of pretty intense sessions with patients. I guess I just need to unwind and talk."

"Well, you've come to the right person," Tim said, sitting down across from her in the other leather chair.

"I keep thinking about my current patients, the ones that could be suspects."

"Have you told the detective about them?"

"Yes and no. I told him about them but not their names. I hate to breach confidentiality. Besides, I don't want them to know about my personal life."

"What do you say we talk over a glass of wine and a quick dinner?" Tim asked.

"I don't want you to change any plans for me. I just wanted to talk for a minute."

"Liz, I'm not changing anything. I'm your friend and right now you need a friend to talk to. I won't take no for an answer."

As much as Elizabeth insisted on being in charge of her own life, it felt good to have someone else take charge for a change. "Okay. Where shall I meet you?"

"You're not going to meet me anywhere. I'll follow you home and we'll take my car. We're not that far from your place."

During the drive to the restaurant, they discussed the phone calls, how little the police had discovered, and the need to give more information to Detective Gualdoni about her patients.

An hour later, Elizabeth and Tim were sitting at a restaurant overlooking the harbor. After talking about the stalking during the drive, it was relaxing to just sit and chat. Tim was one of the few people Elizabeth felt she could be herself with. During their grad school days, Tim, Daniel, and Elizabeth had often gone out for fish and chips or pizza after long hours of studying. Elizabeth always preferred fish and chips, so tonight it was no surprise that Tim had picked a small fish restaurant. A bottle of Chardonnay sat on the table between them and they sipped their wine, waiting for the food to be served.

"Have you talked to Carol lately?" Tim asked.

"No, and I need to give her a call." She and Carol had been friends since their first year in college. The two women hit it off from the start, and when they met Tim, both thought the other was interested in him. As it turned out, neither one was.

"When you do, suggest that she have one of her great barbeques before summer is officially over," Tim said.

"I'll do that. It would be fun."

The fish and chips arrived smelling wonderful. Big pieces of cod dipped in batter and fried to a perfect golden glow and crisp French fries overflowed the plate and along with it, a mound of fresh-made coleslaw. Not the healthiest of meals, but Elizabeth welcomed the comfort food.

Two hours later, Tim had driven Elizabeth home, waited for her to go safely inside, and then left. Thinking about it, Elizabeth realized it was the closest thing to a date she had had in a long time.

CHAPTER EIGHT

Even with police officers watching her home and office, Elizabeth felt uneasy. Their presence made it impossible for her to deny the seriousness of what was happening. She tossed and turned, but sleep evaded her. She would doze off, then awake with a start, thinking she heard something. It was after two when she finally fell asleep, exhaustion replacing fear.

The obscene phone calls continued but the stalker made no visible contact now that the police surveillance had started. She knew he was still out there, somewhere. Her routine left little room for variation. If this man had been watching her for very long, he would not have to follow her to know where she would be — her office, the university, and the Rape Crisis Center — she seldom changed her schedule.

Despite the phone calls, Elizabeth felt safest in her office. Hours spent with patients and paperwork filled her day, and she had little time to worry about her own problems. Today would be no exception. Still tired from a restless night filled with dreams, no, nightmares that she couldn't quite remember, she looked out at the ocean in the distance, hoping for a few more minutes of quiet time before her first patient. No such luck; the buzzer rang and Joanne announced that Mary Ellen had arrived for her session.

Elizabeth tried to hide her surprise when Mary Ellen walked into the office. She looked terrible, even worse than the last time Elizabeth had seen her. Her clothes were wrinkled, she wore no makeup, dark circles were prominent under her eyes, and her face had a look of hopelessness.

"What's been happening this week, Mary Ellen?"

"Dr. Wing, the nightmares are back. I'm afraid to go to sleep because I don't want to have those terrible nightmares."

Elizabeth knew all to well about nightmares.

"Tell me about the dreams," Elizabeth said, intentionally changing the word from *nightmares* to *dreams*.

"I wrote them down like you told me to. My sister and I are playing. We're skipping hand in hand. There's a shadow. We're frightened and start to run. I hold Sue Ann's hand tighter and we run faster. Then the dream gets weird."

"Just tell me what happens," Elizabeth prompted.

"Sue Ann can't keep up with me. My arm stretches longer and longer but she still can't keep up, and I can't stop running."

"And then…"

"And then she lets go of my hand. I hear her screaming, 'Mary Ellen, Mary Ellen.' Her screams pierce the air. I can't go back. I can't stop running. And all I can hear is Sue Ann screaming."

Mary Ellen sat in front of Elizabeth, visibly shaken, her hands trembling, fear filling her eyes. A look of panic at what the dream might mean settled on her face.

"You've mentioned Sue Ann several times while under hypnosis. Why don't you tell me more about your sister?" Elizabeth asks.

"She lives in Arizona, in a small town outside of Phoenix where we grew up. She married her childhood sweetheart. They have a little boy and another baby on the way."

"Are you and Sue Ann close?"

"We were as kids. After I left for college, we drifted apart. Sort of lost touch for a while," Mary Ellen says softly, her head down.

"Do you think that's what the dream is all about, you and Sue Ann losing touch?"

Elizabeth asks.

"Maybe. But Dr. Wing, why is she screaming?"

"I'm sure we'll figure that out. While you were in college, did you go home to visit?"

"The first two years I did. But then I got really busy with school and a part-time job. I didn't want to give up my new life, so I didn't go very often. When my mother died, I went back for the funeral, but after that I didn't go back at all."

"What happened to Sue Ann and your brothers after your mother died?"

"They stayed with Al at first. It took almost four months for them to find my father. Then the boys went to live with him and his wife."

"And Sue Ann, did she stay with Al?"

"No. She moved in with her boyfriend. My father didn't care, but Al was furious. The day after she graduated from high school she got married."

"How often do you see Sue Ann now?"

"Not very often. I don't think she wants to see me. She called and told me Al had died. I went to the funeral, but I don't know why."

"Did Sue Ann go to the funeral, too?" Elizabeth asked.

"Yes. She said she wanted to make sure he was really dead. At first, I thought she wanted us to be close again, but when I couldn't seem to remember all the things she wanted to talk about, she got really angry."

"What did she want to talk about?"

"What it was like when we were kids. How we shared a room and did things together. How we both hated Al. But I told her I couldn't remember much after Daddy left. That's one of the reasons I came to see you. If she can remember our childhood, why can't I?" Mary Ellen put her head in her hands and started to cry.

"The mind is very complex," Elizabeth began. "Sometimes we don't remember things because they are insignificant; sometimes, because the memories are painful."

Mary Ellen lifted her head. "If Sue Ann is so upset about what happened, it must be something really important."

"Do you think what happened to you and Sue Ann may be something too painful for you to remember?"

Mary Ellen buried her face in her hands again and wept. "I don't know. I can't remember."

"Your memories are hidden under the surface. They're available when you're ready to receive them but it may take time."

"I hope you're right, Dr. Wing."

The session was more emotional than usual for Mary Ellen. Elizabeth felt the repressed memories were probably getting closer to the surface. At the end of the session, she tried to encourage her patient.

"If you have any more dreams, Mary Ellen, make sure to write them down. You don't have to read them, just write them down. Continue writing any memories from your childhood in your journal as well. All of this information is helpful. I think we're very close to understanding why you're depressed. We'll talk more about it when we meet next week."

After Mary Ellen left, Elizabeth sat writing progress notes and wondered how her patient would handle the information that had been revealed during the previous hypnosis sessions. Elizabeth had planned to start discussing some of the incidents during this session but Mary Ellen's fragile condition today had changed her mind. Elizabeth feared she already knew what was to come either from the dreams or the next hypnosis session. She had seen too many incest cases not to suspect what could be hiding in the subconscious of this distraught patient.

That afternoon, when Elizabeth arrived at the university for her third class of the semester, she found a note from the department chair in her mailbox. It wasn't unexpected. Each semester, Peter Brewer would summon her to his office and demand that she allow more students into her classes. *Damn, here we go again.* She glanced at her watch, one hour until class time.

Getting off the elevator, she saw Brewer walking down the hall.

"Dr. Brewer, you wanted to see me," she called after him, trying to sound cheerful.

He waited for her to catch up to him, and they walked around the corner toward his office.

"I'll be with you shortly," he said to the group of students waiting outside his office door. He beckoned Elizabeth inside.

She closed the door behind her and sat down on the only chair that wasn't covered with books and papers and waited.

Dr. Brewer placed his overflowing briefcase on the desk, took off his jacket, and hung it on the back of his chair, but didn't sit down. The tall lanky man seldom sat during these meetings, he paced. In an office already crowded with a desk, bookcase, and three chairs for visitors, he managed to find room to pace back and forth. His constant motion annoyed Elizabeth.

He pushed his wire-rimmed glasses higher on his nose, stuck his hands in his pockets, and stopped briefly in front of her.

"Dr. Wing," he said, clearing his throat. "We've had this conversation before. Your Psych 408 class is in demand, and your insistence on only accepting thirty students is unreasonable." He continued pacing and added to the distraction by jangling the coins in his trouser pocket.

"You're right. We have had this conversation before. And, as I've told you before, the reason the class is in demand is because with only thirty students, they not only get individual attention, but the opportunity to work with several patients at the clinic."

"If you refuse to add more students to the existing class, then add another class," he said.

"No, I'm not adding another class. You teach the other Psych 408 class, and you know how hard it is to schedule time at the clinic, especially when *you* have up to fifty students in *your* class."

"Dr. Wing," he said, his voice rising and the pacing getting faster…

"Dr. Brewer," Elizabeth interrupted, "I think our discussion is over." *No way do I intend to let him yell at me with a group of students waiting outside his door.* "I will not accept any more students into my class, lower my standards, or add another class. You have students waiting, and I have a class to teach." She stood up and headed for the door.

"Bitch," she heard him say under his breath as she opened the door.

Did he really say that! Refusing to dignify his statement with a response, she kept walking, but hearing him use that word, she flashed on the phone calls she had been receiving. The voice on the phone usually ended his message by calling her a bitch. She hadn't seriously considered Peter Brewer as the caller, but now, she realized it was possible.

Maybe Detective Gualdoni is right. Maybe I am too close to the whole situation to be able to think clearly about who's capable of harassing me. She thought about other staff at the university who could possibly be considered suspects and came up with no ideas. The calls had started during the summer break so students in her current classes weren't suspect. Last semester she hadn't failed anyone. She couldn't think of any former students who had been unstable, upset with their grades, or angry with her. *Could it really be Peter Brewer?*

Back in her office, she went over the paperwork for each student requesting enrollment in her class. Thirty-two students had fulfilled all of the requirements. Breaking her own rules, she listed all thirty-two names on the final enrollment sheet. *Why am I allowing extra students into my class? Are the harassing phone calls affecting my judgment?* She posted the list on her office door and sent a copy to administration. Then she divided the class into four groups of eight and posted that list. The student groups would work together for the semester, critiquing each other during clinic sessions. But even as she did this she questioned her own reasons.

Hurrying to class, she made a mental note to tell Detective Gualdoni about the incident with Peter Brewer. *I know he doesn't like me, but would he really make those calls?*

CHAPTER NINE

Elizabeth usually stayed in her office at the university after class to prepare for the following weeks classes, but today, thinking that Peter Brewer could be the man stalking her, she felt ill at ease sitting there alone.

She didn't want to think about Peter or whoever was doing this to her, and she didn't want to think about what he might do next. She knew that the best way to forget about her problems was to immerse herself in work, preferably helping someone else. At the Rape Crisis Center, there were always women who needed private counseling. *At the crisis center, I won't be alone.*

"I'm so glad you're here," Barbara, the director of the center, said as Elizabeth entered the shabby government office. "We have a new client who could really use an individual session, if you have time. One of our counselors was with her at the hospital last night, and this morning, the reality of what happened set in."

"Of course I have time. I have the whole afternoon. Which office is open?"

"Remember the Women's Club you spoke to last month? They gave us a generous donation. We were able to fix up the back office. You'll be the first to use it."

The director walked Elizabeth to the office, smiled, and opened the door. The room had been painted a cheery yellow; new curtains hung at the windows instead of the battered old Venetian blinds; the worn-out government-issue metal furniture had been replaced with a new bookcase and desk, and a couch and chairs had been added to the room.

"This looks fantastic. Schedule me for a few more speaking engagements. Maybe we can get the whole clinic redecorated."

"I already have. You next performance is the first week in October," the director said, grinning. "By the way, our next volunteer training will be that week as well; can you fit them both into your schedule?"

"I'd be glad to. Call Joanne with the dates and times. She's a whiz at arranging my appointments."

Training of both staff and volunteers was an important part of Elizabeth's responsibilities at the clinic. Burnout, especially among the volunteers, caused many women to discontinue their work at the center. A poorly trained volunteer could easily become overwhelmed witnessing the intensity of pain the victims experience. Part of the training covered the necessity for debriefing after spending hours in the emergency room or in court with a victim.

Elizabeth spent the next two hours with the center's newest rape victim. Kelly, a seventeen-year-old high school senior, had been attacked and brutally raped about seven-thirty the previous night on her way home from her job. It had still been light when she started to walk home and she thought it would be safe to take a shortcut. She'd been found several hours later hovering in some bushes near the entrance to the park, her clothes torn and bloody. The police called the Rape Crisis Center after they took her to the hospital. *A woman can't even walk alone in the park. At every talk, I tell them not to be alone in isolated places, but I do it all the time and I know better. I've got to be more careful.*

As difficult as it was to hear the pain these women shared with her, Elizabeth was drawn to working with this population. She connected with them emotionally and often cried with them during sessions, unlike the patients in her private practice where she tried to remain neutral to their emotional trauma. She didn't understand this connection; it had to be more than being a woman herself or her training as a therapist.

Two more women Elizabeth had seen on previous occasions came in for follow-up sessions and filled the afternoon hours. *Working with rape victims is as therapeutic for me as it is for the victims.* Four and a half hours after Elizabeth arrived at the center, she closed the door to the counseling room. She hadn't thought about her own problems at all. Seeing a light on in Barbara's office, Elizabeth stopped to say good night.

"Working late tonight?" Elizabeth asked as she paused at Barbara's door.

"I'm afraid so. You look tired, tough session?"

"No worse than usual," Elizabeth said, trying to sound casual. *I don't want Barbara to worry about me and my problems, she's got enough on her mind.* "What are you working on?"

"Just routine reports. We didn't get a grant I'd been counting on and without the extra funds for an administrative assistant I need to take on more of the paperwork."

"How much was the grant?" Elizabeth asked. *Money. Everything is always about money.*

"Well, I'd been hoping for fifteen thousand dollars. That would cover a part-time position with a little left over for supplies. There's another grant pending, but it doesn't look good."

"I think I know someone who'd be willing to make a donation to the center. She's been looking into several charities and she's impressed with your work here at the clinic."

"That would be a miracle. Let me know what information this person needs and I'll prepare it."

"I can tell her anything she needs to know. Don't worry about the money. Put your energy into helping the women."

"You're an angel, Elizabeth. You've done so much for us. It's people like you who make our work possible," Barbara said as Elizabeth left her office.

The parking lot behind the crisis center was well lit. In the past, Elizabeth had never been worried about the short walk to her car. But tonight, feeling like she was being watched, she listened intently for footsteps, looked over her shoulder to see if there was anyone around, and hurried to unlock her car and get safely inside. It wasn't hearing the graphic details of Kelly's ordeal that brought on the uneasy feelings. She'd heard the tragic stories of rape victims before. She knew, in the very depths of her being, that the fear coming from the pit of her stomach was caused by the reality that she too was now a victim.

The strength these women showed after experiencing such traumatic events amazed her. She wondered if she'd be able to give such explicit details, go through the rape examination, testify in a courtroom filled with people, and worst of all, face the rapist.

Shaking off the eerie feelings as she drove home, she concentrated on how she could be of further help to the center. She already volunteered at least eight hours a week. Financial assistance; what they really need is money! *I've got money. More than I need. Probably more than I'll ever spend, but I don't want Barbara to know it comes from me.* Donating the money without Barbara and the staff at the center knowing that it came from her could be arranged if the money came from one of her trust funds. Her grandparents had each left her a considerable amount, the contribution could easily come from one of the accounts without her name appearing on the check. *I'll call my accountant first thing in the morning.*

CHAPTER TEN

Elizabeth opened her eyes with a start. Something didn't seem right. The red numbers glowed from the clock on her nightstand, 5:00 A. M. The early morning light cast shadows across her bed. Feeling uneasy, she listened for sounds that may have awakened her. She heard nothing. *No point in trying to go back to sleep, I might as well get an early start on my day.*

In the kitchen, she brewed a pot of coffee. Retrieving the paper from her front step, she sat at the kitchen table and skimmed the front page while she waited for her morning dose of caffeine to work its magic. Because Detective Gualdoni felt it might be dangerous, she no longer jogged in the morning. Although she had a treadmill, Elizabeth considered it a poor substitute for her run so she skipped her workout and headed for the shower.

Thoughts of her day, and the weekend ahead, milled through her mind as she dressed for work. *No classes at the university. A short day with patients. I should call Carol and see if she can do an early dinner.* The stalker had shaken her self-confidence more than she cared to admit. She fought off the fears that remembering the phone calls and pictures aroused in her.

As she left her bedroom, she glanced toward her dresser. *The picture...where was it?* Her father had given her a picture he had taken of her with her mother just before she left for college twelve years ago. The photograph, in an antique silver frame, always sat on her dresser. Walking back into the room, she looked all around the dresser. It hadn't fallen on the floor and it wasn't anywhere else in the room. The picture was gone! The cleaning lady hadn't been at the house in over a week. If she had moved it, Elizabeth would have noticed it before this. She looked around the room again. *Everything else seems to be in its proper place.* She checked her jewelry box. *Nothing missing.* The uneasy feeling that she had experienced when she woke earlier this morning returned. Her stomach tightened, and an involuntary shiver went through her body.

Hurriedly, she went through the house checking each room. Nothing else seemed out of place. As she walked by the guest bathroom near the front door, a smudge on the mirror caught her eye. *What's that?*

Flipping on the light switch, she looked into the seldom-used powder room. Scribbled across the mirror, in bright red lipstick, the word B I T C H looked back at her. A tube of her own lipstick lay on the counter. She stood motionless. Then, terrified, she ran to the phone and punched in the number to the police department.

When Detective Gualdoni arrived a few minutes later, Elizabeth was still upset. Her hands trembled as she poured him a cup of coffee and her voice quivered as she spoke.

"Dr. Wing, did you have the alarm system turned on?"

"I think so. Yes, I'm sure I turned it on before I went out yesterday."

"How about last night? Did you have it turned on last night?" he questioned.

"My God! Do you think he came into my room while I was sleeping?"

"It's possible."

"No, it's not possible. I'm sure I would have heard him."

Elizabeth's whole body began to tremble.

"I feel violated," Elizabeth said more to herself than to Gualdoni.

"I want you out of here," Detective Gualdoni said, taking charge. He walked her out onto the back patio. "Your house may be bugged," he said quietly. "Is there somewhere you can go for the weekend? A friend you can stay with?"

"I have a beach house in Laguna. I can go there."

"I don't think it's a good idea for you to go alone. Do you have a friend who could go with you?

"I can go alone. Very few people know I have a house at the beach. I'll be fine."

"Absolutely not! Either you find a friend or I'm sending police protection with you."

"I'll ask Tim if he can join me after he finishes with patients."

"Someone other than Tim Henderson," Gualdoni said emphatically.

"Tim wouldn't do this to me. I know Tim."

"Well, I don't," Detective Gualdoni replied in a cold voice.

"I'll call my friend Carol. Maybe she can go with me."

Still on the patio, Elizabeth used Gualdoni's cell phone in case her phone line had been bugged and called her office. Without telling Joanne any of the details she asked her to cancel all of today's appointments. Then she phoned Carol and briefly explained what had happened and asked her to spend the weekend with her at the beach. Following Gualdoni's instructions, Elizabeth packed a few things and checked the house again to see if anything else was missing or out of place.

"While you're gone, we'll check for any sign of forced entry. See if we can figure out how this guy got in. I'll have the place dusted for prints, too," Detective Gualdoni added.

"I can't believe this is happening to me," Elizabeth said.

"If this man is watching you, we don't want him to follow you to Laguna." Gualdoni proceeded to instruct Elizabeth on how they would cover her tracks. "Drive your car to the police station, I'll follow you. I think he'll back off if he sees you're in police protection but we won't take any chances. I'll arrange for a rental car for you to drive for the weekend."

Elizabeth couldn't seem to stop her hands from shaking. She'd never felt so afraid or out of control in her life. A few hours later, as planned, Carol met Elizabeth at the Long Beach Police Station.

When both of their cars had been stored in the police impound lot, Elizabeth and Carol headed south on Pacific Coast Highway for Laguna Beach, driving the rental car arranged by Gualdoni. It took longer than the freeway but Elizabeth had always found the scenic route along the coast to be more relaxing.

"Thanks so much for helping me out, Carol. I hope Andrew doesn't mind you going away for the weekend?"

"My pleasure. You know I love Laguna. I'm glad you called me. As for Andrew, it will do him good to be alone once in a while. Do you have any clues as to who might be doing this? Is it one of your patients?"

"I don't know. Detective Gualdoni has been working on the case all week but so far we really don't have any idea who's doing it."

"That detective of yours is pretty good looking. I didn't see a wedding ring; is he single? Has he asked you out yet?" Carol teased.

"Our relationship is strictly business. I haven't asked him about his personal life."

"Everything is business with you. Gualdoni, sounds Italian to me. A tall, handsome Italian and you don't even know if he's single? You're slipping, Liz, you should find out if he's available. It's time you started having some fun. First school and now your practice; give yourself a break."

"When the right man comes along I'll know it."

"He'll walk right by if you don't open your eyes and look."

"I guess you're right, but this doesn't seem like a good time to start dating somebody, if you know what I mean," Elizabeth added.

It was late afternoon when they arrived at the house in Laguna. Quickly, they changed into their bathing suits and headed for the beach, hoping the water would still be warm enough for a swim. They played in the surf for over an hour, the ocean briefly wiping away the fears and concerns that had plagued Elizabeth for weeks. Back at the house, they dressed in casual outfits and walked into town. They hoped they could get a table on the patio at the Hotel Laguna for dinner.

Cash ordered another round of drinks and waited. From the bar, they were able to watch the customers sitting on the patio and entering the dining room.

"What makes you think she'll be here?" Squirrel asked again.

"When she leaves town she comes to Laguna Beach."

"Laguna's got lots of restaurants. Why this one?"

"Trust me. She'll be here. She always comes here when she's in Laguna."

"Have you followed her here before?"

Impatient with Squirrel's questions, Cash downed his beer. "Yeah, I've followed her here before. Now shut up." He slapped a twenty on the bar and motioned to the bartender for another round. *They sat in silence, drinking their beers and watching the crowd.*

"Look, out there on the patio. I see her," Cash said, nudging Squirrel.

"Where?" Squirrel asked, shading his eyes from the glare of the sun bouncing off the ocean.

"Over by the railing. Behind that group of people that are just leaving."

"Yeah, I see her. Look at her hair. It's even prettier than last night when it was spread out on her pillow."

"I told you she'd be here," Cash said, ignoring his friend's comment.

"Liz, you should be sitting here on the patio watching the sunset with a date."

"Don't start that again," Elizabeth said.

"I mean it; you should have a man in your life. I love coming to the beach with you, it's a real treat for me, but..."

"But nothing. Relationships take time. Besides, we're old friends. I like being with you."

"I like being with you too, but it's time for you to get a new man in your life and forget about Daniel."

"What makes you think my ex-husband is still on my mind?"

"Because you're a romantic. You think he'll come back and sweep you off your feet. Tell you he never should have left. Liz, he was never right for you. You just couldn't see it back then."

"And you could?" Elizabeth asked.

"We all could. Especially Tim."

"Carol, Tim had eyes for you back then."

"Tim's never been interested in me, but he's like a little puppy around you."

Anxious to take the focus off herself, Elizabeth changed the subject. "What about you and Andrew? When are you two going to tie the knot?"

"I'm an artist and so is Andrew. We've always been unconventional. We may never get married but that works for us. It wouldn't work for you."

"Maybe one of these days I'll meet someone. I'm in no hurry," Elizabeth said.

They sat quietly for a while as the sun dropped out of sight behind Santa Catalina Island. For dinner they had both chosen baked sea bass with a mango salsa. It had been served with fresh asparagus and garlic mashed potatoes.

"What a delicious dinner," Carol commented.

Lingering over coffee, Elizabeth had to agree. But as she sat there her thoughts drifted back to Frank Gualdoni. *I wonder if he is single.* She had never considered dating him, but she had to agree with Carol's comment earlier in the day; he was good looking.

Romantic music floated out onto the patio as the band began to play. Couples started to dance, the bar filled with people waiting to be seated in the dining room. They left the hotel and headed down the hill toward Main Beach. The streets were getting crowded with more people arriving for the weekend.

Carol and Elizabeth sat on a bench along the boardwalk and watched as Laguna came alive. Teens played volleyball in the sand, children begged to go higher as their parents pushed them on swings. White phosphorescent surf beat against the sand, the roar of the waves drowning out the sound of the cars as they inched along Pacific Coast Highway. The full moon shone high and left its path on the dark blue ocean waters. On the horizon, the lights of a cruise ship could be seen as it headed south. The magic of Laguna was all around them.

"We should do this more often, Carol. I love being in Laguna." *Tonight I will sleep. Here in my most favorite place, known only to my closest friends, I feel safe and I will sleep. There'll be no nightmares tonight.*

Chapter Eleven

Elizabeth awoke to the sounds of the ocean roaring gently in the distance, as waves beat against rugged rocks jutting out along the coastline. She stretched and opened her eyes. The bright orange glow of the morning sun painted a mural across the wall and onto the ceiling. The aroma of freshly brewed coffee drifted into the room. She lay peacefully absorbing the new morning, but the reason she was in Laguna crept slowly into her consciousness. *I'm hiding, not on a weekend vacation.*

Climbing out of bed and putting on sweats, the smell of coffee lured her into the kitchen. She stopped long enough to pour herself a cup and then, mug in hand, she walked out onto the porch where Carol sat on the steps, sketching.

"Good morning, sleepyhead," Carol teased, looking up from her sketchpad.

"Thanks for making the coffee," Elizabeth replied. She sipped the hot liquid watching her friend continue to draw. "I'm going for a run on the beach."

"Do you think you should go alone?" Carol asked, concern apparent in her voice. "I could come with you."

"Carol, you hate to run. Stay here and sketch." Elizabeth finished her coffee and put her mug on the steps. "I won't be long," she called over her shoulder as she jogged down the hill toward the beach.

It had been over an hour when Carol, sketchbook in hand, headed for the beach as well. In the distance Elizabeth walked slowly along the shore, a stray dog playfully dancing at her heels. She picked up a piece of driftwood and tossed it into the water. The dog eagerly ran into the surf to retrieve it. A few minutes later, Elizabeth reached the spot where Carol sat sketching. Dropping to the sand, she sat down next to her.

"Sorry I took so long. It felt so good to be running on the beach again that I ran all the way to the point."

"I was beginning to get worried that…"

"Carol, you promised you wouldn't talk about the stalker," Elizabeth interrupted.

"Okay, okay."

The two women sat in silence for a few minutes watching sailboats glide through the gentle waves.

"I've always loved Laguna," Elizabeth murmured.

"When we were in college, we used to come down here and study whenever your grandfather would give you the key," Carol reminisced.

"It's a wonder we ever graduated. Our idea of studying was to relax in the sun, listen to music, and share a bottle of wine," Elizabeth added, watching a sailboat disappear over the horizon.

"Did you ever wonder why your grandfather left you this place?" Carol asked.

"He knew I loved it in Laguna as much as he did. Besides, I used the beach house more than anyone else."

"What about your cousin Eric? He used to come down here and party with his friends."

"Grandfather didn't much like his lifestyle," Elizabeth replied, a hardness in her voice.

"What is it with you and Eric?" Carol asked.

"I don't much like him. He teased me unmercifully when I was a kid. He wanted to date my friends when I was in college, and the last I heard he failed his latest attempt at drug rehab."

"Did I ever tell you that I had a crush on him back then?"

"You've got to be kidding! Eric?" Elizabeth asked.

"I was only nineteen," Carol replied defensively. "Didn't you ever have a crush on an older man?"

"Oh, I had more than a crush. I dated an older man."

"You never told me about it. When did it happen?"

"The summer before I moved to California," Elizabeth replied.

"Someone in Europe? Who was it?"

"His name was Miguel and we broke up when I left Spain. He was history by the time we became best friends."

"You've got to tell me all about him."

"I'd just turned eighteen and he was thirty. He was a friend of my parents and a real Latin lover. I'd seen him at several parties and he always asked me to dance. He was gorgeous and I felt so grown up with him."

"And your parents let you date him?"

"Not exactly. When I graduated from high school, I planned to stay in Spain for the summer since I'd be moving to L.A. in the fall for college. Previous summers, I'd visited my grandparents in California. Two friends who'd graduated with me were going to spend the summer traveling in Italy and they asked me to join them. When I told my parents I wanted to travel with my friends, they were concerned. That's when Miguel stepped in. He told my parents not to worry, he planned to travel to Italy himself that summer and he would look out for us. My parents agreed to the trip because he said he would be nearby if we had any problems. Miguel invited my friends and me to start off our trip spending a week with him at his villa on Costa del Sol. My parents thought that was a great idea. I don't think they ever dreamed that he actually meant *with* him."

"Don't stop now. What happened?" Carol urged.

"The first night at Miguel's villa, he invited two of his friends to join us. He served a gourmet dinner, fabulous wine, and made it very apparent that I was his date, and as they say, 'The rest is history.'"

"Oh no you don't. You've got to tell me everything that happened. This is a side of you I've never seen."

"Carol, some things are private."

"Come on, Liz, don't leave me hanging. What happened?"

"My friends were happy having escorts and the six of us spent two weeks on the coast of Spain. I fell madly in love. I'd been a virgin when I arrived but by the end of the first week, my status had changed. Miguel was gentle, romantic, and very experienced. He was my first love. I doubt if I will ever forget him. I know I've never regretted it, and I've never been with anyone whose lovemaking could, shall I say, compare."

"Wow! Liz, I met you that fall and you never even mentioned him."

"As I said, some things are private."

"Why did it end?"

"After two weeks in Spain, my friends left the villa and traveled on to the French Riviera and then to Italy. My parents didn't know that I traveled to Italy with Miguel, not my friends. It was wonderful for me, but I think Miguel began to realize just how young and naive I really was. He treated me like a princess, showing me off to friends, buying me presents, but he knew that when the holidays were over I'd be leaving for the States and he'd be back at his job. He needed a wife, or a companion, who was sophisticated, mature, someone who could entertain with him. I didn't fit the image, at least not then. He said he loved me, but the timing was all wrong. I grew up a lot that summer, and I'll be forever grateful for the experience."

"That's so sad. Did you ever hear from him again?"

"He wrote me brief notes while I was in college. He'd mention people that I knew; tell me about the parties he'd attended, that sort of thing. When he heard from my parents that I had married Daniel, he sent me a short note. He sounded angry, or hurt. I got the impression from the note that he was waiting for me to finish college and come back to Spain, and to him."

"Did he ever marry? Does he know your marriage didn't work, that you're divorced?"

"I don't know. My parents mention him from time to time. That he asks about me, that sort of thing."

"Did your parents ever find out about the affair?"

"No. I'm sure they would have said something if they knew."

"I can't believe you never told me about him."

"When I came to L.A. I needed to forget about Miguel and concentrate on my studies. I became engrossed in college life and, worked hard at getting good grades. It was a wonderful affair, but I needed to move on."

"And move on you did. You buried yourself in schoolwork, had a disastrous, and very short, marriage, and now you work all the time. It's time for you to find another 'Miguel' to win your heart; Daniel certainly didn't do it."

The two women sat in silence again, each in their own thoughts. The waves gently lapped against the shore; finally, Carol broke the silence.

"I'm starving. Let's go into town and have one of those wonderful omelets at the Cottage."

After breakfast, Elizabeth and Carol visited the latest exhibit at the museum, a one-man show by a local artist who Carol loved. Before returning to the beach house, they wandered through several shops, browsing but not buying. The remainder of the afternoon they swam, relaxed in the sun, and talked, two old friends enjoying their weekend in Laguna. Elizabeth had to admit she needed to do this more often. Her life had been focused on work for too long.

"Where shall we go for dinner?" Elizabeth asked.

"I feel like Mexican food. How about Las Brisas?"

"Sounds good to me. I'll call for reservations."

They decided to drive rather than walk to dinner and after circling the block a couple of times, gave up trying to find a parking space and valet parked.

Inside the restaurant they sat by the window overlooking the coastline. They ordered margaritas and munched on tortilla chips with guacamole and salsa while they scanned the menu trying to decide on an entrée. Elizabeth heard a familiar voice and looked up but she didn't recognize anyone in front of her.

"I know that voice. The man sitting at the table behind me," she whispered to Carol. "What does he look like?"

Looking over Elizabeth's shoulder, Carol attempted to describe the man facing her. "Early to mid-thirties, light brown hair, wire-rim glasses, slender, he might be tall, his two front teeth overlap slightly."

Elizabeth listened intently to the voice behind her. "Oh, no," she whispered again.

"Oh, no, what?"

"Can you see who he's with?"

"Another man. Looks like he may be younger."

"Just my luck. It's got to be Peter Brewer. I come to Laguna to get away and run into someone I know," Elizabeth lamented.

When Peter Brewer left the restaurant, he walked past Elizabeth's table, nodded, and gave her a condescending smile.

"I guess he didn't want to talk to you either," Carol commented. "Do you know who the guy was with him?"

"No, and it was obvious he didn't want to stop and introduce him."

Elizabeth relaxed once Peter had gone. She and Carol enjoyed their dinner of shrimp fajitas that were served on sizzling platters, listened to the mariachi music, and topped off their meal with a delicious flan.

"I'm stuffed," Carol said as they left the restaurant.

"Me too, but how often do we get to do this? I'll have to run twice as far tomorrow to make up for it."

The weekend came to an end all too quickly and when Andrew arrived to pick up Carol on Sunday afternoon, they all planned to meet at the beach house the following Friday. Elizabeth promised she would invite Tim to join them.

"What time are you leaving, Liz?" Carol asked.

"Soon. One more run on the beach and then I'm on my way."

"Do you think you should?"

"Don't worry so much, Carol. I'll be fine."

"Liz, promise you'll call me when you get home."

"Okay, okay I promise. Now you two get going before traffic gets any worse. You have a much longer drive than I do. See you both next weekend." Elizabeth waved as her friends drove away, then ran towards the beach. A run before watching the sun set and she, too, would be on the road.

When Andrew turned onto the 405 freeway Carol looked at him. "We should have stayed. We shouldn't have left her alone."

"You heard her, she said she'd be fine and she'll call us when she gets home," Andrew replied, and he continued driving towards L.A.

At eight that evening Carol began to worry. She hadn't heard from Elizabeth and there was no answer when she phoned her house. By nine she was frantic. She tried Elizabeth's home, cell phone, the beach house, and her office. The office line had a message saying Tim was on call, but when she tried to reach him, she could only reach his voice mail. In desperation, she called Detective Gualdoni and left a message. Shortly after ten he returned her call.

"This is Detective Gualdoni returning..."

Before he could finish the sentence, Carol interrupted him. "Detective, this is Carol, Elizabeth Wing's friend. I'm worried about her."

Carol explained to the detective that they had left earlier than Elizabeth and that she had promised to contact them when she arrived home.

"Thanks for calling me," Gualdoni stated briskly. "I'll check it out."

When Gualdoni heard that Elizabeth had not called her friend, he was worried about her as well. He had a bad feeling about this case. Calls to both her residence and cell phone were not answered. The number Carol gave him for the beach house didn't answer either. He tried to reach Dr. Tim Henderson and finally got through to his answering service. After being told that Tim was at the hospital with an emergency, he left a message that he needed to be contacted as soon as possible. Then he called and requested that a patrol car check out Elizabeth's residence. There were no real leads on the case, and now the victim was missing. He didn't like the way things looked.

At 3:00 A. M., when the call from Tim Henderson finally reached him, Gualdoni had gone through a pot of coffee, a half a pack of cigarettes (even though he'd stopped smoking over a year ago), and every bit of paperwork he had on the case.

"Detective, my service said it was important that I call you. What's up?"

"Do you know where Elizabeth is?"

"She went to Laguna on Friday. I haven't heard from her since. Why?"

"Elizabeth never made it home. Carol called me earlier; we don't know where she is. I thought you might know."

"Oh, God," Tim whispered into the phone. "I have no idea. Did you try to reach her in Laguna? Maybe she stayed there for the night."

"I tried. There's no answer."

Sunday night Cash waited in the hotel room for Squirrel. It was late; Squirrel should be here by now, he thought, as he drank another glass of bourbon. He looked out the window for the third time but saw no sign of his friend.

"*Man, it was bitchin','" Squirrel blurted out as he burst into the room.*

"Where the hell have you been?" Cash demanded.

"She went running just like you said she would," Squirrel said, ignoring Cash's question. "She is so beautiful. I followed her for a while but she didn't notice me. Her hair was in a ponytail, swinging back and forth as she ran. I got real close; so close I could smell her. I reached out and grabbed her hair. She started to turn so I hit her. Not very hard. I swear I didn't hit her hard but she fell down."

"What the fuck do you mean, you hit her?" Cash yelled.

"Well, she started to turn around. You said not to let her see me."

"Did she see you?" Cash asked as he started measuring out the cocaine Squirrel had brought with him.

"No. She was out of it. You know, unconscious or something."

"Unconscious? You stupid fool! What'd you hit her with?"

"Just my hand. I didn't mean to knock her out."

"Then what happened?"

"I nudged her with my foot but she didn't move. We were near the water so I pulled her by her arm up onto the beach so she wouldn't get wet. I kicked her a little harder but she still didn't wake up."

"You didn't kick her hard enough to really hurt her did you?" Cash asked, starting to get concerned. This was a mistake. Sometimes Squirrel got a little out of control.

"No. Why would I want to hurt her?"

"Then why'd you hit her so hard?" Cash asked again.

"I didn't mean to."

"What happened next?" Cash asked as he snorted a line and passed the mirror to Squirrel.

"She looked so beautiful, her red hair against the white sand. I wanted to fuck her."

"You what?" Cash yelled.

"I didn't. I couldn't fuck her if she wouldn't wake up." Squirrel opened up an envelope and dumped out the contents. A mass of red curls fell onto the table and Squirrel ran his fingers through them. "I couldn't resist that pony tail so I pulled out my knife and cut it off."

"You weren't supposed to hurt her, just scare her. What were you snortin' to hurt her like that?" Cash asked accusingly.

"I wasn't snortin'! I smoked a couple of joints, that's all."

"I don't believe you!" Cash yelled.

"Okay. I popped some E. What's the big deal?"

"Ecstasy! Why the hell did you do that?"

Cash put his head in his hands. Oh God. This had gone too far. The game didn't seem like fun anymore.

Tick, tick, tick, click. Tick, tick, tick, click. *What's that noise?* Tick, tick, tick, click. Tick, tick, tick, click. *What is that irritating noise?*

Muffled footsteps, hushed voices, rubber wheels, muted by carpeted floors, squeaking as they rolled along the hallway...*Where am I?*

Elizabeth struggled to open her eyes. A dim light shone through a maze of white gauze. She tried to raise her arm, move the gauze to see more clearly, but pain radiated from her shoulder and down her arm. She tried to turn her head, more pain. The voices came closer, then moved away again. Tick, tick, tick, click. Tick, tick, tick, click. The IV machine sang to her as she drifted back into darkness...

"Good morning. Can you hear me?"

Somewhere from the darkness, Elizabeth heard someone speaking to her. She tried to respond but she couldn't seem to form the words.

"I'm Dr. McCormick. You're at South Coast Medical Center in Laguna. The police brought you in last night."

She opened her eyes and tried to focus on the figure standing before her. A hand gently moved the bandages away from her eyes and the face of a man standing next to her bed came into view.

"I'm Dr. McCormick," he repeated. "Can you tell me your name?"

"Elizabeth," she whispered. It hurt to talk. "Elizabeth...Wing."

"Elizabeth, is there family I can call for you?"

"What happened to me?"

"The police brought you in last night. You'd been beaten," the doctor replied. "Is there someone I can call?" he asked again.

"No," she whispered, then, as an afterthought, "Yes, call...Detective... Frank Gualdoni...Long Beach Police."

"Rest now, Elizabeth. I'll be back a little later."

The man with the soft voice and gentle hands moved away from her bed. She moved her head, trying to follow him with her eyes, but the pain engulfed her and she drifted back into darkness.

CHAPTER TWELVE

"Detective Gualdoni, this is Dr. McCormick at South Coast Medical Center in Laguna Beach. The police found a woman on the beach last night. This morning, when she regained consciousness, she told me her name is Elizabeth Wing and she asked me to call you."

"Is she okay?"

"Her condition is stable but she was badly beaten. Are you a relative?"

"No. I'm the detective on her case. Someone has been stalking her."

"Well, it looks like he found her."

"I'll be there as soon as I can. Thanks for calling."

Frank Gualdoni slammed the phone down. "Damn it!" he said out loud to no one in particular.

Heading for Laguna Beach, he couldn't help but wonder what had gone wrong with the plan. *How had the stalker found her in Laguna?* The morning traffic seemed heavier than usual. Impatient to get to the hospital he pounded the steering wheel and cursed at the traffic, all to no avail. The doctor had given him very little information on Elizabeth's condition and he was anxious to find out what injuries she had sustained. It had only been a week, but already he had grown fond of this woman. Elizabeth Wing intrigued him. He'd never met a woman quite like her: successful, bright, beautiful, self-assured, and very charming. This case was more than an assignment, it was becoming personal.

Both as a courtesy, and to obtain more information about the case, Gualdoni stopped at the Laguna Beach Police Department. Briefly, the officer who had been called to the scene gave him what little information they had been able to gather. The crime scene gave them no clues. Anything that may have been present had been washed away with the tide. Late Sunday night, a 911 call had alerted them to a body lying on a deserted stretch of beach. When the police arrived, they found a woman unconscious and badly beaten. She had been taken to South Coast Medical Center, seen in the emergency room, and then admitted. She carried no identification and there had been no calls for a missing person. Gualdoni provided the officer with her name and address, informed him of the ongoing case pertaining to this woman, asked for directions to the hospital, and quickly left.

When Gualdoni arrived at the hospital, he paged Dr. McCormick for an update on Elizabeth's condition.

"Take it easy on her," Dr. McCormick advised. "She's not in very good shape. Interesting thing, whoever did this, could have killed her, but he didn't. It looks like he wanted to hurt her, teach her a lesson, or make her suffer."

"Someone's been stalking Dr. Wing for a month or more," Gualdoni said.

"She's a doctor?" McCormick asked.

"A psychologist. We've been checking out her patients, friends, everyone she would give us information about. So far we have nothing concrete."

Dr. McCormick escorted him down the hall toward Elizabeth's room. "Just a few questions, please. She needs to rest. There'll be plenty of time to question her later. I expect she'll be with us for a few days."

When Detective Gualdoni walked into Elizabeth's darkened room, he could hardly believe what he saw. The strong, self-confident woman he met just one week ago had been transformed. Lying in the hospital bed, her head bandaged, she looked like a fragile porcelain doll. Battered and bruised, one arm in a sling, the other connected to an IV, his heart went out to her.

"Elizabeth," he whispered. "It's Frank Gualdoni."

She opened her eyes and looked up at him. At that moment, he vowed he would do whatever it took to find the man who had done this.

"Did you see who attacked you?" Frank asked.

She answered with a raspy whisper, "No."

"Did you see anyone? Hear anything?"

Again she whispered, "No."

"Did anything unusual happen over the weekend?"

"No," she sighed.

"Why were you alone? Why did you stay after Carol left?"

Before Elizabeth could answer, Dr. McCormick came back into the room. "Enough questions for now."

"Can this hospital provide the best possible treatment?" Gualdoni asked, hoping his question wouldn't offend the doctor.

"We could transfer her to the trauma center at Mission Hospital but a neurologist has checked her head injury, and an orthopedist went over the x-rays of her shoulder, ribs, back, and ankle; we can handle it here."

"What about UCLA Medical Center?"

"No," a shaky voice from across the room interrupted. "I...want...to stay...here."

Surprised that Elizabeth had heard their discussion, Gualdoni moved out into the hall with the doctor.

"Money is no problem. Give her whatever she needs. Put her in the best room you've got, one with a nice view. Hire a private nurse, and I'll be putting an officer outside her door; this man might try again and I want her protected."

Money is no problem. Whatever made me say that? From the look of her house and office she must be doing okay, but who am I to make these decisions?

When Detective Gualdoni got back to the city, he went directly to Elizabeth Wing's office. He wanted to see Tim Henderson's face when he told him about the attack. For several hours last night no one had been able to contact him, Gualdoni wondered just where he had been.

Dr. Henderson and Joanne were both at the office when he arrived. As soon as he walked through the door, Tim started questioning him.

"Have you found Elizabeth?" Tim asked. He looked tired and concerned.

"Yes. I've just come from South Coast Hospital in Laguna."

"Hospital? Is she okay?"

"A Dr. McCormick called me this morning. He told me she was admitted last night. She's in pretty bad shape. Somebody beat the crap out of her."

Joanne started to cry but it was Tim's reaction that interested Frank.

"Detective, get the bastard who did this to Liz," Tim said through clenched teeth.

At five till seven, Gualdoni pulled into a parking space at South Coast Medical Center for the second time that day, a day that had been very long and unproductive. He had checked out every bit of information Elizabeth had given him regarding patients, students, and friends. Nothing added up. He hoped Elizabeth would be able to speak with him tonight, give him something more to go on. Walking past the gift shop, he stopped, looked over his shoulder as if someone might be watching him, then turned and went in.

"A pack of gum, and aah…that plant over there. The one with all the purple flowers."

What's gotten into me? I've never taken flowers to a crime victim before. But Elizabeth was no longer just another victim. Awkwardly, he carried the flowers down the hall and into the elevator. An officer sat outside Elizabeth's room reading a magazine. Gualdoni flashed his badge and asked if anyone had been here to see her.

"Some doctor's in there now."

Expecting to see Dr. McCormick, Gualdoni entered the room. While Elizabeth slept, Tim Henderson sat by the bed holding her hand and tenderly caressing her fingertips. That morning, when Gualdoni had told Henderson about the attack on Elizabeth, Tim had appeared shaken and angry. Now, as he looked up and his eyes met Gualdoni's, there was no mistaking the love and concern in his eyes. At that moment, Gualdoni knew Tim Henderson had not done this to Elizabeth. He loved her.

Gualdoni looked around the room for a place to put the plant. The dresser held a bouquet of long-stemmed red roses, the nightstand overflowed with medical equipment. Silently, he walked to the window, glanced at the fading embers of the sun setting over the Pacific, and put the violets on the ledge.

Maybe Henderson could be of help. "Can we talk?" Gualdoni whispered and beckoned toward the door.

Outside the room, the two men stood awkwardly for a few seconds. "How about some coffee?" Gualdoni suggested.

They headed for the first floor without speaking. Once inside the coffee shop, seated at a small corner table, Gualdoni began his questions.

"Dr. Henderson, Elizabeth hasn't given me much to go on. Can you tell me about her family, friends, anyone who might want to hurt her?"

"She likes to keep her personal life private, but I'll tell you everything I can. Her parents live in Spain. That's where she spent a good deal of her childhood. Her mother has no relatives that I know of. Her father has a sister, married with three kids, but they're not close. Her grandparents are dead and when they died Elizabeth's inheritance was considerably more than the other grandchildren. I think there were some hard feelings at the time."

"Well, I guess that could cause some family problems," Gualdoni commented. "Are we talking about a lot of money?"

"Yes. Elizabeth once told me that she didn't have to work; there's a couple of trust funds, and as I understand it, she could live off the interest on her investments if she wanted to. I think that's true of the other grandchildren as well."

"Do you know why Elizabeth received the biggest piece of the pie?" Gualdoni questioned.

"Not really. But I think it had something to do with Elizabeth's drive, her work ethics. They all received sizeable trusts, but Elizabeth is the only one who chose to have a career, do something with her life. I think her grandparents wanted to reward her for her accomplishments; that, and she was her grandfather's favorite."

"Wow! Who was this guy?"

"Her grandfather was Edward Worthington of the Worthington Development Company and the law firm of Worthington & Associates. Her father and his sister are the primary shareholders. There's plenty of money to go around."

"Okay, who else is there that she may not have mentioned?" Gualdoni continued.

"Did she tell you about Daniel?"

"Her ex-husband. Yes, but he's still in Mexico. I checked with the pharmaceutical company he works for."

"How about Peter Brewer? She probably wouldn't say anything against him, but the two of them have had an ongoing feud for several years."

"He's on her list of colleagues. What's their connection?" Gualdoni asked.

"Dr. Brewer chairs the psychology department at the university. When the position opened up a couple of years ago, he really wanted it. It would have been a close call but Elizabeth didn't want it, so it went to him. Then he started pressuring her to date him. She'd heard rumors of his affairs with graduate students and she wouldn't even consider dating him. They barely speak now."

"Is he capable of hurting her like this?" Gualdoni asked.

"Capable, oh yes. But I don't think it's his style. He'd rather put her on the spot at faculty meetings, embarrass her in front of the other professors."

"Tell me more about her ex-husband."

"Not much to tell. Daniel wanted the divorce. It suited his needs." Tim said sarcastically. "He's always been very...selfish. His needs came first. They probably still do. Besides, I thought you said he was in Mexico?"

"He could have hired someone to do the dirty work for him."

"I don't think so. Even though they're divorced, I think Daniel still loves her in his own way. He just wasn't willing to make any compromises to stay married."

The two men sat drinking their coffee. Finally, Gualdoni broke the silence.

"Dr. Henderson, thanks for your time. If you can think of anyone else, please call me. Here's my card. In the meantime, I've got to go over every possible bit of information again. Maybe there's something I've missed."

Gualdoni left the coffee shop, mentally adding Dr. Peter Brewer to his list of people to check out and dropping Tim Henderson to the bottom of his list of suspects.

CHAPTER THIRTEEN

Three days after the attack and Gualdoni still had no clue as to the identity of the assailant. If he could only discover why Elizabeth had been the target of the stalker, maybe he could figure out his identity. Sitting at his desk, Frank poured through the paperwork on the case looking for anything he might have missed. The long hours he spent on the case and his driving desire to find the perpetrator caused his co-workers to hassle him about the real reasons for his diligence.

"Hey, Gualdoni, you got the hots for this broad?" Lieutenant Brooks teased as he sauntered past Gualdoni's desk. "You sure are spending a lot of time on this case."

"I spend a lot of time on all my cases," Gualdoni replied through clenched teeth.

"He's obsessed with her. She's a real looker," the detective sitting across from him chimed in.

"You've been on this case for two weeks. You dragging your heels or just losing your touch?" Brooks added.

He was one of the best detectives on the force, he knew it and, furthermore, Brooks knew it. He'd spent his entire career tracking down perps like this one. Comments that the reason he was still working the case had to do with Elizabeth's looks were ridiculous.

Gualdoni refused to consider not giving every minute of his time to finding the man who had attacked Elizabeth, but to pacify his boss he arrived early every morning to handle routine paperwork before driving south to Laguna. He believed that Elizabeth knew her attacker and that the right question would trigger the memory of what happened that night. He just had to figure out what the right question was.

Frustrated by the time he arrived in Laguna, he stood in the corridor outside Elizabeth's hospital room talking quietly with Dr. McCormick. He had expected that once she had regained consciousness, she would be able to identify her attacker, but when she was conscious she was heavily medicated.

"How much longer before she's able to stay alert?" Gualdoni asked McCormick.

"In cases like this, it's hard to tell. Her body needs to rest and heal, and her mind has shut down to allow the body's natural healing abilities to do their job."

Frank paced the corridor with the impatience of an expectant father. Elizabeth's condition concerned him. He could feel himself becoming involved, overly involved in this case. Personal feelings could get in the way at a time when he needed to be thinking with a clear head.

Walking down the hall, Dr. McCormick stopped at the nurses' station. "Let me know if there is any change," he ordered.

As he headed toward the elevator, a nurse called out to him, "Her brother called again. When do you think she'll be able to speak to him?"

"Tell him she's still unconscious. Tell him it will be several days before she can talk on the phone."

The elevator door opened and Dr. McCormick stepped inside, pushed the button, and looked down at the file in his hand. The door started to close but Gualdoni's foot stopped it.

"That phone call, you were talking about Elizabeth, right?"

"Yes, her brother called inquiring about her condition," Dr. McCormick replied.

"She doesn't have a brother. It's got to be the attacker. He's the only one who would be calling."

The doctor looked anxiously at Gualdoni. "How do you want us to handle it?"

"I'll take care of everything. It will take a couple of hours to put a tracer on the line and get a policewoman in here to answer the call, but maybe this time the bastard will make a mistake and we can catch him."

The two men rode down to the first floor together, the doctor puzzled about what would happen next, and Gualdoni excited about a possible lead on the case.

Gualdoni arrived at the office even earlier than usual. He sat and stared at the stack of paperwork on his desk that was growing as out of control as the front lawn of his neglected house. He knew if he didn't complete all of it, Lieutenant Brooks would chew him out. Anxious to get back to Laguna, he hurried through the routine forms needing his attention. He wanted to know how Elizabeth was doing. He wanted to know if the attacker had called the hospital again. He wanted something to go on to help him solve this case. The morning meeting was about to start but he had little interest in hearing about the robberies and car thefts that had taken place during the nightshift. He just wanted to get to Laguna.

"Gualdoni, get in here," Lieutenant Brooks bellowed. "Just because your case lets you lounge at the beach doesn't mean you can ignore roll call."

The sarcastic tone of the lieutenant's voice grated on Frank's nerves. *Hold your temper! Just finish this semester, and I'll be out of here and in law school. In a couple of months, I won't have to deal with Brooks any more.*

Gualdoni walked into the meeting room and sat in the back, barely listening to the officers drone on about their cases.

"Drug bust on Fourth Street...Got the mugger in the park...Found black Mustang in underground parking structure..."

"Hold on," Gualdoni interrupted. "What was that about a black Mustang?"

"Avis reported a black Mustang overdue. We found it in the parking structure connected to the medical building on Long Beach Boulevard. It's in impound; they're dusting it for prints."

"The stalker in my case drove a black Mustang and the victim's office is in that building. Who rented it?" Frank hoped they would have a name, a person he could hunt down.

"The guy used a stolen driver's license and credit card. Sorry."

"I'm going over to impound and check it out," Gualdoni said.

Anxious to follow up on the newest lead, he sat impatiently waiting for the meeting to end. He had to sit through the meeting. Lieutenant Brooks would like any excuse to write him up.

Once out of the meeting, Frank could feel the adrenaline rush at the possibility of finding out the identity of the stalker. At the impound lot, he flashed his badge and walked through the gate looking for the black Mustang. Spotting it still in the garage, he hurried to question the crew before they moved on to another car.

"What'd you find?" he asked, taking out his notebook and pen.

"We just finished logging in the evidence. Some traces of white power, several strands of long red hair, and red stains on the front passenger seat, samples of everything are going to the lab for testing. The results should be ready by tomorrow morning."

"How about fingerprints?" Gualdoni asked.

"Not a one, this guy either wore gloves or wiped everything down very carefully," the evidence crew chief answered.

When Frank heard that no fingerprints had been found anywhere in the car, he was disappointed but not surprised. The creep hadn't left any prints at Elizabeth's home either. This guy was smart, but he'd make a mistake. They all did, and Frank was sure it was only a matter of time before the attacker would make a mistake as well.

Gualdoni went back to his office and talked to the officers working the stolen car case. After going over their notes, he wanted to interview the Avis rental clerk again. He needed a better description, more details. Maybe he could get enough information for a composite drawing.

CHAPTER FOURTEEN

Beverly Moore had been a private duty nurse for many years and she had never seen a patient respond like this. She adjusted the IV, regulating the drip, and checking the needle site for redness and noted that it had been several hours since her patient had used any pain medication. The morphine had been set up to allow Elizabeth to push a button whenever she needed relief from the pain. The nurse watched her patient take slow, but steady breaths; she appeared to be conscious, but not aware of what was happening around her or in any pain.

Being touched, the slightest noise, any movement in the room, disturbed Elizabeth. It took every bit of concentration for her to breathe at a steady pace, allowing her mind to escape from the pain that racked her body. She focused on her breathing, instructing her mind to remember a time and place where she felt safe. Drifting back, back to her childhood...drifting, until a feeling of being very small and safe encompassed her...

Sitting on the floor studying the pattern of the lace tablecloth as the afternoon sun shone through it...feeling the plush carpet warm against her bare legs...she studied the curved legs of the table she sat under as they rested against the carpet like the paws of a kitten...and near her on the floor, the call-button, just beyond her fingertips. The first time she had hidden under the table, she pushed the button not knowing what it was, and her mother had instantly appeared. At dinner parties, her grandmother would push the button with her toe and someone would come to clear the table or bring dessert. Pushing the button always brought help in an instant...She felt safe under the table, warm and safe.

Tim Henderson arrived at the hospital and went directly to Elizabeth's room, only stopping briefly to show his identification to the uniformed police officer outside her door.

"Anyone try to see her?" Tim asked.

"Only the priest."

"Priest! I know Elizabeth and she won't be asking for a priest. Did you tell Detective Gualdoni?"

"No. The priest didn't go in because she was asleep. I didn't think it was important."

"Well, it might be. Tell Gualdoni."

Before going into Elizabeth's room, Tim went back to the nurses' station. He wanted to ask the nurses why a priest had tried to see Elizabeth. When he discovered that it wasn't the usual priest, but a substitute filling in this week, he grew more concerned. Unfortunately, no one could describe him.

"Tell Detective Gualdoni about him, and don't let that priest near Elizabeth," he instructed the nurses.

Tim went back to Elizabeth's room and spoke briefly with the private duty nurse before she went to dinner. Alone, he sat next to Elizabeth's bed beginning his nightly vigil by her side. He paid little attention to the passing of time.

When Detective Gualdoni entered the room, Tim looked up; surprised that darkness now obscured the ocean view. Gualdoni walked over to the window and looked out at the moon rising over the hills surrounding Laguna. Tim joined him and they stood in silence for a few moments. Trying not to disturb Elizabeth, they talked in hushed tones.

"Good call on the priest, Tim," Gualdoni said. "But what makes you think she won't be asking for a priest? I got the impression she was Catholic."

"She is, or was. It has something to do with a bad experience her mother had. I know Elizabeth hasn't been to church since her grandfather died."

"Thanks. I gave that cop a few pointers on how to protect a victim. He won't be letting anyone in without proper authorization."

"Do you think the priest is the attacker?"

"I don't know, but I put in a call to St. Catherine's Church to see what I could find out. They're going to get back to me. You can never tell what this guy might try."

The two men walked back to the bed and sat side by side in straight-back chairs watching Elizabeth. Tim, as he had been for years, was content just to be near her. Gualdoni fidgeted, looked around the room, then stood up and walked to the other side of the bed. Finally, after a long silence, he spoke to Tim in a whisper.

"Do you think she's unconscious again or just drugged?"

"Neither," Tim replied. "My guess is she's using self-hypnosis rather than the morphine to alleviate the pain. She's in a self-induced altered state. Watch her eyes. See them moving under the lids?"

"No kidding. She can do that?"

"Absolutely. She's used hypnosis with her patients for years. I have no doubt she can hypnotize herself," Tim responded.

"When will she come out of it?" Gualdoni asked. "I really need more information."

"I can bring her back, but don't say anything until I give you a nod." Tim's voice changed. His words were commanding, but had a rhythm and tone different from his usual speaking voice. "Elizabeth, it's time for you to come back. It's Tim and I'm going to take your hand if that's all right. Give me a signal. Is it okay for me to touch your hand?"

Gualdoni stood and watched, not knowing what he was watching for.

Tim sat patiently waiting for the familiar sign. Seconds passed. Slowly the index finger of Elizabeth's right hand lifted up and then fell back down.

"Good," Tim said, taking her hand gently in his. "Elizabeth, take a deep cleansing breath."

Again the two men waited. Elizabeth's breathing continued in a slow and shallow pattern as if she were deciding whether or not to follow Tim's instruction. The shallow breathing became deeper and they watched her chest rise and fall with a deep breath.

"Good girl. Take another deep breath, Elizabeth."

She followed his command.

"When you're ready, you can open your eyes. You will feel comfortable, safe, and relaxed. Comfortable. Safe. Relaxed."

Elizabeth continued to take deep breaths. Her eyelids fluttered, and then opened. Her eyes met Tim's and she smiled.

"Welcome back." Tim squeezed her hand. "You feeling okay?"

"I'm okay."

Tim continued to hold her hand. "Liz, we need you to be alert for a while. Can you do that for us?"

"Yes."

"Detective Gualdoni is here and wants to talk with you. Is that okay?"

Her gaze left Tim and she saw Gualdoni standing by her bed. Elizabeth squeezed Tim's hand tighter but gave a slight nodded.

Tim looked at Gualdoni. "Go ahead."

"Do you remember the attack, Elizabeth? Anything at all?"

"No. I was running on the beach, that's it. Then I woke up, here, in the hospital."

"Have you thought of anyone who might do this to you?"

"No. No one."

"Just one more thing, Elizabeth. I don't know if anyone has told you yet but…aah, this guy, he aah…he cut off your hair."

A look of alarm crossed her face. Her breathing became rapid and she reached for her head.

"Elizabeth," Tim said in the rhythmic tone he had used earlier. "Your head is bandaged. He didn't cut off all your hair, it's just…shorter now. Elizabeth, breathe with me. Breathe. In…and out…in…and out…Good girl."

Her breathing became steady again, her eyes calmer.

Gualdoni continued, "I just need to know if this hair thing might be something one of your patients might do?"

"No. I don't think so," she said softly.

Tim looked at Gualdoni. "That's enough. No more questions right now."

"I'll be leaving," Gualdoni said. "See you tomorrow."

Tim walked the detective to the door.

"I've never seen anyone who could leave their body like that. She can really make the pain go away?"

"Yes, for herself and she can do the same thing with patients," Tim replied.

"That's amazing, absolutely amazing." Gualdoni left the hospital room shaking his head in wonder at what he had just witnessed.

Tim went back to Elizabeth's bedside and sat down. He took her hand in his as if it were a fragile orchid, tenderly stroking it with his fingertips.

"You're going to be all right, Liz."

She looked up at him, questions filling her eyes. He gave her hand a tender squeeze.

"You'll be fine. All you need is a little time, and you'll be fine."

Dr. McCormick entered the room on his evening rounds and smiled when he saw Elizabeth awake.

"Feeling better?" Without waiting for an answer he continued. "As soon as you start eating a little, I'll take the IV out."

"I'll wait outside while the two of you talk," Tim said and started to leave.

Elizabeth held his hand tighter. "Please stay, Tim. I want you to hear whatever the doctor has to say."

Dr. McCormick sat down on the edge of Elizabeth's bed.

"When you came in, we did a series of x-rays, a CAT scan, and an EEG. You were badly beaten but I have every reason to believe that you will recover completely."

"What are my injuries?"

"The most serious is the skull fracture. You were unconscious for several hours. When the swelling in the brain started to go down, you regained consciousness but our main concern has been that you keep slipping back. I need you to take an active role in your recovery. Stay with us. Talk to us. I know you need a lot of rest but I need to know if there are memory lapses, if you're in pain, and how much you can physically do."

"What other injuries do I have?"

"Your left shoulder was dislocated. It's been reset, that's why your arm is in a sling. You have three fractured ribs and bruises on your lower back. Your legs are badly bruised but there are no broken bones. That pretty much covers it."

"Is there…any…anything else…I need to know?"

"The IV contains antibiotics, and morphine is in the IV pump for pain. You have a catheter until you're able to be up an around. That's about it."

"That's it?"

"Oh, the hair. Unless you had a really strange hair cut, it looks like this guy cut chunks of hair from the back of your head."

After listening to the doctor describe her injuries, Elizabeth closed her eyes. She took a deep breath, opened her eyes again, and looked directly at Dr. McCormick.

"Was I raped?"

Tim squeezed Elizabeth's hand. He looked at the doctor and anxiously waited for his reply.

"No. There were absolutely no signs of sexual assault."

Elizabeth let out a deep breath. "Thank you."

"Tomorrow," Dr. McCormick said, "I want you to have another CAT scan and EEG. If there are no problems, I want you to begin getting up and moving around. The longer you stay in bed, the harder it will be for you to get your strength back." He patted her hand and smiled. "Get some rest now."

Tim walked Dr. McCormick to the door and thanked him. Elizabeth had asked the question that he had worried about since the attack. She had not been raped.

CHAPTER FIFTEEN

Pain awakened Elizabeth; sharp, gripping pain in her ribs and back. She had allowed herself to use the morphine for relief during the night but now, as the first rays of the morning sun shone through the opening in the drapes, the spasms became so intense that any movement caused her to cry out. Reluctantly, she pushed the button and waited for relief. Once the muscle spasms were under control, she would again use hypnosis rather than drugs to keep herself comfortable. She concentrated on her breathing, the morphine pushing her into a hazy state of limbo, not asleep, but not really awake.

When the breakfast tray arrived, the nurse aroused Elizabeth. She attempted to eat the bowl of liquid the nurse said was chicken broth, but it had no taste. She pushed it aside. The hot tea tasted good. She could feel it warming her chest and stomach as she drank, but she could barely chew the toast and gave up after only one bite. As much as she wanted to follow Dr. McCormick's request and remain awake, the unrelenting throbbing in her lower back forced her to rely once again on hypnosis to tolerate the pain. She focused on her breathing. Breathing that would allow her to slip back into an altered state of relaxation and freedom from the pain.

Elizabeth drifted from the hypnotic state into peaceful sleep. An hour later, the orderly arrived to transport her downstairs for the CT scan and x-rays. They lifted her onto the gurney and pain once again radiated through her body. Pain, waves of pain like the ocean beating against the rocks in a storm, caused her to again cry out.

The nurse reached for the morphine button. "You'll need it," Beverly said. "They'll be moving you around for the x-rays."

The orderly pushed her into the hall, bumping the gurney against the side of the doorway as they passed through. The nurse was right; even with the medication, each bump sent searing pain through her body.

Accompanied by the police officer and the nurse, Elizabeth was taken to the radiology department. The officer remained outside the door but the nurse stayed with her inside the room. Detective Gualdoni had given them both strict orders that Elizabeth was not to be left alone.

After what seemed like hours, the tests were completed and she was again pushed over the bumps in the floor, banged against elevator walls, and lifted back onto her bed. She pushed the button for medication, praying for sleep.

"She's one lucky woman," the radiologist commented as he went over the CT scan, the MRI, and x-rays with Dr. McCormick. "She's young and healthy; she should recover completely from her injuries."

"Lucky is right. From what the detective tells me this wasn't a random attack. Some sicko has been stalking her for several weeks."

"The swelling has gone down in her shoulder, that's good. The ribs are healing nicely; no apparent damage to the vertebrae in the lower back; she'll do just fine," the radiologist said, putting the x-rays away.

"What about the EEG?" Dr. McCormick asked.

"Everything is normal there as well."

Dr. McCormick breathed a sigh of relief. "I hope she does as well emotionally."

Back in his office after completing his rounds at the hospital, Tim Henderson sat at his desk and shuffled through his stack of messages. Requests for speaking engagements, patients needing reports written, the usual calls to be returned, but the message to call Dr. McCormick at South Coast Medical Center stood out above all the others. He knew Elizabeth had had tests taken this morning, and the doctors would evaluate the test results sometime this afternoon to decide on her course of treatment. He expected Elizabeth would tell him the plans this evening when he visited her. *Why does Dr. McCormick want to talk to me? What's wrong?*

After several unsuccessful attempts to reach McCormick, Tim started his afternoon therapy sessions, leaving explicit instructions with Joanne to interrupt him if McCormick called. Three hours later, and no return call. Concern mounting by the minute, Tim told Joanne to cancel his remaining patients. He couldn't wait any longer. He was going to Laguna.

Afternoon traffic crawled slowly along the 405 freeway but he didn't care how long it took; if Elizabeth needed him, he would be there. In his mind, he conjured up one scenario after another about what could be wrong as he headed south.

Tim finally reached Laguna Canyon Road and turned off the freeway; he pulled over, stopped his car on the shoulder, grabbed his cell phone, and dialed the hospital.

"Page Dr. McCormick. Tell him Dr. Henderson will be there in 30 minutes and wants to see him," Tim barked at the switchboard operator.

He heard the woman reply, "Yes, Doctor," before he pushed the button to disconnect the call. *This behavior is not like me but I need to know what's wrong.*

Thirty minutes later, Tim walked up to the information desk, told the woman his name, and asked for Dr. McCormick.

"He's waiting for you in the cafeteria, Doctor."

At a table in the corner, Dr. McCormick sat drinking coffee; he smiled when he saw Tim.

"Didn't mean to scare you, but I would like to discuss Elizabeth's condition. Please, have a seat."

Tim sat for a long time listening to Dr. McCormick. From time to time, he would nod his head or ask a question. An onlooker would have thought they were in total agreement but then Tim shook his head.

"No," Tim said. Then even louder, "No, I won't do it. I won't go against Elizabeth's wishes."

Dr. McCormick persisted. "I think her family should to be called. Her physical condition is improving but I'm worried about how this attack has affected her emotionally. I think she needs her family with her."

"That's her decision."

"As long as she's using self-hypnosis or morphine to hide from reality she's not capable of making good decisions."

"I won't call them. If she doesn't want them to know what's happened then I won't go behind her back," Tim said as he stood up. He wanted to see Liz.

"Tim," Dr. McCormick said gently. "You're her closest friend. I think she'll listen to you."

"Okay, I'll talk to her about calling her parents."

"What about the other issue?"

"Psychotherapy? I'll talk to her about that too." Tim started to walk toward the elevator. He stopped, turned around, then walked back and sat down again with Dr. McCormick.

"You don't know the real Elizabeth Wing. All you know is the wounded little bird lying upstairs in that bed. She's a strong, independent woman; a highly respected clinician."

McCormick sat for a moment before answering. "You're right. But what I see is a woman who is using her unusual skills to suppress the truth. I think she knows more than she's telling us about the attack. She may even know who the attacker is and can't face it."

"Then she'll face it when she's ready."

McCormick waited again before he replied, choosing his words carefully. "Use your skills, her skills with hypnosis, and find out the answers."

"Elizabeth is an expert in her field. She has strong feelings, theories, about how to work with victims. I believe her theories. I won't go against what she believes and treat her differently. For whatever reason, she needs to keep that information buried for now. When the time is right, when she feels safe again, then I'll help her, if she wants my help."

When Tim walked into Elizabeth's room, he was surprised to see her sitting up watching the afternoon news on TV.

"Hi, Liz, nice to see you awake."

"Hi, yourself. What are you doing here this time of day?"

"I've rearranged my patient schedule since you've been in the hospital. Are you feeling better?"

"I'm still hurting, but I don't want to use the morphine if I don't really need it. It makes me so groggy I lose track of time."

Tim realized Elizabeth had no idea how long she had been in the hospital. Gently, he went over the events that had taken place. Although she remembered most of what had happened since her admittance, the days had run together.

"How long have I been here?"

"Four days."

"What about my patients, my classes?"

"They're being handled. Don't worry about those things now. You just get well."

Tim sat by her bedside and they talked for a while before Elizabeth fell asleep. For the first time since the attack, she seemed like herself. He understood Dr. McCormick's concerns, but Elizabeth seemed so much better today. She hadn't been close with her family since the death of her grandparents. If she didn't want to contact her parents, worry them when they were so far away, then he intended to honor her decision. He turned off the TV and sat watching her as she slept. He couldn't bear to leave now that the Elizabeth he knew was back.

CHAPTER SIXTEEN

Follow the money. It wasn't a new concept, and it certainly wasn't something Gualdoni had figured out himself. He'd heard it repeated many times in the police science classes he had taken over the years, but he'd also seen it over and over again in murder cases he'd worked. You look for who would benefit from the death of the victim. This wasn't a murder case but it might have been. If the beating had been worse, if the attacker had intended to kill her, Elizabeth would be dead. But Elizabeth isn't dead, and the attacker is still out there. The same theory might apply; what else did he have to go on?

Gualdoni didn't want to burden Elizabeth with more questions while she was still in the hospital. He already knew she was wealthy, expensive house beautifully furnished, high-end office, designer clothes, new car; it all spelled success, and money. What he didn't know was who would benefit from her death? Tim Henderson knew her as well as anyone. He'd been helpful when questioned a few days ago. But more important, after watching Tim's concern at Elizabeth's bedside, Frank no longer considered him a prime suspect. Gualdoni picked up the phone and made an appointment to see him.

That afternoon, flipping through magazines in Henderson's waiting room, Gualdoni sat anxiously waiting for the last patient of the day to leave. At ten after six, the door to Tim's office opened, a young woman walked out wiping tears from her eyes, and Tim beckoned the detective inside.

"Sorry I kept you waiting. Running behind this afternoon. When you called you said you needed my help. What can I do?" Tim asked as he ushered Gualdoni into his office.

"I have some questions about Elizabeth that I don't want to ask her right now. I thought you might be able to answer them for me," Gualdoni replied, sitting down in one of the leather chairs. He looked around the office and made a mental note of his surroundings; expensive, probably professionally decorated.

"Be glad to, if I can," Tim replied.

Gualdoni proceeded to explain the concept of following the money, then asked Henderson what he knew about Elizabeth's finances.

"I can tell you about our financial arrangements here at the office," Tim said without hesitating. "We each incorporated to prevent personal loss from malpractice suits and for tax purposes. If either of us died or became disabled and unable to practice, the only gain to the other person would be from taking over some of the patients. Assets held by our individual corporations would become part of our own estate in the event of death."

"Both of your corporations are the same?"

"Yes. We incorporated at the same time using the same attorney. Unless Elizabeth has changed something without telling me, they're identical."

"What do you know about her estate? Who gets that money?" Frank questioned.

"We talked once about our wills, or rather she talked. At the time, I didn't have much to leave to anyone, with school loans and all. Elizabeth said she wanted to leave a significant amount to the Rape Crisis Center. She also mentioned establishing a scholarship fund in her mother's name at the university. I don't know if either of these things have been set up, but Elizabeth is very organized when it comes to financial matters. She isn't one to leave loose ends, I would assume it's been taken care of."

Frank kept pushing Tim for more information. "Who else is aware of her intentions?"

"Only her attorney as far as I know."

"Can you tell me anything else? Anything that might motivate someone to want Elizabeth out of the picture?"

"I think I mentioned before, there's a lot of family money, trust funds, that sort of thing. In the event of her death, if she died leaving no spouse or children, the trust fund established by her grandparents would revert back to the family trust. That would mean more money to be divided among the other grandchildren, I presume. Her three cousins would, of course, be aware of the trust fund regulations, as I assume their trust funds are set up the same way."

Gualdoni sat back in the chair, stretched his long legs out in front of him, crossed his ankles, and folded his arms. "Sure doesn't give me much to go on. Do you know anything about the family?"

"Not very much. Elizabeth doesn't like to talk about them. All I know is there has been an ongoing family feud between her father and his sister for a very long time. I think that's why her parents live in Spain."

"The ex-husband, Daniel, does he have any claim on her estate?" Gualdoni questioned.

"They weren't married very long, less than a year. I doubt if he is even mentioned in her will."

Gualdoni noticed a tightening of Tim's jaw as he talked about Daniel. He wanted to question Tim further about his intentions towards Elizabeth but decided to wait until another time. Tim had been helpful, he didn't want to make him defensive.

Gualdoni stood up. "Thanks for your help. I wish we had more to go on." With a brief handshake, he left the doctor's office. His next stop: the university and a surprise visit to Dr. Peter Brewer.

Brewer kept Gualdoni waiting while he finished office hours with his students. There were no chairs in the hall and Frank stood leaning against the wall, impatient for his time with the professor. After a long wait, he entered Brewer's office.

"Well, who are you and what do you want?" Brewer asked rudely. "You're not one of my students."

Gualdoni flashed his badge, passed Brewer his card, and sat in the straight-back chair without being asked to sit down.

"I'm Detective Frank Gualdoni, Long Beach PD. I'm working on Dr. Elizabeth Wing's case." Before he could continue, Brewer interrupted him.

"She probably got what she deserved," Brewer said, tossing a pen across his desk. "That pushy broad needs to keep her nose out of other people's business, you know, follow the rules."

Gualdoni, surprised at Brewer's hostility, stared at him. "Well, do I take it that the two of you don't get along?" Gualdoni asked, dislike for this man growing by the minute.

"I guess you could say that," Brewer replied as he stood and began pacing back and forth behind his desk.

"Do you know of others who have difficulty with Dr. Wing?"

"Students often complain about her, maybe some of the staff have problems as well," Brewer said not being specific.

"What kind of problems?"

"Problems!" Brewer shouted.

"Anyone who would hurt her physically?"

"How would I know?" Brewer snapped.

This guy is definitely not being cooperative.

"She's arrogant, thinks she's smart. People just have a problem with her." Brewer paced, jingled the change in his pants pocket, and then sat down at his desk.

"What people? Give me some names."

"Just people. Detective, I've got work to do. I don't have time for this."

"Thanks for your time," he said sarcastically, as he stood to leave. "I'll be back."

Walking to his car, Gualdoni had a bad feeling about Dr. Peter Brewer. *That asshole goes to the top of my list.*

CHAPTER SEVENTEEN

The morning sun glistened on the ocean and Elizabeth watched from her hospital bed as a sailboat caught the wind in its sail and glided through the waves. *That's where I'd like to be, out in the ocean in a sailboat.*

"Ever do any sailing?" she asked Beverly, her nurse, as she cleared away the breakfast dishes.

"No. I never had any desire to. I'd just as soon stay on dry land."

"You don't know what you're missing. When you're out there sailing, it's just you and the ocean. It's great therapy."

The nurse put the tray of dishes outside the door. "Are you feeling up to sitting in a chair while I make your bed?"

"Up to it or not, I've got to start moving around or I'll never get out of here."

"Come on, I'll help you."

An hour later, when Dr. McCormick came in on his morning rounds, Elizabeth was still sitting in the chair watching the ocean.

"Mesmerizing isn't it?" he asked as he sat down next to her.

"Yes. I love the ocean. My fondest memories as a child are sailing with my grandfather. It was our special time together. He taught me how to sail when I visited here every summer."

"Do you sail much now?"

"I never seem to find the time. But I think the attack, this whole stalking thing, has given me a different perspective. I need to do more of the things I enjoy."

"I'm glad to hear you say that. I've been worried about you. The way you used hypnosis to withdraw and all."

"I wasn't using the hypnosis to run away from what happened. I used it to escape the pain. I don't like taking drugs if I don't really need them."

"How's the pain now?" the doctor asked.

"I'm doing better. My legs don't hurt and my shoulder is tender but not bad. Most of the pain is in my lower back."

"That's where the severe bruising is. It may take a few weeks but I expect you'll be good as new."

"When can I go home?" Elizabeth asked.

"That's the question that tells me a patient is feeling better. How about we take the IV out and see how you do? If all goes well, you can go home tomorrow."

"That sounds good to me. I'm sure you'd like to get the police out of your corridor."

"I'll come by tonight and check on you and bring a prescription for pain medication and something to help you sleep in case you need it," Dr. McCormick said as he left her room.

"Would you like me to take the IV out now?" Beverly asked.

"Please do," Elizabeth said as she lay back down on her bed. She watched as the nurse slid the needle out of her arm, applied pressure to the site with a cotton ball, and stuck a Band-aid over it.

"Get some rest. After lunch I'll get you up and walk you around a bit," the nurse said, wheeling away the IV bottle with the tubes attached.

But sleep evaded Elizabeth. Her mind kept returning to the beach, her afternoon run, and the sounds of footsteps behind her. *Why didn't I turn around? Who did this to me? Will I ever feel safe again?*

She gazed out at the ocean. There were several sailboats skimming across the water, their sails full in the wind. Memories of her grandfather and the hours they'd spent sailing and talking filled her mind. *If only Grandfather were still alive, he'd know what to do about this stalking thing.* Elizabeth had made very few major decisions in her adult life without asking her grandfather's opinion. The first was her decision to become a psychologist and not a lawyer. Even though she knew he was disappointed she would not be taking over the law firm someday, he encouraged her in her choice. She could almost hear his voice: "You have a keen mind,

Jamie, you'll succeed in whatever you do." Her grandfather had been right; she was a success in her work. Grandfather was the only person who called her Jamie. She had been named Jamie Elizabeth, but when she and her parents moved to Spain they had stopped calling her Jamie, saying only that they preferred Elizabeth. The second decision she made without consulting Grandfather had not turned out well at all; in fact, her decision to marry Daniel had been a disaster. *If only I could ask Grandfather one last question.*

Muffled sounds from the hall interrupted her thoughts. The voice of the police officer outside her room got louder. "No one goes in without authorization," she heard him say. Another voice responded but she couldn't hear what he said. "I don't care who you are. You're not on the list and you're not going in that room."

A voice over the intercom paged security to the third floor. *What floor am I on?* Elizabeth could feel her stomach knotting up. "Please see what's going on out there," she asked the nurse.

Beverly opened the door just in time to see a young man rush by her and around the corner. She slipped out and closed the door behind her. Elizabeth heard more muffled voices. She strained to hear what was being said. The nurse came back into the room, closed the door, and leaned against it.

"What's going on?" Elizabeth asked, seeing the frightened look on Beverly's face.

"Everything's under control," the nurse replied.

"Who's out there?" Elizabeth asked, louder than she had intended.

"No one. He's not getting in. He's gone."

"Who? Who's trying to get in?" Elizabeth was becoming more frightened.

"Security is after him. Says his name is Jackson or Justin or something. Says he's your brother."

"I don't…"

"I know. You don't have a brother. Detective Gualdoni told me about the phone calls."

"What phone calls?" Elizabeth asked. *Oh, God. What else don't I know?*

"Oops. I guess he didn't tell you. Some guy has been calling the hospital saying he's your brother. They tried to trace the calls but didn't have any luck."

"Did you see the guy outside the door?"

"Leave it to the police. They'll handle it."

"But did you see him?"

"Yes, but he's hard to describe. Average height, average weight, brown hair, needed a shave. But I could ID him in a lineup. Detective Gualdoni's been called. Now you leave this to the police and get some rest."

Rest! Will I ever rest again? Elizabeth could feel her body tremble, she hoped the nurse didn't notice. She kept trying to tell herself that she was safe but she didn't feel safe. Not if this guy had the nerve, or the stupidity, to try to get to her in the hospital. *What would he do next?* For the first time, she thought about calling her parents. She never called them with her problems, she'd always asked Grandfather for help. *But Grandfather is gone. What could my father do, he doesn't have the connections that Grandfather had? Tim is a good friend but not for something like this. I've lost control of my life.* For the first time since the attack, Elizabeth let herself cry. Tears slid down her face. Tears of fear, frustration, and loss of control. She rolled over on her side, buried her face in her pillow, and sobbed.

Lunch came but Elizabeth didn't feel like eating. She pushed the food around the plate then put the cover back on the dish. She drank some hot tea and ate a cracker.

"That's not lunch," Beverly said with a look that reminded Elizabeth of her mother. "How do you expect to get your strength back if you don't eat?"

"You're right, I can't let this guy get to me." Elizabeth took the cover off her lunch again, picked up her fork, and took a bite of chicken. She still didn't feel like eating but she forced herself to take another bite. "Yummy," she said, making a face at the nurse.

"Gourmet it's not, but it's nourishing. Eat or you'll be here forever," the nurse said with a smile.

Doing as she was told, Elizabeth ate the chicken and mashed potatoes; the green beans tasted like rubber bands and she pushed them to the side. Dessert consisted of red Jell-o of undetermined flavor. She'd never cared much for Jell-o but she ate it anyway.

Detective Gualdoni arrived as she finished the last of her lunch.

"I hear you had an unwelcome visitor," he said as he sat down next to the bed.

"I wish I could have gotten a glimpse of him. Maybe I could identify him."

"Well, something's strange. He doesn't fit the description the Avis clerk gave us at all. His hair is brown, not blond, his clothes were shabby, not expensive, nothing matches."

"So where does that leave us?" Elizabeth asked.

"No where. It leaves us right back where we started with no idea who this guy, or guys, could be."

"Guys? Two? Do you think there could be two men stalking me?" The thought made her shudder. She pulled the sheet tighter around her.

"After today, it seems like a possibility. The descriptions are totally different. Another thing, I picked up the tapes from your office, Joanne gave them to me. I've listened to the voices several times and until today I just thought the guy was trying to disguise his voice, but now, it seems like two different men could be calling you."

"I couldn't even think of one person who would do this to me. Now I'm supposed to think of two?"

"Don't worry about it; they may not know you at all."

"Yes, they do. At least one of them knows me. He knows way too much about me to be a stranger," Elizabeth said.

"On a brighter note, I hear they're going to let you out of here tomorrow."

"Yes, I thought I might go to the beach house and rest for a few days before I go back home."

"Not on your life. He knows about Laguna. You're not safe here. Your house in Long Beach is much more secure."

Elizabeth sighed. "I guess you're right." *No control. I have absolutely no control over my life!*

"I've taken the rental car back. Your suitcase and purse were in it so I brought them here. I'll bring them up before I leave."

"Thanks. At least I'll have clean clothes to wear."

"To be on the safe side, I'll pick you up tomorrow and drive you home. About this time if that's okay. I'd like you to hire a bodyguard for the next week or so."

"Are you serious?" Elizabeth could feel her stomach tighten up again.

"Absolutely. I know several policewomen who'd be good. It's not unusual for them to earn extra money doing security work when they're off duty."

"I guess if this guy tried to see me here, he might try anything. Okay, arrange whatever you think is best."

"Consider it done," Gualdoni said as he stood to leave. "See you tomorrow."

"That is one handsome man," Beverly said to Elizabeth after Gualdoni had left.

"Yes, I suppose he is."

"You suppose! You were hit on the head, you're not blind. He is drop-dead gorgeous, and no wedding ring. If he's coming to take you home tomorrow, we've got to fix you up."

"Fix me up?"

"Well for starters, the hair. My hairdresser can do wonders with a pair of scissors. If I call him he'll come to the hospital and give you the full treatment. Shampoo, cut, blow dry, whatever you need. He's a bit expensive but worth every dime."

"I don't care about the money. I've got to get this hair fixed; call him. What else can I do?"

"If you don't care about the cost there are several restaurants in town that will deliver anything on their menu. We need to get some good food in you. You aren't eating enough to keep a bird alive."

"Really? I can do that?"

"Of course you can, you're the boss. I'll get a phone in here and you can call your favorite restaurant."

Beverly was out the door before Elizabeth could object. She'd never been hospitalized before and had no idea special services could be arranged for patients. Even though she had been raised with money, her family had not indulged in extravagant spending. All except her Aunt Nancy and her spoiled cousins, that is.

"It's all set," the nurse said as she hurried back into the room. "Marcus will be here at four o'clock. I told the police outside to expect him, and I guarantee that you'll be thrilled with what he can do."

"Great," Elizabeth said. But in her head she had doubts. She'd taken years to develop the professional look she wanted and a short haircut was not what she envisioned as part of her image.

"Now, up up up. You need to be walking around, getting used to being on your feet. Usually I walk my patients up and down the hall, but we can't do that, so around the room a few times will have to do."

The nurse hustled Elizabeth out of bed, helped her into the paper slippers provided by the hospital, and took her arm. "Stand up straight. Take a good deep breath. Now, let's get some exercise."

Elizabeth didn't resist. She simply let her nurse take charge.

At ten minutes past four, Marcus sashayed through the door and stopped. He eyed the room, and Elizabeth eyed him. Tall and slender dressed in black leather pants and a white shimmering silk shirt, he could pass for an Elvis look-a-like. Loaded down with a glitzy tote bag in each hand, he had come prepared for any emergency.

"Fashionably late, as usual," Beverly said, introducing Elizabeth to Marcus.

"Of course," Marcus said, putting down his tote bags and giving Beverly a hug. "If I'd come early I may have caught you with your boyfriend and I would be very jealous. I'm in between lovers right now." Marcus busied himself, opening his bags and meticulously arranging combs, brushes, shears, clippers, and a variety of bottles on the table.

"Sweetheart, are you comfortable sitting in that chair? I could do you in bed if you'd rather," then he giggled. "Well, not *do* you, you're not my type. But you can lie down while I shampoo you if you'd be more comfortable."

Elizabeth smiled and tried not to laugh. "I'm fine in the chair," she replied.

"Now does anything hurt? I don't want to hurt you, I'm not into pain."

"My shoulder is tender, and there's a bump on my head, right here," she pointed to the back of her head, "that still hurts quite a bit."

"I will be ever so gentle, trust me." Marcus said as he ran his fingers through Elizabeth's hair. "Curls," he exclaimed. "And I bet you try to straighten them don't you?"

"Always," Elizabeth replied.

"And the color, you're a natural redhead and you've been coloring it to make it darker. No, no, no. Never go darker. Always lighten, and highlight, much sexier."

Marcus kept playing with Elizabeth's hair, combing it with his fingers, first to the left then to the right. "Oh my, that bad man took a big chunk right out of the back of your hair!"

Elizabeth sighed. "Can you do anything to fix it?"

"Don't you worry, sweetheart, Marcus will fix it. I'm a diva with shears. Let's get you shampooed."

Marcus escorted Elizabeth into the bathroom, where he had attached a plastic tray to the sink. Moving the chair just under the tray, he asked Elizabeth to sit down. Next he draped a large white towel around her shoulders, followed by a shampoo cape.

"Comfy?"

"I'm fine," Elizabeth said.

"And the water temperature? Not too hot, is it, honey?"

"No, it's just right."

Ever so tenderly Marcus soaked, lathered, rinsed, conditioned, and rinsed again, his fingers never seeming to touch the bump on Elizabeth's head.

"I didn't hurt you, did I, sweetheart?" Marcus asked as he helped Elizabeth sit up.

"No, not at all. You're very good."

"I sure am! And just wait till you see what I can do with the shears," Marcus replied, walking Elizabeth back to the bedroom. "Now you sit right here and get yourself all relaxed." Marcus removed the plastic cape from around Elizabeth shoulders and replaced it with a silky cloth cape. Again he ran his fingers through her hair, letting the curls fall into place. His picked up one of several pairs of shears and began snipping and trimming, finger combing her hair, and then snipping and trimming again.

Elizabeth wished she had a mirror in front of her. She wanted to say, "Not too short, I don't like my hair short." But she sat, putting her trust in a man she'd never met, without saying a word. After what the attacker had done to her, what choice did she have? She looked down at the floor and saw pieces of her hair lying all around her.

"Don't you fret. It's going to be just fine," Marcus said, as if he could read her mind.

When Marcus finally passed Elizabeth the mirror, she hardly recognized herself. The short hair seemed to change the shape of her face. Her blue eyes looked bigger, and she definitely looked younger. For years she had been trying to look older, wanting her patients and students to take her seriously. But this new look, this young, playful, sexy look, made her appear to be a totally different person.

"Don't you just love it?" Marcus asked.

Before Elizabeth could answer, he continued. "Now this is only the beginning. Next we're going to do something about all that dark color."

"No. The cut is fine. I don't think I want to…"

"Marcus knows best. You'll look marvelous! Trust me."

Elizabeth looked at herself in the mirror again. It was a great cut. *Why not go for a whole new look?*

"Okay, Marcus. You're the expert. Let's go for it."

"Ooh, you're going to just love it, I promise."

Marcus pulled the mirror out of Elizabeth's hand and tossed it on the bed. He started opening bottles and mixing the ingredients together. Before Elizabeth knew what was happening, Marcus had painted the concoction on sections of her hair and wrapped them in pieces of silver paper.

"There, that was easy. Now we just wait. It won't take long and the new you will be complete."

He started cleaning up the mess of bottles, pulled a hair dryer out of one of his bags, and packed away some of his other paraphernalia. A few minutes later, Marcus took Elizabeth back into the bathroom, rinsed her hair, and wrapped it in a towel.

"No peeking," he said, as he escorted her back to the bedroom chair.

Brush in one hand, hair dryer in the other, Marcus styled Elizabeth's hair. At one point, he grabbed the shears and snipped a bit and then went back to brushing and drying.

"Ooh, you're going to love it," Marcus said, putting down the dryer and brush. He passed Elizabeth the mirror again and stood back admiring his work.

"Wow. I never would have believed it. I look like just like my mother. I always thought I looked like my father's side of the family."

"And…" Marcus asked.

"You're right. I love it!"

"Wait till your boyfriend sees it. He's going to love it too."

"I don't have a boyfriend but it's a great cut and I really like the highlights too," Elizabeth said, as she wrote out a check for Marcus that included a generous tip.

"She may not have a boyfriend but that detective that's working her case is a hunk," Beverly chimed in.

"Ooh, a policeman. Don't you just love men in uniform," Marcus said as he finished packing up his two bags. "Now you come see me in about a month and I'll trim it up a bit." He gave a wave, picked up his totes, and was out the door.

"That was an experience," Elizabeth said, after he had left. She picked up the mirror again, ran her fingers through the new cut, and smiled. "I look like a new person. Even better, I feel like a new person."

CHAPTER EIGHTEEN

More and more paranoid, Cash had changed hotels again. He worried more and more about undercover cops busting him. He worried that street people or other druggies might steal his money or his stash. Not wanting to attract the attention of the police, he hadn't tried to contact Elizabeth in days.

"Damn you!" he yelled at the empty room. "Where are you?" Almost out of drugs, he needed Squirrel to make the buy and get back here. He turned the TV up louder but didn't watch the screen, poured himself a bourbon, and paced, first to the window then to the door. He listened for footsteps in the hall.

Just as he picked up his cell phone to call his connection, he heard the familiar knock on the door.

"Cash, you there?" Squirrel said from the hall.

Cash threw his phone on the bed and hurried to unlock the door. "What the hell took you so long?"

"Cool it, I'm here," Squirrel replied.

Cash didn't like the smirk on Squirrel's face. "What have you been up to? Did ya make the buy?"

"Here." Squirrel pulled the bindle out of his shirt pocket and tossed it to Cash. "I've been to Laguna," he added.

Cash, busy with the cocaine, didn't really listen to Squirrel. He spread some of the powder out on the mirror and compulsively started to make neat little lines. Suddenly, what Squirrel had said registered. "You went where?" he yelled.

"I went to Laguna. I wanted to see Elizabeth."

"Are you crazy? The cops will be watching her."

"Yeah, they even got some cop sittin' outside her room. He got all pissed off when I tried to go in and he called security."

"You're out of your mind! You're fucking out of your mind!" Cash snorted two lines in rapid succession.

"Hey," Squirrel said, taking control of the conversation. "I got away. Besides, you're the one who started all this. She's so beautiful, why'd you want to scare her anyway?"

"It's none of your business."

"Fuck you. I'm in this now, we're partners."

"Like hell we are."

Squirrel grabbed the mirror from Cash and snorted a line.

"You keep doing dumb things like showing up at the hospital and you're going to get caught," Cash said, taking the mirror back. "You'll get caught and give me up and we'll both end up in jail."

"Hey, I don't give nobody up. We're partners, buddies, I would never give you up."

"Right," Cash said. "I should never have let you call her."

"What is it with you and her anyway? She refused to date you or something?" Squirrel said and took back the mirror.

"It's not her I want, asshole. It's her mother. You know, the woman in the picture you stole."

"Hell, I just thought you wanted the silver frame. You wanted the picture of her mother! What do you want some old broad for?"

"Watch your mouth," Cash said.

"I don't get it. If it's her mother you want, why are you following her?"

"Pay attention, idiot! I scare Elizabeth, she calls her mother. Kathleen comes from Spain to help her daughter." Cash took the mirror and poured another pile of cocaine onto it. Again he divided it into neat little lines and snorted the first line.

"And then what?" Squirrel asked, confused.

"She loves me, that's what! Once she's here and we talk, she'll remember she loves me and leave David. We'll be together just like we were before."

"You've had way too much of that stuff," Squirrel said, taking the mirror back. "You're living in fantasy land."

"Fuck you!"

"I'll be back," Squirrel said heading for the door. "I'm not the idiot here."

"Don't bring another coke whore up here," Cash yelled after him.

"I'll do anything I want."

Squirrel's words were like a slap in the face. Cash knew he had crossed over the line. Up until now he had been in control. He had the money. But now, Squirrel had the information that could end it all.

CHAPTER NINETEEN

Six days after Elizabeth had been admitted to South Coast Medical Center, Frank Gualdoni wheeled her through the halls of the hospital and out into the afternoon sun. Directly in front of the entrance to the hospital, the unmarked police car Frank had driven waited in the red zone at the curb.

"Special treatment for me?" she asked, trying to make light of his apparent concern for her safety.

"Absolutely."

Elizabeth was glad she had taken the pain pill Dr. McCormick had prescribed. Getting from the wheelchair to the back seat of the car turned out to be more painful than she had expected. During the drive home, Frank made small talk but she said little. The closer they got to Long Beach, the more nervous she became. For the first time in her life, the thought of being alone frightened her.

"Did you arrange for the policewoman?" she asked, hoping he hadn't forgotten.

"It's all set. She'll be there when we arrive."

Elizabeth knew she'd feel safer with police protection, but the thoughts of having someone baby-sit her in her own home felt like a violation of her privacy. *I guess my safety is more important than my privacy.*

"Dr. Wing, are you okay?" Gualdoni asked.

"I'm fine, just a little uncomfortable with all the bumps. I never realized this road was in such bad condition."

"Sorry about the construction. We're almost there. I just took a few detours in case we were being followed," Gualdoni said.

Elizabeth had noticed the detective had kept his eye on the rear-view mirror, now she knew why.

Once home, Elizabeth met Jody Randall, the female police officer who had taken the day shift. Before Gualdoni left, he explained the rotation of in-house protection as well as the schedule of drive-by surveillance cars.

Elizabeth didn't feel like socializing with her bodyguard. She walked through her house trying to reacquaint herself with her surroundings. The police had removed the lipstick from the bathroom mirror, but in her mind she could still see "B I T C H" written across the glass. A shudder went through her body. In the den, she tried to sort through the stack of mail that had piled up since she'd been gone. She couldn't concentrate. *I'll tackle that tomorrow.*

"I'm going upstairs," she told Jody.

"Do you want me to come with you?"

"No, I'll be fine. I think I'll rest for a little while and then take a bath." *Just pretend everything is okay.*

Each step, as she walked up the stairs, caused spasms in her lower back like she had felt earlier getting into the car. She considered taking another pain pill but decided to wait and see if she felt better after her bath. *I can't drug myself to make all this go away. I've got to get through it.*

Her bedroom looked just the way she had left it. She stared at her dresser and the empty spot where the picture of her mother should be. *Damn him!* She retreated to the bathroom and turned on the water. *This is what I need.* She poured Fresh Vanilla Bubble Bath into the water and watched as the bubbles filled the tub, the delicate fragrance filling the room. She lit several candles around the tub, and turned off the bright overhead lights, the last rays of the afternoon sun mingling with the flickering candles as her only light. Next she found her favorite Richard Clayderman CD and turned on the stereo. The piano music of "Lara's Theme" filled the room.

As she peeled off her clothes, she tried to avoid looking at herself in the mirror. Even in the dim light, she could see the purple bruises beginning to fade, but still evident, on her thighs and back. She had lost too much weight in just a few days, her slender body looking more like a starving child than an adult woman. The reflection screamed "victim." She wanted to deny she was the person in the mirror, but the image looking back at her held a reality that she had to face. Someone hated her. Hated her so much that they had stalked her, beaten her, and could have killed her. The questions remained. *Who is he? Why does he want to hurt me? Why didn't he kill me when he had the chance? What is he going to do next?*

Pushing these thoughts aside, she stepped into the hot water, feeling it ease her sore muscles as she slid down and rested her head against the back of the tub. She closed her eyes and let the clean sweet aroma of vanilla occupy her thoughts. She breathed in long, slow breaths. She tried to relax. The soft piano music in the background switched to "Que Sera, Sera, Whatever Will Be, Will Be," and she tried to convince herself that whatever will be is what is meant to be. She opened her eyes and watched the flickering candles fill the room with a mellow glow; for the moment, here in her own house again, she almost felt safe.

She stayed in the tub until the water turned tepid, then, she carefully stood up, pulled the lever to let the bathwater swirl down the drain, and turned on the shower to rinse off. The hot water had relaxed her body and she felt less pain as she moved. She wrapped herself in a warm towel, stepped out of the tub, dried off, and put on her terrycloth robe. Back in her bedroom, she stretched out on her bed for a short nap, but even after the relaxing bath she couldn't stop her mind from focusing on the attack. Thoughts that the attack had been different than she had been told persisted. Even though Dr. McCormick had assured her there had been no sexual assault, a clouded memory of her arms being pinned against the ground, the weight of someone's body on top of her, and the sour smell of alcohol, refuse to go away. She needed to know the truth. She wanted to talk with Tim; she knew he wouldn't lie to her.

Unable to sleep, she dressed in a comfortable velour sweat suit, went downstairs, and poured herself a glass of wine. *I much prefer wine to pain pills.* Elizabeth could hear the TV in the living room, the newscaster reporting a gang drive-by shooting, a convenience store robbery, a hit-and-run accident. Violence, everywhere violence, even in her own house, a policewoman was keeping watch, a constant reminder of her own danger.

Elizabeth told the policewoman a friend was bringing dinner at seven and invited her to join them. When she accepted, she called Tim to ask him to bring enough for three. As expected, he had planned on bringing Chinese for dinner.

As usual, Tim was right on time and the police woman answered the doorbell when it rang. She showed Tim into the den and took the bags of take-out into the kitchen.

"Wow," Tim said. "You look like a different person."

"Oh, the hair cut. I had to do something. I couldn't leave it the way it was. My nurse called a hairdresser she knew in Laguna, he came to the hospital and did it all. It's really different but I think I like it short."

"So do I. They'll think you're one of the students at the university. We'd better eat before the food gets cold. I brought Mu Shu Shrimp, Kung Pao Chicken, Beef with Broccoli, and both steamed and fried rice."

"Tim, I can always count on you to cook a great meal," Elizabeth said, teasing. Tim didn't cook but he had a long list of great restaurants that provided take-out meals.

Elizabeth, her trusted friend, and her bodyguard sat in the kitchen eating dinner and making small talk. Even if it did feel like she was under house arrest, it felt good to be home, much better than in the hospital.

After dinner, Jody went back into the living room and Elizabeth and Tim went into the den. Life was beginning to feel normal again. Tim poured each of them a brandy and he absentmindedly swirled the amber-colored liquid around in his glass.

"I love to watch you do that," Elizabeth commented. "It reminds me of my grandfather. When I was a little girl, I would wait patiently for him to finish his brandy before asking him to read me a bedtime story."

"I didn't know you lived with your grandfather."

"Only until I was about five, then we moved to Spain. But we visited every summer."

"Were you and your grandfather close?"

"Yes. I was the last grandchild, and I think I was his favorite. Each evening after dinner, William would pour brandy for Grandfather and a small goblet of ginger ale for me; each time Grandfather took a sip, I would too. The summer I was fifteen, he allowed me to have a small bit of brandy with him. It was watered down but it was still a big deal. When I was older, we sat for hours discussing international politics, philosophy, and, of course, law. He was an attorney and wanted me to become one too, just like my father."

"Who's William?"

"My grandparent's butler, driver, and all-around house manager; he was with them for years. After my grandmother died, there were just the two men in that big old house. When my grandfather died, it was in the will that William was to stay on in the house for as long as he wanted. He's still there. He doesn't work now, but he does manage the house, arrange for caterers and household help whenever Aunt Nancy has a party there or when my parents come for the holidays."

"Speaking of your parents, when do you expect them this year?"

"In about six weeks."

She and Tim sat quietly, each deep in thought, sipping their drinks. Tim broke the silence.

"Liz," he began softly. "Dr. McCormick assured me that you're going to be fine physically, but you haven't talked about the attack. I'm concerned about your emotional health. You know you can't just ignore what happened."

"I'm not ignoring it. I've told you and Detective Gualdoni everything I can remember about the attack, and I told you about the flashbacks and nightmares."

"I'm not talking about the facts, I'm talking about feelings. The flashbacks may have been triggered by the attack," Tim said, "but I don't think they're related to it. Besides, you said you were having nightmares before the attack."

Elizabeth could tell Tim had automatically switched from concerned friend to therapist. "Tim…"

"They go further back, possibly something from your childhood. My diagnosis is PTSD."

"Post-traumatic stress disorder! Tim, I respect your clinical skills, but it just doesn't feel right."

"Remember what Detective Gualdoni said? You're too close to be objective."

"Maybe you're right, but PTSD?"

"I think you experienced some kind of trauma as a child and don't remember it. The stalker has awakened the same fears you experienced then."

"No, I don't think so," she said defensively. "I had a wonderful childhood living in Spain with my parents and summers here with my grandparents. They all treated me like a princess."

"Do you think it's possible that something happened to you as a child and you repressed the memories?" Tim asked.

Elizabeth shuddered. There were lapses in her childhood memories. She knew Tim was being careful not to upset her. "Of course it's possible. But I don't really think my parents would have kept something like that from me for all these years."

"Liz, you need to work this out in therapy. If you like, I'll work with you. We can use hypnosis. If we haven't figured it out when your parents come for the holidays, we'll ask them."

"I know you're right, Tim. I need to find out what the nightmares and flashbacks are all about, but…"

"But what? Do you want to go to another therapist?"

"No, that's not it."

"Then what is it?"

"Maybe I'm a little scared of what we'll find out."

"It's okay to be scared. We'll take our time; I'll even tape the sessions so you can listen to them later if you like."

"It's time I figured this all out, isn't it?" Elizabeth asked without really expecting a reply. "Let's do it. Hypnosis is fine, but let's see what we dig up before we make any decisions about discussing anything with my parents."

"It's a deal. We'll start on Tuesday in my office, my last patient will be done at five. Take the next couple of days to relax and feel comfortable being back home, then we'll get to work."

Tim poured each of them a bit more brandy. He swirled his brandy slowly then touched his glass lightly against Elizabeth's.

"Here's to sorting it all out." He downed his brandy, kissed her tenderly on the cheek, and said good night.

Elizabeth was still sitting on the couch when the doorbell rang a few minutes later. She listened as the policewoman answered it and greeted her replacement for the night shift.

"Dr. Wing," Jody said, entering the den. "This is Officer Tina Munroe. She'll be with you tonight. If you don't mind, I'll take her on a walk-through of the house so she knows the layout."

"That's fine," Elizabeth answered. *The changing of the guards!* She could hear the two women go upstairs and then come back down again. Next they went through the living room, dining room, and kitchen, checking doors and windows as they went. She heard them walk outside to the backyard and saw the motion-activated security lights come on. Back in the house, they checked the doors leading to the laundry and to the garage. Cocooned in her house, she wondered if they were keeping her in or keeping an intruder out.

"Everything's secure, Dr. Wing. I'll see you tomorrow."

Sipping the remainder of her brandy, Elizabeth pushed the possibility that Tim could be right about a childhood trauma out of her mind. *I had a great childhood!*

CHAPTER TWENTY

For the first time since the attack, Elizabeth, accompanied by the police officer, went to her office, the place where the perpetrator had always contacted her. Fear was an emotion that she hadn't felt until recently, and she didn't like the feeling. Intellectually, she knew that she was safe, but her stomach was tied in knots. It was only a short drive from her home to her office but she had gripped the stirring wheel so tightly that her hands ached. Getting out of her car, she scanned the parking lot. Detective Gualdoni had assured her they had the black Mustang. She looked for it anyway. It wasn't there. Once in the elevator, she practiced the relaxation techniques that she knew so well. *I'm not alone. Tim is in the office.* She was determined to regain her self-confidence. *Thank God I won't be seeing patients today.*

The police officer escorting her checked out the office and then sat in the waiting room. Elizabeth looked over notes written in the files by Tim and her intern. It had only been a week but it felt like a long time since she had seen her patients.

Sitting at her desk, she waited for Tim to finish his last patient of the day, the last one before her. She hadn't been a patient since her internship days. To fulfill her graduation requirements, she had completed twenty hours of mandatory therapy. The therapist had not been looking for pathology, and Elizabeth had intentionally avoided discussing her childhood or her family. She and Daniel had just decided to end their marriage, and the therapist had been satisfied to spend her time in therapy discussing the breakup of their marriage. *This time it will be different. Tim won't put up with my avoidance tactics.*

Elizabeth trusted Tim's judgment, but she didn't want therapy. Maybe a few sessions would help her remember something about the attack. *But what if I can't remember anything?* Maybe she could find the missing pieces of her childhood. *Maybe I don't want to! Could it be a childhood trauma that's causing the nightmares and flashbacks? Do my patients have such ambivalence about therapy?*

She heard Tim's last patient leave and wondered if her patients were this nervous. Tim is a good therapist, just relax, she told herself as she walked into his office and sat down. It felt strange sitting in Tim's office as a patient, uncomfortable. She took a deep breath and tried to relax.

"Liz, I'll tape the sessions if that's okay. That way we can go over them together if there are any significant areas of concern."

"Let's get started. I'm as ready as I'll ever be," she said, taking another cleansing breath.

"You're really nervous about this, aren't you?"

"I'm used to being in your chair," she said with a weak smile.

Only a short induction was necessary. Elizabeth had been hypnotized many times during her training as a hypnotherapist. She continued to take long slow breaths while Tim watched.

"Listen to my voice while you continue to breathe. I will count backwards and guide you into your subconscious. Memories will surface and you will describe them. Ten...nine...eight...deeper and deeper into your subconscious. Seven...six...you are relaxed. Five...four...very relaxed. Three...two...Tell me what you remember about the last time you were on the beach in Laguna."

Elizabeth took a deep breath and began to speak softly. "It's late in the afternoon. I'm near the water's edge where the sand is hard. It's low tide. I can see Catalina Island. The sun feels warm."

"What are you doing?"

"I'm walking, and then I begin to jog. I stop and take my sweatshirt off and tie it around my waist. I start to run again. The sun will be setting soon."

"Do you see anyone on the beach?"

"An old man with a dog is walking toward me."

"Do you recognize him?"

"No."

"Does he walk past you?"

"No. He walks over to the rocks and sits down."

"Do you see anyone else?"

"No."

"What do you do now?"

"I run past the man and the dog. I keep running."

"Then what happens?"

"It's time to go back. I'll run to the next outcropping of rocks and then turn around. I can hear someone running behind me." Elizabeth stops talking, her hands are shaking, and her breathing becomes rapid.

"Elizabeth, breathe slowly."

She follows Tim's instructions.

"Good. You're safe, Elizabeth. Take another deep breath. What happens now?"

"He's too close to me."

"How do you know it's a man? Can you see him?"

"No. I start to turn my head. I see a hand. A man's hand."

"Is there anything unusual about the hand?"

"No."

"What happens next?"

"He grabs my hair. I reach up, try to pull away, to see who's there… My hand touches his. I can feel a ring. There's a ring on his right hand. Something hits me. Ooh. Pain. Sharp pain. I'm falling…" Elizabeth stops talking.

"Elizabeth," Tim asked, "Can you describe the ring?"

"No."

"Can you remember anything else? A smell, a glimpse of anything?"

"No. It's dark, quiet, I'm not on the beach; I don't know where I am."

"Elizabeth, take another cleansing breath. I'm going to bring you back to the present. When you open your eyes, you won't remember anything you have told me. I will count backwards from five to one. When I reach one, you will open your eyes. You will feel relaxed and rested."

Tim started counting backwards and when he reached one, Elizabeth opened her eyes and took another deep breath.

"Do you know all my secrets now?"

"Not really but I did get some information that may be helpful."

"About the attack?"

"Yes. You didn't see the attacker but you did see his hand, feel it. He was wearing a ring. We need to tell Gualdoni about this bit of information."

"Did I tell you anything else? Am I a cooperative patient?"

"You did just fine, Liz. The ring may be a good lead."

Elizabeth wondered what else she had said but decided not to ask. There would be plenty of time to discuss it all later. Suddenly she was very tired. She wanted to go home and have a quiet evening and a good night's sleep.

"Liz, I think we should have another session. Are you up to coming in tomorrow at the same time?"

"Do you think there may be more I didn't tell you?"

"I don't know for sure but I think we need to try and dig a little deeper."

"Okay, tomorrow it is. At least it gets me out of the house."

The following evening Elizabeth arrived at the office more relaxed and ready to find out what other hidden memories could be uncovered. Detective Gualdoni had assured her that if they find a suspect, the ring could be an important piece of evidence.

Just as the night before, Tim rapidly went through the induction procedure with Elizabeth. He took her back to the beach, and her description of the events was very much the same as during the last session. No new bits of memory were revealed.

"Elizabeth, can I take you back to your childhood?" Tim asked.

He watched for Elizabeth's response. Slowly the index finger of her right hand lifted up and dropped back down again.

"Allow me to guide you," he began. "The years will slip away as I count. Twenty-five...twenty-four...twenty-three...relax and go back through the years, eighteen...seventeen...sixteen...You are a child again, nine...eight...seven...six...how old are you?"

"Four."

"Elizabeth, can you..."

"My name is Jamie Elizabeth O'Reilly."

"Hello, Jamie Elizabeth. My name is Tim. Do you know your daddy's name?"

"David Worthington."

"Can you tell me what you're doing?"

"I'm baking cupcakes with Mommy," Elizabeth stated in a childlike voice. "I like to cook with Mommy."

"What else do you like to do?"

"I like it when William carries me on his shoulders."

"Are there other things you like to do?"

"I like to swim in Grandfather's pool."

Tim saw a frown on Elizabeth's face and her body tensed. "What's happening, Jamie Elizabeth?"

"I'm going outside to play in the pool."

"Are you allowed to do that by yourself?"

"Eric is there."

"Who's Eric?"

"My cousin and he's shouting at me."

"What's Eric saying?"

"He says, 'Go away, you can't swim in my pool.' He's in the pool and I want to swim too."

Tim watched as the tears welled up in Elizabeth's eyes and rolled down her cheeks.

"Why won't Eric let you swim?"

"He doesn't like me and he yells at me again."

"Is Eric older than you are?"

"He's eleven."

"What's he saying?"

"He says, 'Get out of here, you're a bastard.'"

The hurt look on Elizabeth's face showed Tim how painful these memories must be for her. "Then what happened?" Tim asked.

"I yelled back as him, 'I am not.' Then he said 'Your mother's a whore and you're a bastard.'"

Elizabeth sat quietly sobbing the way a child sobs, trying to catch her breath.

"What's happening now, Jamie Elizabeth?"

"Grandfather comes out of the house and yanks Eric out of the pool by his arm. He tells him to sit in a chair and be quiet."

"Jamie Elizabeth, do you know what those names mean?" Tim asked.

"No, but they sound bad and Grandfather is really mad."

"What does your grandfather do?"

"He picks me up in his arms. He says Eric is being mean and saying naughty words. He carries me into the den and gives me some jellybeans from his desk. He calls Grandma from the other room and she comes in and we sit together in Grandfather's big chair. Grandfather goes back out to Eric; I can hear them talking through the open window."

"What are they saying?"

"Eric says I don't belong here. Then Grandfather says he doesn't like his behavior and it's time for him to leave. He calls William to take him home."

"Then what happens?

"Grandma takes me out to the pool and sits with me while I swim. That night I get to talk to Daddy on the phone. He says he's coming home soon."

Tim isn't sure what any of this means but it might have something to do with the ongoing family feud that Elizabeth has mentioned regarding her father and her Aunt Nancy.

"Jamie Elizabeth, please take a big breath." He watches as Elizabeth follows his instructions. "I'm going to bring you back to the present. When you open your eyes you won't remember anything you have told me. I will count backwards from five to one. When I reach one, you will open your eyes. You will feel relaxed and rested."

Tim started counting backwards and when he reached one, Elizabeth opened her eyes and took another deep breath.

"How'd it go?" Elizabeth asked.

"Pretty much the same as yesterday," Tim replied.

"Something's different," Elizabeth said. "I can tell by the look on your face that I told you something you didn't know."

"We went into your childhood a bit. I didn't know your first name was Jamie."

"Wow, you went way back. Nobody but my grandfather has called me Jamie since I was about five."

"Well, I thought since you were under I might as well start trying to figure out the nightmares."

"Any luck?"

"No, but we'll talk about the childhood stuff later. Right now we need to concentrate on the attack."

Elizabeth knew Tim was avoiding the question but she let it go. She didn't want to get into her childhood right now either.

CHAPTER TWENTY-ONE

Elizabeth was nervous about her first day back at the university but the plain-clothes police officer would be at her side all day. Except for her new hair style, there were no visible signs of the assault. In the clinic, she pulled patient files for her class and tried to ignore the persistent back pain that still plagued her. Regardless of her suspicions about Brewer, she wanted to get back to teaching. Seeing Peter Brewer in Laguna could have been a coincidence, but the feeling that he could somehow be connected to the attack weighed on her mind. She hoped she wouldn't see him today.

The students from her Practicum class were scheduled to start patient interviews today, and she wanted to be the one to guide them through this important step of their training.

A group of anxious students milled around in the hall outside the University Clinic observation room. Rumor had it that the "ice queen" used the first student interview as an example of all the things that are done wrong in a counseling session. The unanswered question, who will be the first student to interview a patient, hung like a thundercloud in the air.

Dr. Elizabeth Wing walked out of the clinic office, down the hall, and toward the group of students. She carried a file containing the intake forms that had been filled out.

"This is our first patient," she said holding the file. She unlocked the door and led the students into the small, dark observation room.

"Her name is Betty Jo. She is fifteen years old and works at a fast-food restaurant."

Elizabeth shuffled through the file, closed it, and then stood for a moment looking into the faces of the students, as if reading their minds.

"Find a seat where you can see the patient through the one-way mirror. Watch her body language and her facial expressions. There's a microphone in the counseling room and you will be able to hear everything that is said. She will not be able to see or hear you, but she knows she is being observed by students." She paused, "Are there any questions?"

Silence echoed in the room. A nervous voice from the shadows asked the dreaded question, "Who's going to interview her?"

After a long pause, Elizabeth responded. "I will. Watch and learn." She saw the surprised looks on their faces as she turned and left the room. *This is the first time I've ever demonstrated an intake interview for my students.* Since the assault and her narrow escape with death, Elizabeth had been doing a lot of things differently.

Through the one-way glass, they watched as Dr. Wing led the young woman into the counseling room. She knew they would be expecting to see a typical teenager, not the young girl, looking more like twelve than fifteen, and obviously pregnant, who walked in and sat down across from her.

An hour later, Elizabeth ended the interview with the patient and joined the students in the observation room.

"What did you learn?

The students just stared at her. Finally, one young man blurted out, "Wow, that was great."

"How'd you get so much information so fast?" uttered another student.

"By asking the right questions," Elizabeth replied. "Never assume anything. Even if you think you know how the patient will answer, ask the question. And remember, if the patient hasn't told you something, then you don't know it. Just because most people may believe something is true, doesn't mean your patient will believe it."

"How will we know what questions to ask?" a shy young woman wanted to know.

"That's where experience comes in. Now, what did you learn from the intake?" Elizabeth repeated.

"She's..."

Elizabeth interrupted. "The first thing for you to learn is to make the patient real. Use her name. Start again."

"Betty Jo," the student began, "was raised in a small, isolated town in Arkansas. She was the third of nine children and the family didn't have much money."

"Good." She pointed to another student. "What do you remember?"

"Betty Jo was the first in her family to attend high school. She was more interested in school than boys. She didn't want to be like her mother and aunts and have a bunch of kids."

"Yeah," another student added. "Betty Jo wanted to leave the hick town in the mountains and make something of herself."

Dr. Wing used this student's comments to make a point. "Be respectful of your patient, their family, and their background. It's okay if the patient wants to badmouth their own life, but they may become offended if you do it. What else do we know about Betty Jo?"

"A neighbor boy forced her to have sex against her will," the shy young woman said quietly.

"Why don't you say what really happened?" surfer boy stated. "She was raped and now she's seven months pregnant."

"Yeah. And when her brothers found out she was pregnant, they tried to get the creep to marry her," another young man added.

"Her brothers shouldn't have told her what he said," an older woman in front added. "That was cruel, telling her he said she was no good at sex and that the creep was going to marry someone else."

"We know Betty Jo has pride, and guts," the black woman with the braids said. "She left home because she was ashamed of her condition and the rejection by her baby's father. She didn't intend to let the town or her family humiliate her."

"Good point," Elizabeth added. "Now that you can see her strengths you can use them. Okay, you know the facts. Now what have you learned and how are you going to help her?"

The students mumbled among themselves.

"I hope you've learned never to take a patient for granted. Don't assume anything. For example, not all fifteen-year-olds are rebellious teens. Not all teenage pregnancies are the result of promiscuity. Remember to always ask the questions, even if you think you know what the answer will be. Find out where a patient is in their emotional and intellectual development."

Notebooks opened, papers rustled.

"What will be the next step to take with this patient?" Elizabeth continued.

Comments flew.

"Get her in touch with her anger..."

"Charge the guy with rape..."

"Deal with her guilt..."

"Wait," Elizabeth ordered. "You have to start with her basic needs. Doesn't anyone remember Maslow's Hierarchy of Needs?"

An eager young woman raised her hand and started to explain.

"Draw it on the board," Dr. Wing instructed.

Going to the board, the student drew a triangle and divided it into quarters. She filled in the appropriate categories starting with the top quarter, Self-Actualization, Self-Esteem, Belongingness, and Love, Safety, Physiological Needs.

"Now, let's look at where Betty Jo fits in," Dr. Wing said.

Pointing to the bottom of the section of the diagram, Safety and Physiological Needs, Dr. Wing explained, "Betty Jo needs to feel safe, secure, and out of danger. She needs prenatal care, money, probably welfare because she won't be able to work for a while after the baby comes, and a different place to live. She may need legal advice to become emancipated since she's only fifteen. Everything else will come later."

"It looks like we're her social worker," one student commented.

"You need to find out what the patient needs and start there. You can't have your own agenda. Betty Jo will be coming back next week for her first counseling session. Think about how you can help her, because one of you is about to become her therapist."

Elizabeth dismissed the class and sat alone in the observation room. *That was a good intake. The class responded well.* She looked at the diagram of Maslow's Hierarchy of Needs still on the board. *I'm just like Betty Jo, stuck at the lowest level of needs trying to achieve personal safety. That bastard may have bruised my body but he's not going to stop me!*

Driving home, her bodyguard still at her side, Elizabeth realized how exhausting the week had been. She had worked only one day but her body ached and she no longer had the stamina that had driven her before the attack. She was tired of police escorts, of being suspicious of her patients and friends, and of doubting her own judgment. Most of all, she was physically tired. Thoughts of how soothing a hot bubble bath would feel comforted her as she drove toward home, then she remembered that she had told Detective Gualdoni he could come over this evening to discuss her case.

A brief shower substituted for a leisurely bath. Refreshed, she dressed and hurried downstairs for a quick dinner. The doorbell rang but Elizabeth didn't bother to get up. She knew the police officer would answer it and show Gualdoni in. When Frank walked into the den, she noticed, perhaps for the first time, his physical appearance. Well-built, probably from years of working out; dark curly hair; brown eyes that held a look of sadness. *I could have been attracted to this man if only we had met under different circumstances...I am attracted to him.* Clearing her mind of these thoughts, she stood to greet him.

"Thanks for letting me come over this evening, Dr. Wing."

"You said it was important. Have you figured out who attacked me?"

"No, I'm sorry to say I haven't. But I do have several bits of information about him that I'd like to go over with you."

As they sat down, Elizabeth noticed her wine glass still half full on the table. "Detective, would you like a glass of wine?"

Before he had a chance to answer she added, "I'm sure there's coffee made if you'd rather. My 'babysitters' keep a pot going all the time."

Gualdoni smiled. "I'm officially off duty, I'll take the wine. Thank you."

Elizabeth poured a glass of wine for the detective and sat down beside him on the couch.

He took a sip, then proceeded. "This is what we've got so far. We talked to the cleaning lady who put the pictures in your office. She gave us a description of a young white male. She thought he was trying to look Mexican with a black wig and fake mustache but his Spanish wasn't very good. The Avis rental clerk described a male about thirty-five to forty. The description is limited but he is Caucasian, blond we think, and dressed in expensive clothes but wrinkled, like he might have slept in them. He had the car for a week before your report of harassment. A few days after the attack, we found the car in a corner of the underground parking at your office building. There were no fingerprints in the car. What we did find were crumbs and red stains identified as Mexican food, powder that turned out to be cocaine, and pieces of your hair."

A shiver went through Elizabeth, a flash of memory that vanished before she could identify it, and then, a sickening feeling in her stomach.

"Does this remind you of anyone?" the detective asked.

"Thirty-five to forty and blond fit dozens of men I know."

"Do you have any friends or patients with drug problems?"

She shook her head. "My friends don't use cocaine and I don't see patients with drug problems."

"Can you give me any hint as to who this might be?" Gualdoni asked.

"I'm afraid I can't help you," Elizabeth said.

Gualdoni took another sip of wine and placed the glass carefully on the table. "I wish I had more to go on, but this guy is smart and cautious," he said with sadness in his voice. "The information about the attacker wearing a ring may be helpful if we can catch him but I'm afraid we have very little to go on."

Elizabeth looked into his eyes. He seemed troubled at not being able to identify the attacker. The therapist in her wanted to lessen his pain. She was surprised at the intensity of her attraction to Frank Gualdoni. *He may be a bit rough around the edges, but there's a sensitivity that I do find appealing.*

"Dr. Wing," Gualdoni said, standing to leave, "if you can think of anyone who might fit this description, give me a call."

"Please stay," she heard herself saying, "I'd like to discuss something else with you. And please, call me Elizabeth. You know more about me than most of my friends."

Gualdoni sat back down, and Elizabeth filled his wine glass again.

"I think it's time to stop the police escorts," Elizabeth began. "I feel smothered by their constant presence. Sooner or later, I'll need to be on my own."

"Not yet. This guy is out there and I'm afraid he might try to hurt you again."

"You can't protect me forever," Elizabeth said.

"How about a compromise? We'll stop the guard at your office and here at the house. But we will continue to escort you everywhere else as well as the hourly drive-bys. We'll meet you every night after work and escort you home. Once you're safely inside, and the security system turned on, we'll leave."

"That sounds like something I can live with," Elizabeth said with a smile. "It can start tonight. Tell the officer she's got the night off."

Gualdoni went into the living room and discharged the officer on duty, then returned to the den where Elizabeth sat finishing her wine.

"Mission accomplished. You're on your own."

"Thank you so much, Detective Gualdoni," Elizabeth said as she walked him to the door.

"The name's Frank," he replied, smiling.

He closed the door, tried it to be sure it was locked, and then walked to his car.

CHAPTER TWENTY-TWO

Elizabeth had been unable to see her patients for two weeks, but for some, that could be an eternity. She feared Mary Ellen was one of those patients. They had missed four sessions, and although she had been seen by Tim, Elizabeth still worried about how she was doing. Tim had reported that the sessions went smoothly, but Mary Ellen didn't trust men, and Elizabeth worried about any setbacks her absence may have caused in her patient's therapy. She need not have been concerned. When Mary Ellen came in, it was obvious that something had changed. The dress she wore showed off her slender figure, her makeup had been carefully applied, and her hair hung in loose curls on her shoulders.

"You're looking very nice today," Elizabeth said, trying to hide her surprise.

"Dr. Henderson told me I needed to take better care of myself—pretend I had an important person to meet, act as if I were important. I tried it. No matter how I feel, when I wake up, I pretend."

"Well, it looks like it's working."

"Dr. Wing, are you and Dr. Henderson…a couple?"

"No. We're not."

"He's so nice, and good-looking, too. Why, if he weren't my doctor…well you're my doctor, but I guess he is too, sort of…I would give anything to go out with a man like him."

Elizabeth thought about Tim and how attentive he had been since the attack. *He is a nice man.* Mary Ellen was right about him being good-looking, as well. Tall and athletic with blond hair that he kept cut short, Tim could pose for *GQ Magazine*. He could turn heads, even in L.A. They had known each other for a long time, and she knew Tim would like to be more than friends. *It's too bad I could never think of him as anything but a friend.*

"Yes, Mary Ellen, he is very nice. It's important for you to know that there are nice men who won't hurt you or take advantage of you. It sounds like the sessions you had with Dr. Henderson were very helpful."

"We didn't talk about the nightmares. Mostly, we talked about me taking control of my life."

Elizabeth could tell that Mary Ellen had developed transference issues with Tim. That could be a useful tool for her patient in forming relationships with men. Mary Ellen seemed to have weathered her absence very well. She looked better and sounded better than she had in months.

"Mary Ellen, you seem to be doing quite well. I think it's time to talk about some of the things you told me under hypnosis, what do you think?"

"Did I tell you awful things?"

"You told me about your adolescence. About things that Al did and how you tried to protect yourself and your sister."

"Do I need to hear them?"

"I think it's important for you to understand that no matter what happened to you and your sister, you showed a lot of strength for a young girl."

"Okay, I guess I'm ready."

"We'll take it slow. I'll discuss an incident; if any conscious memories come up for you, we'll talk about them. If you like, I'll play back the tape so you can hear your exact words and anytime you want, we can stop," Elizabeth assured her.

Elizabeth revealed one scenario at a time that Mary Ellen had talked about while under hypnosis. Some she had memories of, others she didn't. At times Mary Ellen cried, at other times her body tensed as she remembered the events. During the hour, only a few of the many incidents she had revealed were discussed.

"I think that's enough for today," Elizabeth said near the close of the hour.

"I can remember at lot of what you're telling me. Why can't I remember Al trying to molest me?" she asked.

"For you, these memories are too painful. But, now that we have discussed them, you may start to have conscious recollections."

"No wonder my sister is so angry at me. She remembers what Al did to her."

"You're beginning to understand some of the things Al did; the time might be right for you to call your sister and discuss these events from the past."

"Dr. Wing, that feels really scary. I don't know if I can do it."

"Remember what Dr. Henderson told you? Take control of your life. You can do it, Mary Ellen. I know you can."

Mary Ellen smiled. "Yes, I can. I'll do it."

The session went by quickly and after Mary Ellen left, Elizabeth realized that no matter how fragile her patients may seem, they all have inner strengths.

Sandra Cunningham hadn't faired as well. She canceled her appointment when Joanne called to inform her that Dr. Henderson would be seeing her because of Dr. Wing's hospitalization. This week, she called to see if *her* doctor had returned.

When Sandra walked into Elizabeth's office, she showed none of the self-confidence present during their last session.

"I'm so glad your back, Dr. Wing. I need to talk and I just couldn't talk to a man about how I'm feeling."

"You don't seem like yourself today, is there something in particular you would like to discuss?"

"Yes. Yes, there is. Roger has changed." Sandra spent a great deal of time explaining the incidents of the past two weeks. "He's agitated, angry, and very unpredictable most of the time. Sometimes he goes out at night. He never used to do that. He hits me in front of the children without giving it a second thought."

Sandra pushed up the sleeves of her blouse and showed Elizabeth the newest bruises.

"Is he hitting the children?" Elizabeth asked, knowing that she would need to make a child abuse report if this was happening.

"No, just me. But they're scared."

"How are your plans to leave coming along?"

"I've done the intake interview at two shelters. I just hope that if they call my friend and tell her there's an opening, I'll be able to get away. Timing is so important for me," Sandra said with a sigh.

"How long will they hold the space?" Elizabeth asked.

"One shelter said three days, but the other one will only hold the space for twenty-four hours."

Noise from the waiting room disrupted their conversation, and the sound of something hitting the office door startled them.

"Tell the doctor her time is up," Roger Cunningham's voice bellowed.

"See what I mean?" Sandra said as she rose to leave. "He's getting worse."

"Same time next week, Sandra," Dr. Wing called after her as her patient hurried into the waiting room.

Elizabeth's secretary walked into the office and closed the door. "That man is terrible," Joanne said. "He makes me nervous, sitting there staring at me. Why can't he just wait for his wife in the car?"

"I don't think we'll be seeing too much more of him," Elizabeth responded. She knew Sandra would need to leave her husband soon. She just hoped that the shelter called before it was too late.

Elizabeth called the police escort, informing him that she was ready to leave. As she straightened her desk and started to put away her last two patients' files, Tim came into her office.

"Do you have a minute?" he asked as he walked over to the window and stood with his back to Elizabeth, looking out at the city lights.

"Probably more than a minute; my escort is stuck in traffic."

"I'd like to talk to you about Mary Ellen," Tim said without turning around.

"You did a great job with her. She came in today and looked better than I've seen her look in months. I think it was good for her to have a positive experience with a male."

"I enjoyed working with her." Tim left the window and sat down in the chair next to Elizabeth's desk. "She's...sweet..." Tim said softly, leaving the sentence hanging.

Elizabeth stopped what she was doing and looked at him. "And…" she questioned, hoping Tim wasn't contemplating what she thought he might be.

"And I just…just wanted to know how she's doing…" Tim stammered.

"Do you want to keep her as a patient?" Elizabeth asked. She hoped that was it. That he wanted to continue working with Mary Ellen professionally.

"No!" Tim said emphatically. "No, not at all."

Elizabeth didn't like what Tim's question was leading to. "Well, what is it?" She would make him say it. Make him verbalize out loud, just what he wanted.

"Is…do you think…does she trust men enough to…date?"

"Tim, you can't. You saw her as a patient. It's a dual relationship and you know it!"

Tim sat up straighter in the chair, taking a defensive posture. "She was never really *my* patient. I filled in for you during an emergency. She's your patient."

"You're trying to rationalize," Elizabeth said, slamming the file in her hand down on her desk. "The Board of Psychology would have you before the Ethics Committee. They would see it as a dual relationship."

"Liz, I find her very attractive. I'd like to go out with her," Tim said quietly.

"Don't put me on the spot, Tim. The rules are very clear on this one: three years. You can't date someone you've seen as a patient without a time lapse of three years."

"I know you're right, but she really wasn't my patient."

"Don't take this any further. You've got too much to lose."

"Okay, Liz, I won't do anything stupid." Tim stood up and walked to the door then stopped, "Liz, I haven't shared my feelings with Mary Ellen, and I won't. At least not until I think it through. Maybe I'll run it by legal counsel anonymously and get their take on the situation. Either way, I won't say anything to her without discussing it further with you."

Tim left Elizabeth's office without looking back. *Poor Tim, he always picks the women who are unavailable to him.*

CHAPTER TWENTY-THREE

Cash was in a foul mood. He hadn't been able to find Squirrel and didn't dare make another buy himself. His stash was gone. The police were watching Elizabeth. And now, the night manager had given him a room in the rear of the hotel instead of the one overlooking the street that he usually rented.

By the time Squirrel arrived, Cash was agitated and ready to pick a fight.

"Where the hell have you been? I've been trying to find you for days."

"I don't have to answer to you."

"You do when I'm the one supplying the coke."

"You supply the money. I'm the one who takes all the risks. Why don't you just buy your own stash?"

Cash knew Squirrel was right and he backed off, keeping his anger under control. He needed Squirrel as much as Squirrel needed him.

"Here," Cash said, holding out a handful of bills. "Go make the buy." He shoved Squirrel out the door.

Cash paced the floor waiting for Squirrel to return. He couldn't watch the buy go down because of the location of the room. Ten minutes. Fifteen. It shouldn't take this long. Had that creep taken off with his money? He heard footsteps in the hall and then a rap on the door.

"It's me."

The chain still fastened, Cash peered through the crack. Squirrel was alone. He pulled off the chain and hustled Squirrel inside, then looked down the hall to make sure Squirrel hadn't been followed.

"What took you so long?"

"I met a friend."

"What the hell do you mean, you met a friend?" Cash yelled.

"A girl. I haven't seen her for a while. I invited her up."

"I told you before, nobody comes to the room. I don't want anybody to see me here."

"Stop being so paranoid. It's only a girl," Squirrel shouted back. "She'll give me a blow job, I'll give her a little snow and she's out of here. She's good. If you give her some coke she'll do you too." Squirrel smirked, knowing Cash wouldn't do it.

"I don't need some coke whore doing me." Cash grabbed the buy and started his ritual of preparing the powder.

"Damn, you're uptight. When do we pay another visit to 'your doctor'?"

"Thanks to you, the cops are watching her day and night."

"Well, let's call somebody else," Squirrel suggested, taking a snort from the lines of coke on the mirror.

"I don't want somebody else. I want her, and what she can get for me," Cash responded. He took the mirror from Squirrel and snorted a line.

"You don't have enough women in your life," Squirrel said as someone knocked on their door.

"And you've got too many. Get rid of her."

Cash snorted another line, turned on the radio full blast, shut off the overhead light, and walked to the window. The girl at the door made him nervous. The activity in the alley down below made him nervous. Squirrel's careless attitude made him nervous. He wanted things the way they were before Squirrel messed it all up by attacking Elizabeth.

The door closed and the girl giggled as she followed Squirrel into the room. Turning slightly, he saw Squirrel sit on the side of the bed and the girl drop to her knees in front of him. Oh, God, he thought, I'm just like that whore. I'll do anything to get my fix. All that time in rehab and look at me.

CHAPTER TWENTY-FOUR

Frank didn't know what to do with himself. This was the first weekend he'd taken off in months and he missed his kids. His ex-wife had moved them to New Mexico. She wanted to become a painter, or maybe she just wanted to punish him. She blamed him for the divorce. She said he worked too much overtime and didn't spend enough time with the family. Well, she was right, he did work too much, but why New Mexico?

He thought about doing something with a friend but the few friends he had were cops. If they had a weekend off, they certainly didn't want to spend it with another cop talking cases; they wanted to be with their families.

He'd paid the bills, run a load of wash, and done what little housework the typical bachelor does; the cleaning lady would do the rest. He'd gone for a long run. For years he stayed in shape running; at forty-two he could still keep up with the new recruits. After he retired from the department in January, he'd need to keep running. Sitting all day in law school would put on the pounds for sure. Lately, he'd spotted a few gray hairs among the black curls but it didn't bother him. He figured it would make him look distinguished as an attorney.

Bored, Frank headed for the back patio with his coffee and the morning paper. Looking around the yard, he realized it had been weeks since he'd done any yard work. *I'm not that bored!* Settling down to read the paper, a CD of Kenny G playing classical jazz in the background, he promised himself he would spend more time on the yard after he retired.

A half hour later, he worked diligently on the crossword puzzle. Fifteen down, British gun…sten, he knew that one. Twenty-six down, a seven-letter word for Greek money…

Startled by a sharp knock at the front door, he looked at his watch. Only eight-thirty. Too early for salesmen, maybe it's a neighborhood kid selling candy. *Maybe whoever it is will go away.* The loud knocking persisted.

Frank didn't want to get up. He didn't want to be disturbed. He wanted his day off to be relaxing. But he got up anyway and headed for the door. When he looked through the side window he could see a man with a close-cropped mustache, dressed in a cheap, ill-fitting suit. *Looks like a cop. Now what?*

"Frank Gualdoni?" the man asked as Frank opened the door. "Frank L. Gualdoni?"

"Yes. I'm Frank L. Gualdoni."

The man thrust the paper he had been holding into Frank's hand. "You've been served."

"I shouldn't have answered the door," Frank mumbled more to himself than to the process server as he looked down at the paper in his hand.

"Doesn't matter. I'd have found you sooner or later."

"Yeah, I guess so."

The man shrugged his shoulders, turned, and walked away as Frank slammed the door.

Frank knew who the papers were from, but he read them anyway.

"Damn her," he muttered. His ex-wife had taken most of the furniture, a cash settlement for her share of the house, and now she wanted more child support and alimony.

"That bitch." His dream of early retirement and law school seemed to be slipping away. Kicking at a pile of magazines, scattering them across the living room floor, he swore again. *I'll call her. Ask her why the hell she needs more money. Tell her to get off her lazy ass and get a real job.* But he didn't. He knew better. It would only make matters worse.

Back on the patio, he tried to work on the crossword puzzle again but he couldn't concentrate. Thoughts of how to handle his ex-wife had taken over. First, hire an attorney; not the nice guy he'd used for his divorce;

look what he'd lost with him. No, this time he'd get a real barracuda, someone who would protect his rights. *Damn. I might as well go to work; the day's shot now anyway. At the office, there's always paperwork to do and someone to talk to.*

Driving toward the station, Frank thought about Elizabeth. He hadn't seen her in a week. No reason to since the department had arranged an escort for her and he had no new information on her case. *I wonder how she got along this week without a full-time bodyguard. I'll just stop by for a minute and see how she's doing.* He changed lanes, made a sharp left turn, and drove toward the high-rent district where she lived. *If I ever get involved with a woman again, it will be someone like Elizabeth. Someone with class. Someone who is smart, beautiful, rich…Just how much did she inherit from her grandfather?* Pushing these thoughts out of his mind, he turned onto Elizabeth's street. *Forget it; she's out of your league, Gualdoni.*

Frank rang the bell and waited. He rang again. He was about to leave when he heard footsteps. It had taken Elizabeth a long time to answer the door and when she did, she looked like hell. *She looks like a different person.* The first time he'd seen her, smartly dressed, makeup and perfect hair, he was impressed. This morning she looked tired, liked she hadn't slept well in days. She wore no makeup and her hair, now a short mass of curls, looked like it hadn't been combed. *The stress is really getting to her. She looks like she could use a friend.*

"Good morning," Frank said, trying not to show his surprise at her appearance. "I hope I didn't catch you at a bad time?"

"No. It's…it's fine. I'm an early riser. Would you like some coffee? I just made a fresh pot."

Frank followed Elizabeth into the kitchen. After an awkward silence, they both started to speak at once. Laughing, Elizabeth let Frank continue.

"I just stopped by to see how the week went without the bodyguard."

"It went well," Elizabeth said, trying to act cheerful. She looked down, and then back at Frank. "No, no it didn't go well. I'm surprised at how nervous I've been all week."

"Do you want me to arrange for another officer to be with you?"

"No. I've got to get used to being on my own again. I can't have a babysitter forever," Elizabeth said, stirring her coffee. "Are you working on a Saturday?"

"Nothing official. I was just on my way to the station to do a little paperwork and thought I'd see how you were doing."

"I wish I could say everything was great, but I miss my routine. I wanted to go running this morning, then I realized it probably wasn't a good idea to be out there alone."

"I run most mornings. We could jog together sometime if you'd like," Frank suggested.

"I'd like that."

Frank told Elizabeth about his plan to retire from the police force and how anxious he was to start law school. She told him how her grandfather had discussed points of law with her when she was a teenager.

"My grandfather and I would go sailing and he would start talking about a case he was researching. He said the sea air cleared his mind and helped him plan his strategy."

"My brothers and I went to sailing camp on the Jersey coast when we were boys," Frank responded. "I was never very good at it."

"We could go sailing sometime. I could give you a few pointers if you want to try again," she suggested.

They laughed and talked. Frank couldn't believe how comfortable he felt with her. At lunchtime, when he started to leave, she asked him to stay and offered to make lunch for them.

In the kitchen, Elizabeth stared into the refrigerator. She hadn't been shopping in over a week. She pulled out a loaf of bread and discovered it had mold on it and tossed it into the trash. She found some tomatoes, an onion, celery that was a bit limp but would pass in a salad, and a couple of eggs that she put on to boil.

"Can I help?" Frank called from the balcony.

"No, thanks," she replied as she carried out two glasses of ice tea. "I've got everything under control."

Back in the kitchen, she opened a can of tuna fish, chopped the celery and a bit of onion, and mixed them all with mayonnaise. She cut the tomatoes in eight sections, making sure not to cut them all the way through and stuffed them with the tuna salad. The eggs were hard boiled, and she hurriedly peeled them, cut them in half, and mixed the yokes with mustard, mayonnaise, and salt and pepper for deviled eggs. Arranging a plate for each of them, she opened a bag of chips and dumped them into a bowl.

"Surprising what you can whip up from an empty frig," she said as she carried lunch onto the balcony.

"Looks good to me," Frank said.

"Thanks for stopping by, Frank. I've spent too much time alone the past couple of weeks, and it's nice to talk about something besides work."

"Yeah. The only reason I was going to work was to be around people and forget about my ex-wife." Frank paused for a minute then went on, "She had me served this morning. She wants more child support."

"How many children do you have?"

"Two. My son Frankie Jr. is fourteen and Lauren is twelve. I don't mind paying child support, but she can't give them everything they want. I just want to finish law school before they start college."

"I planned on having children when Daniel and I got married but we decided to wait. I guess it's a good thing we did. I hope I have the opportunity to have a family some day."

It was after five when Frank noticed the time. "We've spent the whole day talking," Frank said. "If you're not bored with me, I know a little Italian restaurant on the coast that serves great seafood. If you don't have plans…"

"No plans and you're not boring," Elizabeth responded, without giving Frank a chance to finish.

"Great. I'll go home and change and pick you up in about an hour."

On the drive home, Frank couldn't believe he had asked Elizabeth out to dinner. He knew this wasn't a real date. He knew she just didn't want to be alone. Well, he didn't want to be alone either. A woman like her made him feel alive again. *Screw my ex-wife. It's Saturday night and I'm going out to dinner with Dr. Elizabeth Wing.*

Elizabeth didn't like to admit, even to herself, that the past week without a police officer had been difficult. She had not done well. At work, she'd been able to put her personal life aside and concentrate on her patients, but at home, she had no such diversion. Today, with Frank there, the cloud of denial had lifted and she saw clearly what she had refused to acknowledge. Signs that, as a psychologist, she knew meant trouble. Her appetite hadn't returned since her stay in the hospital, and she had continued to lose weight. She slept poorly. Nightmares awakened her. She dragged herself to work each morning, and had no interest in social activities. *If a patient had told me they had no appetite, couldn't sleep, and had no interest in life, I'd diagnose them as clinically depressed. At my next therapy session, I should tell Tim. No, Tim will insist that I take antidepressants. I know what's wrong, I can handle it. I don't intend to go on medication.*

Frank's visit had been a wake-up call for her to get on with her life. She seldom took the time to just talk with friends. Talking with Frank had been relaxing and enjoyable. Tomorrow she'd call Carol; she hadn't returned her calls. After a date with Frank, she'd have something besides the attack to talk about. *Dinner tonight will be fun.*

Soaking in a hot tub, vanilla-scented bubbles surrounding her, candles flickering, and piano music playing in the background, she felt more like herself than she had since the attack. The phone rang. *Let it ring, Tim's on call, he can handle any emergencies.*

Going through her closet looking for something to wear frustrated her. *I must go shopping for new clothes; shop therapy, that's what I need. Shopping always makes me feel better.* Finally, she settled on a black crepe dress, accented it with a colorful yellow flowered scarf, put on gold earrings, slipped into black pumps, and went downstairs to wait for Frank.

The phone rang again; this time she answered it.

"Hi, Liz," the voice on the other end said cheerily. "I've been trying to reach you. Do you want to join Andrew and me for dinner tonight?"

"Sorry, Carol. I have a date. Well, not really a date, a dinner engagement. Frank Gualdoni is taking me out for seafood."

"I'd call that a date. Go for it, girl. He's all man."

"He came over this morning to check on me and ending up spending the day. It was enjoyable and…well, he invited me out to dinner."

"Call me tomorrow and tell me all the details. Have fun," Carol added playfully.

Elizabeth hung up the phone and caught a glimpse of herself in the hall mirror. It surprised her. This morning she had looked tired and listless. Now she looked relaxed and happy. *Spending time with Frank is good for me!*

For years, Elizabeth had worked on presenting a professional appearance. Her clothes tailored in a business look, her makeup subtle, and her hair usually pulled back to keep the curls under control, all in an effort to appear older. The attacker's desire for locks of her hair had forced her to now wear her hair short. The short haircut gave her a more playful look, a pixie appearance, making her blue eyes look even larger. There was no mistaking the electric blue eyes of the Worthington family. Her grandfather, her father, and even her cousins all had the violet-blue eyes that seemed to be able to both peer into your soul and melt your heart. Her mother told her that it was her father's eyes that drew her to him in the beginning.

My eyes may be Worthington, but this red hair is pure O'Reilly. She had inherited her mother's delicate Irish complexion, naturally curly red hair, and a temper that could flare out of control, if provoked.

Looking into the mirror, Elizabeth vowed to regain the feisty spirit that had once been her trademark. She would not let this attack change her!

CHAPTER TWENTY-FIVE

"Your escort awaits," Frank said with a flourish when Elizabeth opened the door.

He looked handsome. His suit, high end, probably not tailor made but an excellent fit, was not the suit he wore to work. Carol's words echoed in her head, "He's all man." *Definitely good looking! Good looking and he can protect me, if necessary.* He stood over six feet tall and she guessed he topped the scale at about 210. Up until this point, Frank Gualdoni had been the detective on her case. Today, he seemed more like a concerned friend. But now, picking her up for dinner, she realized there could be more to the relationship than she had allowed herself to admit. *This really is a date.*

She smiled up at him. "Why, thank you, Sir." Taking his arm, they walked down the steps to his car.

They made a striking couple, the tall, well-built Italian and the lovely redhead on his arm. Frank had chosen a romantic restaurant on the coast, and when they entered, heads turned. Once seated, Frank looked briefly at the wine list and selected a bottle of Kossler, Pinot Grigio.

"If you like clams, they make an excellent Spaghetti alle Vongole," Frank said, closing the menu.

"I do and it sounds wonderful."

Elizabeth sat back and let Frank order. He seemed to know what he was doing, and somehow she didn't mind letting him take charge. Along with the wine, he ordered an appetizer of Bruschetta al pomodoro and garlic Bruschetta, La Caprese salad, and their main course of Spaghetti alle Vongole.

This man knows his Italian food! The waiter brought the wine perfectly chilled, poured them each a glass, and placed the bottle in an ice bucket. Their appetizer appeared right after the wine, and Elizabeth could easily see why Frank liked this restaurant. The wait staff seemed to fill your needs before you knew you had them.

"You seem to be quite a connoisseur," Elizabeth remarked, as she tasted the wine he had ordered.

"This Pinot Grigio is from the Alto Adige region in northern Italy. There's not too many restaurants that sell it in the States; too bad because it's excellent. I try to follow my parents' philosophy about wine. Always serve the best you can afford. Growing up, dinner may have been just pasta, but it was always accompanied by good wine. What can I say? We're Italian."

"Does your family live in California?"

"No, New Jersey. I joined the Marine Corps right out of high school. After boot camp I was stationed at Camp Pendleton. I loved Southern California, and when I got out after three years I stayed here and joined the Long Beach police force."

"Were your parents upset that you didn't go back home?"

"Not really. They knew I wanted to be a cop and it would be a lot easier for me away from the family."

"Easier, why?" Elizabeth asked puzzled.

A beautiful presentation of Caprese appeared before them, along with hot garlic bread.

Frank paused. "My family is…complicated," he paused again.

"Most are," Elizabeth said, thinking about her own family. Even she didn't understand the complicated barriers that existed in her family. She watched as Frank refilled their wine glasses.

"Not like mine. I'm the oldest of the brood, three girls and three boys, a good Catholic family," he said with a laugh.

"My family is Catholic too. At least both of my grandmothers were. My parents seldom go to church. I guess you'd say I'm not exactly Catholic even though I was baptized in the church."

"My brother would say that makes you Catholic."

"Your brother?" Elizabeth asked a bit confused.

"Yes. My baby brother, Michael, is a priest."

"So, why is it easier to be a cop in Long Beach?" Elizabeth asked again.

"In my family, you're a priest, a cop, or a crook. I'm a cop. I wasn't cut out to be a priest. Michael had the calling and joined the Jesuits. That leaves my middle brother, Johnny. His activities are, shall we say, often against the law. So as you can see, it would be difficult for me to be a cop back home."

Elizabeth sat for a minute, thinking about what Frank had just said. What exactly did he mean when he said his brother's activities are "against the law"?

"A crook," she finally repeated. "Do you mean some kind of white-collar crime or does he knock off neighborhood 7-Elevens?"

"Neither. Let's just say his activities are such that being a cop in my hometown would be more than complicated."

The band had just started playing and they ate in silence, listening to the music for a while. As Frank had predicted, the Spaghetti Alle Vongole was fantastic. It certainly compared to the wonderful food she remembered when traveling in Italy. They hadn't talked about the attack or her stalker. Elizabeth liked that. It made the evening seem more like a date, and she hoped this wouldn't be their only one.

The waiter cleared the dinner plates, then brought a dessert tray.

"Just cappuccino for me," Elizabeth said.

"Make that two," Frank added and waived the tray of desserts away.

Sipping her coffee, Elizabeth looked out at the waves lapping against the sand. She hadn't been to the beach since the attack.

"Would you like to dance?" Frank asked. "The dance floor isn't too crowded and I promise not to step on your toes."

"I'd love to," Elizabeth answered, a bit surprised. "But let me warn you, it's been a while."

Frank led her around the floor with such ease that she had no difficulty following him. He held her close and her body responded willingly to his touch. *I haven't been in a man's arms in a long time.* She closed her eyes and rested her head against his shoulder. The band ended the set with "Arrivederci Roma," and Frank held Elizabeth's hand as they walked back to their table.

"This is a lovely restaurant," Elizabeth said as they ordered another cappuccino.

"One of my favorites; I thought you might enjoy it."

They lingered over the cappuccinos, as if neither wanted the evening to end. On the drive home along the coast, Elizabeth was grateful that they continued to avoid the subject of the stalker. *No need to spoil a perfect evening.*

Lying in bed after her date with Frank, Elizabeth tried to remember the last time she'd been out with a man. Besides an occasional dinner with Tim, she hadn't had a date in months. This evening had been a very romantic first date, nothing pretentious, but definitely more than casual. *I hope tonight was as special for Frank as it was for me.* He had been attentive but not overbearing. He seemed interested in her life for reasons other than the case. A romantic restaurant, very good wine, great food… She drifted off to sleep remembering the music, the candlelit table in the corner, and the deep brown eyes of the man sitting across from her.

A barking dog woke Elizabeth. She tried to go back to sleep but the incessant barking annoyed her. The neighbor shouted at his German shepherd to be quiet. Wide-awake, she sat up in bed. *Someone's out there!* Fear grabbed her. She crept out of bed and went to the window. Her heart pounded wildly. The security lights in her back yard flashed on. The neighbor's dog charged at the six-foot-high chain-link fence. He ran back and forth along the fence, barking out of control. Terror that the man who had attacked her had come back to finish the job filled her mind. Elizabeth reached for the alarm button but the flashing light indicated the silent alarm had already been triggered. The police were on their way. Her hands trembled as she grabbed the cordless phone and ran into the bathroom and locked the door. She dialed Frank's cell phone.

"Elizabeth, is that you?"

"Yes, my alarm went off."

"I know. The station called me. I'm on my way."

"Where are you?"

"Upstairs. I'm locked in my bathroom."

"Stay there until the police arrive. When they get there, I'll call you."

Elizabeth stood, her back against the bathroom door, waiting for the sounds of sirens. *I can't go on living like this. I've got to find out who's after me.*

When the phone finally rang, she answered with a shaky voice. "Frank, is that you?" Elizabeth's fear had all but paralyzed her.

"Elizabeth, the police are at your front door. Go let them in."

Still on the phone with Frank, she unlocked the bathroom door, went downstairs, and let the police in. Snapping on latex gloves, they searched the house and the yard but found no one. Frank arrived minutes after the patrol car and joined the other officers. Broken branches on the bushes outside the living room window indicated the intruder had looked inside and possibly tried to enter through the window. Footprints were visible in the garden. An officer found a note stuffed between the screen and the sliding glass door leading to the kitchen and passed it to Frank.

Scrawled in pencil on a scrap of paper was written, "Don't you think dating a cop is beneath you?"

"Do you recognize the handwriting?" Frank asked, showing the note to Elizabeth.

"No," she answered wearily.

Frank passed the note back to the officer. "Have this dusted for prints. He may have been careless this time."

It was after three in the morning before the police finished their investigation and finally left. Elizabeth made coffee and she and Frank went into the den to drink it. Frank pulled the drapes closed before he sat down next to Elizabeth.

"We know he's still watching you. I just wish he'd make a mistake," Frank said.

"I've decided to buy a gun. Will you teach me how to use it?"

"Yes, of course I will. But are you sure you want to do that?"

"I can't live my life being frightened."

"Elizabeth, carrying a gun will not make you feel less frightened. Believe me, I've carried a gun most of my adult life and I'm still scared every time I think I may need to use it."

"I don't know what else to do, Frank."

"You don't have to make any decisions right now. Why don't you go back to bed and get some sleep? I'll stay here on the couch if you don't mind. We can talk more about the gun later."

She didn't mind Frank sleeping on the couch at all. In fact, if he'd asked to sleep in her bed she wouldn't have minded!

Elizabeth went upstairs, alone. Back in bed, she thought about Frank's comment that a gun would not make her feel less frightened. Tonight, she felt safe in his arms when they danced. His strength, the smell of his cologne, the intense brown eyes, all aroused feelings in Elizabeth. She wanted to call out to him, ask him to hold her again. Hold her and sleep by her side. Ask him. . . *Slow down, don't do it. Not tonight. Not for the wrong reasons.*

Tossing and turning, unable to fall asleep, she thought about how the barking dog had awakened her and chased away the intruder. She contemplated buying a dog; a big, well-trained, mean dog. She pictured herself wearing a Big Dog tee shirt and being dragged down the street by a giant, four-footed bodyguard; she smiled as she fell asleep.

Desperate for some coke, Cash broke his own rule and called the hotel from his cell phone. The same hotel he always stayed in, but this time he insisted on the front corner room that he preferred. He usually used a pay phone even though he had blocked the number on his cell phone. He called Squirrel from his cell phone, too; the two would meet in an hour. When he got to the hotel, he circled the block then parked on a side street a block away and walked. No need to take any chances.

He checked into the room and waited for Squirrel. When he finally arrived, Cash counted out five one-hundred-dollar bills and thrust the money into Squirrel's hand.

"Get an ounce," Cash ordered. "And this time, no girls."

"Yeah, yeah," Squirrel replied.

Cash stood at the hotel window as Squirrel walked to the corner to make the buy, but something went wrong. This time, when Squirrel held out the money, cops surrounded him, pushed Squirrel and the dealer against the wall, slapped cuffs on them, and led them to an unmarked police car. He didn't think Squirrel would give him up but he had to get out of there. Helpless, he watched as his money and his chance to get high disappeared.

Afraid to go out the front door of the hotel, he ran up the stairs to the roof. Now what, he thought. This isn't a movie! I can't leap to the next building and escape. He peered over the edge of the building, no police cars in sight. The streets seemed filled with the usual blend of hookers, street people, and teens cruising by. He walked back down the stairs trying to look casual; at the front door, he stopped and checked the strangers walking by, then walked out hoping no one noticed him.

In his car driving home, he became increasingly agitated over the two near misses. He'd tried to break into Elizabeth's house and leave her a message but the neighbor's dog and motion-activated lights from the security system the bitch had installed alerted her and he barely escaped. Now this! What if he'd tried to make the buy himself? It went okay last time but it could be him instead of Squirrel calling for a lawyer. Damn! Everything is falling apart.

CHAPTER TWENTY-SIX

Frank desperately wanted to ask Elizabeth out again. Two weeks ago, it had seemed natural. They'd spent the day together and dinner followed naturally. Now, with her case still open, he felt that he had crossed professional boundaries. They had talked on the phone, met for coffee, and jogged together, but he had held back on having another date. Without a doubt, he felt a physical attraction. If only he could catch this pervert, then he would feel free to continue the relationship.

He pushed away from his desk and stood up and walked into Lieutenant Brook's office. He dropped the completed file of another case he had been assigned in the center of the lieutenant's desk. Another criminal off the streets, he thought to himself. The satisfaction he felt having the paperwork completed before his boss had a chance to ask for it was a cross between a personal pat on the back and giving him the finger. Lieutenant Brooks insisted on assigning additional cases even though Frank was still spending a good deal of time on the Wing case. *If only Elizabeth's case had been as easy to solve as this one.*

Seven-thirty. He'd skipped dinner to finish up the paperwork. He was hungry, but as he walked to his car, he did not look forward to going home to an empty house and eating alone.

Frank had just reached the parking lot when his cell phone rang.

"Yeah," he barked into the phone, wondering who was calling him when he was supposed to be off duty.

"It's Officer Perez. I'm on patrol in sector three and I just drove by Dr. Wing's. There's a car parked out front. It wasn't here a half-hour ago and it's not on our list of approved cars."

"Did you run the plates?"

"It's a rental. Avis. They're checking on the status."

"I'm on my way."

Frank hung up his cell phone and turned on the police radio. Wednesdays were Elizabeth's early night. She should have been home by six-thirty, seven at the latest. He pulled out of the police parking structure and headed for her house. Impatiently, he tapped his fingers on the steering wheel as he came to a stop at a red light. Using the police radio, he called Officer Perez back.

"Perez, any sign of activity in or around the house?"

"No, sir."

"Go knock on the door. I'll stay on the line."

Gualdoni sped through the residential streets waiting for Perez to respond. Leaving the police line open, he dialed Elizabeth's home number from his cell phone. It rang several times before the answering machine picked up with Elizabeth's cheery voice.

The police radio crackled and Officer Perez came back on the line, "Detective, there's no answer at the door."

"Start checking around outside for any signs of forced entry. I'm a block away."

Gualdoni called the station and asked if Dr. Wing's escort had reported any problems. He was told that she left her office a little after six, and drove straight home. There was no mention of any plans to go out for the evening.

When he pulled up outside Elizabeth's house, Officer Perez gave him a wave and walked up to his car.

"Everything looks fine. No sign of any break-in."

"Perez, check the neighbors. See if this car belongs to anyone in the neighborhood. I'm going to call her office, maybe someone knows where she is."

Frank didn't like not knowing where Elizabeth was. Ever since the attack she had cut back on the hours she spent seeing patients, and her routine had been predictable. Maybe it had been too predictable.

He dialed Elizabeth's office and listened to the rings, hoping someone would answer.

"Dr. Wing's office, this is Dr. Henderson."

"Tim, its Detective Gualdoni. I'm trying to locate Elizabeth. Do you know where she is?"

"She's having dinner with a friend. Is there a problem?"

"The patrol officer spotted a rental car outside her house. He called me and I'm making sure she's okay. You don't happen to know who the friend is, do you?"

"Not for sure. If I were to guess, I'd say it's Daniel. I heard through a friend he's in town."

"You mean her ex-husband, Daniel?"

"One and the same."

"Oh. Well, ah...I guess that's all," Gualdoni paused. "I think I've asked you this before, but do you think Daniel is capable of hurting Elizabeth?"

There was a long silence before Henderson answered. "Daniel is ill-tempered and impulsive. He's been known to get himself in hot water because he doesn't think about the consequences of his actions." Another long pause...

"Do you think...?" Frank started to ask.

"The psychological profile of the man who attacked Elizabeth is someone who plans out his actions. A stalker is patient and waits for a chance to pounce on his victim."

"And Daniel?"

"He doesn't have that kind of patience. He's much more direct and needs instant gratification for his impulses. I don't think Daniel is your man."

"Thank you. If you hear from Elizabeth, ask her to give me a call."

Frank hung up the phone. Her ex-husband? Elizabeth went out to dinner with her ex-husband. He felt relieved, or did he? She was safe but why was she out on a date with her ex-husband? Feelings of anger and jealousy filled his mind. *What right do I have to be jealous? We only had one date.* But at that moment, he knew he had crossed over the line of professional interest in this case. He had become personally involved, and he knew that this could only lead to trouble. A cop who gets personally involved in a case is a cop who doesn't think clearly.

Officer Perez tapped on the car window. "I just got a call back on the car. It's rented to a Dr. *Daniel* Wing. He picked it up two days ago and is scheduled to return it on Friday."

"Good job. He's her ex-husband. Her associate told me they're having dinner. I guess our work is done here. Keep up the half-hour patrols and let me know if anything else unusual happens."

Frank drove away from Elizabeth's house and headed for home. He asked himself the same question over and over. Why had Elizabeth's ex-husband come to see her?

CHAPTER TWENTY-SEVEN

Daniel stood at her door, flowers in hand, and she was taken aback at how little he had changed. He still looked like a struggling student. The baggy jacket was reminiscent of their college days, and he wore the same wire-rimmed glasses.

"For you," Daniel said, as he passed Elizabeth a bouquet of flowers.

She felt awkward accepting them, but it would have been embarrassing for him had she refused. When her ex-husband had called that afternoon saying he was in town, he caught Elizabeth off-guard. She hadn't heard from him in over two years, and it had been much longer since she had seen him. Now he stood at her front door waiting to take her to dinner.

"Let me put these in water," she said, gathering her thoughts as she headed for the kitchen. *Why did I say I'd go to dinner with him? We should have just met for coffee.* When she got back to the foyer, he was still standing in the doorway looking rather ill at ease.

"Can we take your car?" Daniel asked. "The rental is a piece of junk and we're driving up the coast to Malibu."

"Yes, of course," Elizabeth answered, surprised at his choice of location.

"Do you still drive a convertible?"

"Always."

"Good. We can drive with the top down."

Sitting next to Daniel in the car, she still couldn't believe she had accepted his invitation to dinner. The restaurant he picked had been a longtime favorite of hers. She was both pleased and astonished that he had remembered it. She sensed this might not be just a causal dinner when he reached for her hand from time to time as he talked.

On the drive to Malibu, they talked about his research and his attempt to convince the drug company to continue funding his project. Daniel believed that in a few more months he would have a breakthrough in the drug he was researching. She wondered if his motive in taking her to dinner was to obtain money to fund his project.

Oblivious to the stir they caused, Elizabeth followed the maitre d' to a corner table overlooking the ocean. Heads turned as the tall, attractive redhead, escorted by a slender Asian man badly in need of a haircut, took their seats. Elizabeth noticed Daniel seemed even more ill at ease than he had been at her front door.

Five years ago, after she and Daniel had eloped, Elizabeth's grandfather hosted a dinner party for them at this restaurant. Although the place was a favorite of Elizabeth's, that party had been the only time she had been here with Daniel. He talked about taking her back to the restaurant before their divorce, but he never found the time. Tonight, he seemed to want everything to be perfect. Reservations at a restaurant with memories, a table with a view, flowers, and now he ordered a bottle of rather pricey Beaujolais. It was one of her favorites, and she wondered if he had remembered or if he had asked Carol. Either way, he was making an effort to please her. *He's courting me! Are there rules for situations like this?* Rules or no rules, it was obvious he intended to give it his best shot.

Elizabeth didn't need to look at the menu; she'd eaten here many times before and knew the restaurant was famous for its prime rib. They served it in the traditional manner with Yorkshire pudding, mashed potatoes, and creamed spinach.

"I'll start off with a garden salad," she told the waiter, "and prime rib."

"Still carnivorous, I see," Daniel said, looking uncomfortable.

"It's the best thing on the menu."

"I'll have the garden salad as well," Daniel said, "but no cheese, no seasoning, and no dressing. Just bring lemon slices."

"And for your main course?"

"A plate of steamed vegetables, no butter, no seasoning, no cheese, just vegetables, and of course lemon wedges." Daniel closed the menu and passed it to the waiter.

"Will there be anything else, sir?"

"No, that's it."

"Have you become a vegetarian?" Elizabeth asked after the waiter had left their table.

"Vegan. I'm a vegan. Not only don't I eat meat, fish, or poultry, I don't use animal products, eggs, dairy, or any materials from animals."

"Is this for religious reasons or health concerns?" she asked, trying to understand why his eating habits had changed so drastically.

"I'm cautious about what I put in or on my person. I believe my body is a temple and should be respected, but my main concern is for a more humane and caring world."

"Daniel, we could have gone somewhere else for dinner. Somewhere that wouldn't have made you uncomfortable."

"You like this restaurant. I always told you I'd bring you back here."

The waiter arrived with the wine and poured a small bit into Daniel's glass. He stared at it, and then, as if an old memory had suddenly been stirred, he picked it up and tasted it. "Yes, this is fine," he said to the waiter, who proceeded to pour a glass for Elizabeth and fill Daniel's glass.

"Carol and Andrew told me about the attack when I called them from Mexico," Daniel said. "Do you have any idea who did it?"

"No, and I'm frustrated. I don't know who would do something like this to me," Elizabeth said, but in the back of her mind, after hearing Daniel was is town, she had wondered, and then dismissed, the thought that he could be connected to what happened.

"Carol feels terrible that she left you alone."

"It's not her fault I went for a run after she left," Elizabeth said.

"How do you think this guy found you in Laguna?"

"Well, if it's someone who knows me, maybe he knows about the cottage. But if he's a patient, or a stranger, then he must have followed me. The police haven't been able to come up with anything substantial."

"If I'd been here, if we were still married, you wouldn't have been alone."

Surprised by this statement, Elizabeth didn't know what to say. She took a sip of her wine, put her glass down, and stared out at the ocean, an uncomfortable silence hanging between them.

Daniel cleared his throat. "Liz, I miss you. After all this time, I still miss you. I should never have taken that job without consulting you, especially a job where it was impossible for you to come with me. I should have stayed here."

Elizabeth picked up her glass again and took a long sip of wine. She didn't know where he was going with this but she had to make sure he understood where she was coming from. Carefully placing the glass back on the table, she looked into Daniel's eyes.

"We can't go back, Danny."

"Couldn't we start over?"

"It would never be the same. We're not the same as we were in college."

"Liz, I still love you."

The waiter brought the bread and salads and the interruption give Elizabeth a few moments to process what Daniel had just said. There she sat in her favorite restaurant, looking out at the ocean, listening to the band play romantic music, with a man who had just told her that he loved her. The words were right but it was the wrong man. If Frank had said those words… But she wasn't with Frank, and Daniel didn't have the sophistication or the sex appeal that Frank had. As she sat there looking at this brilliant but socially inept man, she wondered why she had married him. Had she been rebelling against her family? Had he always been like this or had she changed so much that someone she once found appealing no longer attracted her? At this moment, what she really wanted to do was to get up and run. She busied herself eating her salad so that she wouldn't have to say anything, but she was distracted watching Daniel dissect his salad.

"Danny, what are you doing?"

"It won't work like this," he said, separating the dark greens from the light greens and the pine nuts from the tomatoes on his plate. "They shouldn't mix the ingredients like this."

Elizabeth offered Daniel a roll from the basket; he shook his head no. She took one, buttered it, and placed it on her side plate all the while watching him move things around on his salad plate. Finally satisfied with the arrangement, he squeezed lemon juice on it and began to eat.

The obsessive-compulsive behavior she was witnessing disturbed her. *Who is this man? He has changed, but not for the better. Could he be the one who stalked me?*

"I still love you, Elizabeth," he said again.

"Danny," she said softly, "it won't work. I'm sorry. It just won't work."

"We can make it work! I'll be finished with my research soon and I can move back here. The company will let me work wherever I want."

"We broke up because our dreams and goals, our whole lives, were just too different."

On cue, the waiter came to their table and poured more wine for them. Daniel hadn't noticed her glass was almost empty. So like him, oblivious to the needs of anyone else. The waiter served Elizabeth her side dishes and Daniel his vegetables, but when the chef rolled the side of beef to their table to carve it, Daniel turned pale. Obviously he had forgotten about the presentation of prime rib at this restaurant. The chef stood by the cart and ceremoniously sharpened his knife. He then explained the different cuts: English cut, thin slices stacked high; California cut, a small cut for lighter appetites; traditional cut, standard thickness; Henry VIIIth cut, an extra thick portion. Elizabeth ordered the traditional cut.

"And how would you like it? Rare, medium rare..."

Daniel stood up, excused himself, and left the table. He didn't return until her dinner had been served and the meat cart wheeled away. She looked down at her dinner, cut a piece of prime rib, and took a bite. Daniel pretended not to notice but Elizabeth could tell he was still uncomfortable with her dinner choice. As with the salad, Daniel separated his vegetables into what appeared to be color categories. He placed them in a circle around the plate and ate one bite at a time from each section.

This is going to be a long evening!

"Is there someone else?" Daniel asked between bites.

She didn't want to hurt him but she couldn't avoid answering the question.

"Yes. Yes, there is."

"You're dating someone else?" he asked again, looking puzzled.

"Yes, Daniel, I'm dating." She pushed the food around on her plate trying to avoid looking at him.

"Is it Tim? Are you dating Tim?" Daniel reached for his wine glass, almost knocking it over.

"No. Tim and I are just friends. You know we've never been anything but friends."

"He loves you, you know. He's loved you longer than I have."

"It's not Tim."

"Who is he?" Daniel demanded, his voice getting louder. He slammed the empty wine glass down on the table and reached for the bottle. Heads turned at nearby tables.

"It doesn't matter," Elizabeth answered softly, trying to keep their conversation private. She put another bite of dinner into her mouth but had trouble swallowing. Putting her fork down, she took another sip of wine. No use trying to eat, she'd lost her appetite.

"Yes, it does. Who's my competition?"

"No one you know. Danny, this conversation isn't a good idea."

"But I have a right to know."

"No, Danny, you don't. We've been divorced for a long time and we have our own lives now."

"But I want to be a part of your life."

"I've recently started dating and I'd like to give it a chance, that's all you need to know."

"Are you sleeping with him?" Daniel asked accusingly, as he took another gulp of wine.

Elizabeth remembered that Daniel had never been able to drink much without getting drunk. She wondered if this had changed but from his outburst she feared he had already had too much to drink.

"That's none of your business."

"I just want to know how much of a head start my competition's got. Are you sleeping with him?" he repeated, his voice getting loud again.

Not wanting a scene, she answered him. "No, I'm not, but even if I was, it's none of your business."

Elizabeth could see Daniel was not going to give up easily. She started to worry about the drive home. *This dinner was a bad idea.*

"If I stay in L.A.," Daniel said, his voice softening, "and work for the company here, do I have a chance?"

At that moment, Elizabeth felt sorry for Daniel. As gently as possible, she tried to answer Daniel's question. Their marriage had been a mistake. She hadn't known it at the time. She hadn't seen how mismatched they were. He was brilliant and she had admired his dedication to his career. Now that time had passed, she could see why their marriage hadn't survived. Why it could never work.

"Danny, you and I had a whirlwind romance. It was fun. It was who we were at the time. But it's not who we are now."

"I'll be whoever you want me to be, Liz."

"It won't work, Danny."

"Are you sure?"

"Yes. I'm sure."

Elizabeth poured herself more wine, finishing off the bottle. She didn't particularly want it, but she didn't want Daniel to drink any more. They picked at the food on their plates in silence, neither one finishing their dinner. Elizabeth ordered coffee for them both and attempted to discuss mutual friends but Daniel didn't want to talk. They had been friends before their brief marriage; it didn't look like they could be friends again.

"I'm driving," Elizabeth said when the valet brought the car.

Daniel didn't object. The drive back home was long and uncomfortably silent. He hadn't been interested in her practice, her teaching, or her volunteer work. He asked about the attack but that was to show how he could take care of her, if they got back together. Now she remembered how self-centered and controlling Daniel had always been. Starting over with him would be a big mistake. No matter how fearful she had become since the attack, or how frightened she felt living alone, she would not go back to him.

Frank grabbed his cell phone after the first ring.

"Detective, it's Perez. I just made a run past Dr. Wing's house."

"Is everything okay?" Detective Gualdoni asked.

"I'm parked two houses away. An Asian man just got into the rental car. He slammed the door and pounded his fists on the steering wheel, gunned the engine, and took off. Do you want me to follow him?"

"Does everything look okay at the house?"

"Yes. The front light just went off and the upstairs lights went on."

"Good. Follow him for a few blocks to make sure he doesn't come back. Thanks, Perez."

Gualdoni breathed a sigh a relief. Elizabeth was home. The pieces of the puzzle lay before him but he still didn't know how they went together. Her ex-husband had left, obviously angry. He wondered if Daniel should still be considered a suspect or was he simply concerned about Elizabeth's safely.

CHAPTER TWENTY-EIGHT

Early this morning, Elizabeth received a call from her answering service telling her that a patient named Sandra was holding on the other line and that she needed an emergency appointment. Elizabeth told the operator to have Sandra come into the office at ten o'clock. The last time Elizabeth had seen her, Sandra Cunningham had been upset by her husband's increasing abuse.

When Sandra arrived, Elizabeth was not prepared for what she saw. Sandra's left eye was swollen shut and purple and red bruises covered most of her face and neck.

"What's happened?" Elizabeth asked, not even trying to cover her shock.

"Last night, Roger and I had a terrible argument. He told me he had a business trip and would be gone for two days. I asked for the car keys and money for groceries. He went into a rage and for the first time, he hit me in the face. He's never hit me where anyone can see the marks."

"Did you call the police?"

"No. The children were watching and they were screaming. I didn't want to upset them further."

"This time you've got to call the police. I can take more pictures but you need a police report."

Sandra sat on the edge of the couch, looked at Elizabeth with a determined expression, and calmly said, "I'm going to do better than that. I'm leaving Roger, today. Hitting me in the face, not caring that the children saw what he was doing, that's too much. Next time he might hit the children."

"Does the shelter have a place for you and the children?" Elizabeth asked, knowing that Sandra had been waiting for an opening at a battered women's shelter for several weeks.

"No, but when I told them we had to leave today they found an opening for us at a shelter in another county. From there I'll make plans to move out of state. Roger left this morning for San Francisco and won't be back until tomorrow night. He may try to call me, but he won't know for sure that we're gone for two days."

"I am so proud of you. I knew you had the strength to leave him. Is your friend helping you?"

"Yes. She's driving me to the local shelter. They'll transport us from there."

"Do you know where you're going after the shelter?"

In the months Elizabeth had been seeing Sandra, she had watched her grow stronger and more determined to leave her husband. She knew if anyone could escape an abusive relationship, Sandra could.

"I have some ideas. I trust you, Dr. Wing, but if you don't know where I am, you won't have to lie to Roger. I know he'll call you. He thinks you'll tell everyone that I'm crazy. That's why he allowed me to see you. He says anyone who sees a therapist is crazy."

"It sounds like you have everything taken care of. Have you been able to put away enough money until you can start working?"

"Roger gave me fifty dollars for groceries and I took a check out of the back of his checkbook while he was in the shower this morning. He put my name on the account years ago even though he never let me have any checks. I'll go to the bank when I leave here and take out as much as I can. That, along with what I've managed to put away, should keep me and the kids going for a while." Sandra leaned back on the couch and sighed. "I'm ready to do this."

Elizabeth looked at the woman who sat across from her. Only a few months ago she had appeared helpless; today, inner strength and determination to leave her abusive husband showed through. Sandra now looked directly at her, sat erect, and spoke with a strong, clear voice. *No matter where Sandra goes she's going to make it.*

"Do the children know the plans?"

"No. I didn't want to take any chances that they would say something to one of their friends. I don't know who Roger will question when he starts looking for us. After I go to the bank, I'll pick up the children from school and then we're leaving."

"Is there anything I can do for you, Sandra?"

"Roger will be looking for me. He'll tell everyone I'm crazy. He'll say that I took the kids and that I might kill them and myself. He'll call the police. Please tell them I'm not crazy. Tell them that I love my kids and would never hurt them. And, I would *never* kill myself. Dr. Wing, I'd kill Roger before I'd kill myself. He's the crazy one."

Elizabeth could tell by the way Sandra kept looking at her watch that she was anxious to be on her way.

"Good luck, Sandra. When you're settled, let me know how you're doing."

"I will. Someday you'll get a letter from someone you have never heard of telling you that all is well. As soon as I can legally arrange it, I'll be changing our identity. I'll never use my old name again."

The two women hugged, like two friends who were parting rather than doctor and patient. Elizabeth had grown very fond of Sandra Cunningham and admired her strength and courage.

Alone in her office, Elizabeth went through Sandra's file page by page. She wanted to make sure the documentation regarding the physically abusive treatment and the hostage living situation was accurate. She also wanted it perfectly clear that Sandra was in no way mentally unstable or a danger to her children.

CHAPTER TWENTY-NINE

As Gualdoni started his car, he heard the call for backup on his police radio. *Oh, God. That's Elizabeth's office.* Looking at his watch, he assumed the police escort had put in the call. He placed the red light on top of his car, turned on the siren, and gunned the engine. His cell phone rang just as he made a sharp right turn and headed downtown. He fumbled for the phone.

"Gualdoni here."

"Frank, it's Elizabeth. One of my patients…he just came after me."

"Are you okay?"

"He threatened me with a gun!"

Frank could hear the fear in her voice. "Is your police escort there?"

"Yes. He came in just after my patient tried to attack me."

"Elizabeth, are you okay?" Frank repeated.

"Yes, I'm okay."

"Who's there with you?"

"Tim and Joanne are in my office. The police officer has my patient in the waiting room and he called for backup."

"I've got my radio on. There's another squad car pulling up out front. I'm on my way."

Frank's concern for Elizabeth grew as he raced through the streets of Long Beach. *Who is this bastard? Why hadn't we suspected him of attacking Elizabeth before this?* He pulled up in front of Elizabeth's office building and saw four police cars lined up. Officers were guarding the front and rear exits not letting anyone in or out. Frank held open his jacket, revealing his badge attached to his belt, and hurried for the elevator. Ned, the building security guard, sat wide-eyed at his desk. He recognized the detective and nodded.

As Frank exited the elevator on the top floor, he met two police officers leading a handcuffed man down the hall. He stared at the tall blond man dressed in an expensive business suit, remembering the description he had gotten from the Avis rental clerk. *That could be the same man.*

"What are you looking at, asshole?" the man bellowed angrily as he saw Frank eyeing him.

"Shut up and keep walking," one of the officers ordered.

Frank flashed his badge at the officer. "Why are you after Dr. Wing?" he asked the man.

"I just want to talk to her," the man shouted.

"Do you always bring a gun when you want to talk?" the officer responded as he pushed the man into the elevator.

The doors closed and Frank watched as the indicator lights blinked the numbers of each floor. When it reached L, he turned and headed for Elizabeth's suite.

A police officer greeted him as he entered the waiting room of Dr. Wing's office. "Hey, Gualdoni, we caught your stalker," one of them boasted sarcastically.

Frank looked around the room at the chair tipped over and the plant knocked off the receptionist's desk, dirt tracked across the light carpet. "Where's Dr. Wing?" he asked, ignoring the snide comment.

"Sergeant Adams is taking her statement," the officer said with a smirk.

Gualdoni knocked and without waiting for an answer opened the door and walked into Elizabeth's office. He looked around the room. He needed to see for himself that she was all right. Elizabeth sat calmly at her desk answering the sergeant's questions. The fear he had heard in her voice earlier had disappeared. Tim Henderson stood by the window, arms folded and a look of frustration on his face, while Joanne sat on the couch nervously biting her nails.

"Dr. Wing," Gualdoni stated, not wanting Sergeant Adams to know how close the relationship with Elizabeth had become. "Are you all right?"

"I'm fine now," Elizabeth said. "I knew Roger would be upset about his wife leaving but I had no idea he would come after me with a gun."

"Well, it's the last thing he'll do to you. We have him now," Frank said.

"Detective," Elizabeth said quietly, "I know it looks like he's the one who's done all these things to me, but I don't think so. It just doesn't feel right."

Tim turned to them, his eyes blazing with anger. "He's the one. Didn't you hear anything he said, Elizabeth?"

Anxious to get the details, Frank addressed Tim. "Just what did he say?

"For starters, he called her a bitch, just like on the phone. Then he started ranting at Joanne about how useless, stupid, and untrustworthy women are. I could hear him from my office, and I came in just as he shoved Joanne out of the way and barged into Elizabeth's office. I'm cleaning the language up a bit, but it's obvious he doesn't like women." Tim started pacing the floor "Elizabeth, why don't you believe Roger Cunningham is the man who attacked you in Laguna?"

Elizabeth paused, and before she could answer, Joanne replied, "Mr. Cunningham has always been rude to me, but today he acted just plain crazy."

Sergeant Adams broke in. "Is there anything else any of you can tell me?"

"No, Sergeant, I think we've told you all we can. Thank you so much for responding so rapidly." Elizabeth was cordial as she dismissed the sergeant.

"I guess you don't need the police escort any longer," the sergeant commented.

"Let's keep him on another day or two," Gualdoni suggested. "Just in case Dr. Wing is right and this guy isn't the stalker."

"Whatever you say," Sergeant Adams said as he left the room.

After the sergeant had gone, Elizabeth turned to Tim and Joanne. "I appreciate your help. I'm fine now, really. Joanne, we don't have any more patients today; why don't you go on home? The cleaning crew can take care of the mess in the other room."

"Thanks, Dr. Wing."

Elizabeth saw the fear on Joanne's face. "Mr. Cunningham is in jail and he won't be back," she said, trying to comfort her secretary.

"Okay," Joanne replied, her voice quivering a bit.

"I'll walk you to your car," Tim said, putting his arm around Joanne's shoulder. After they left, Elizabeth turned to Frank. "I appreciate you coming over. I've never had a patient lose it like that before."

"What makes you think this guy isn't the one who attacked you?" Frank asked, sitting down on the couch.

"He's physically and emotionally abusive to his wife. He came after me today because his wife took his kids and left. He wants them back and he thinks I know where they are. Men like him don't usually stalk or abuse someone other than their own wife or girlfriend. It doesn't make sense that he would have spent the last few months trying to frighten or hurt me. He needs me to confirm that his wife is the disturbed one."

"You're the expert. We'll see if anything happens while he's locked up."

Frank didn't want to leave. There was no reason to stay, no work-related reason, but he wanted to make sure Elizabeth was really okay. Before he could talk himself out of it, he blurted out, "Would you like to go out for a drink? I could be your police escort for tonight."

"I'd like that," Elizabeth answered without hesitating. "It's been a rough day."

CHAPTER THIRTY

Cash walked up and down the street in front of the Royal Hotel where he usually met Squirrel. He'd called everyone he knew. No one had heard from him.

"Hey, have ya seen Squirrel?" he asked a kid on a skateboard who almost knocked him over.

"Not today," the kid yelled back.

Cash kept walking. The neighborhood wasn't the greatest but it was the only place he could think of to look. Here everyone knew Squirrel, or knew of him. He grew up on these streets, knew his way around. But today, no one had seen him. In fact, no one had seen him since the night he got busted buying drugs. Getting busted was nothing unusual for Squirrel. In one day, out the next, he always came up with his bail, and for some reason, he always seemed to get out of whatever jam he got himself into. Something was different this time. Cash didn't know what it was but something was different and it worried him.

Cash paged his supplier and waited; he knew he was taking a chance using his own phone; he'd been taking too many chances. His mind jumped from one thought to the next. Disjointed, irrational, thoughts.

Just one more buy. One more stash and I'll be set.

She'll be here any day. He'd tried to get her here sooner but nothing worked. But one thing he knew for certain, she always came for Thanksgiving and he'd be invited, he always was.

His cell phone rang. He checked the number but didn't know it. He answered it anyway. "Yeah," Cash said into the phone.

"*The usual,*" *he said to the caller.* "*Where to, I'm coming myself?*"
Cash listened for a minute.

"*I haven't seen him. I said I'll come.*" *he replied.*

He listened again.

"*McDonald's…on Cherry…One hour, I'll be there.*" *Cash disconnected the call.*

Damn. He didn't want to make the buy himself. He certainly didn't want to drive his own car. Where the hell was Squirrel!

CHAPTER THIRTY-ONE

"I'll be in Laguna for the weekend if you and Andrew want to join me," Elizabeth said into the phone as the voice mail recorded the call. "If I'm out, the key will be under the red flower pot."

Elizabeth couldn't stand not being able to come and go without a police escort. The depression that had been hanging like a rain cloud over her for the past month seemed to be growing by the day. She'd had it. Tim continued to hover like a mother hen, Daniel appearing and wanting to rekindle a romance that never should have been, and now, a patient's husband threatening her. She just wanted to go away and be herself.

Leaving early Saturday morning, Elizabeth drove down the coast. Amazing how just seeing the ocean lightened her somber mood. Halfway to Laguna her cell phone rang, but she ignored it. Every ten minutes it rang again until she finally pulled off the road and checked the messages.

"What do you mean you're going to Laguna?" Carol's voice echoed in her ear. "Call me." The other messages were more like demands. "Liz, call me."

Elizabeth pushed redial and Carol answered on the first ring. Before she could say more than hello, Elizabeth interrupted her. "I have to get out of my house, run on the beach, eat out, anything but stay home and think about my life. Don't try to talk me out of it, just join me if you'd like."

"I'll be there by noon, Andrew's on a business trip for a week. I can stay as long as you want. Liz, please be careful."

"I'll chill the wine," Elizabeth said as she hung up the phone. She pushed the button to put the top down on her Mercedes. Even though it was November, the sun was warm and she loved to let the wind blow through her hair.

By the time she arrived in Laguna, Elizabeth had already started to feel less depressed. She quickly put away the groceries she had brought and placed two bottles of Pinot Grigio in the refrigerator to chill. The beach called to her and she checked her watch to see how much time she had before Carol arrived. *Just enough time for a short run. I won't let fear take this from me!*

From the beach, Elizabeth could see Carol's car pull into the driveway. Jogging along the water's edge, the ominous feeling that someone was watching her persisted. She tried to blame the eerie feelings on paranoia, but she knew all too well that there were real reasons to be frightened. As she walked back to the cottage, her decision to come to Laguna without telling Frank bothered her. It may have been a dangerous idea.

She saw Carol sitting on the porch steps and she waved, but her friend was engrossed in something she was reading. "Hi, welcome to…" but Elizabeth stopped mid-sentence when she saw the look on Carol's face.

"Liz, who knew you were coming to Laguna?" Carol asked, standing up.

"No one. You're the only one, and I called you from my cell phone on the way down here. What's wrong?"

"This note was pinned to the screen door."

Elizabeth took the paper and read the words neatly printed in bold letters.

You can't get away from me. I know your every move. I know what you're thinking. You can make it all stop. Just do what I want and I won't bother you anymore.

Elizabeth stood motionless on the steps. "Carol, it's like this guy is in my head."

"We're going inside. He could be watching us right now. Then you're going to call Frank." Carol took Elizabeth's arm and all but pushed her into the cottage. She locked the door behind them and headed for the phone.

"No, wait," Elizabeth said. "I need time to think. That's why I came down here. I thought you and I could try to figure out who this could be."

"You're crazy. If the police can't find this guy, what makes you think we can?"

"No. Not find him. Brainstorm all the people I know. I'm sure he's not a patient. I really doubt if he's a student. This creep has got to be somebody I know. Someone I've known for a long time. He knows too much about me to be a stranger."

"I think we should call Frank," Carol said, sitting in the chair next to the phone.

"I've got a plan. You and I will do all the things we usually do in Laguna but we'll take lots of pictures."

"Pictures. Why?" Carol asked.

"I know this may sound weird, but if you and I take pictures of each other showing lots of background, he may show up in one."

"Liz, stop trying to *play* detective, just call the real one!"

"Please, Carol. Just for the weekend. We'll both keep our eyes open for someone we recognize. I promise I won't leave your side."

"I'll go along with it on one condition. You call Frank and tell him where you are and what we're doing."

Elizabeth started to object but Carol cut her off. "Either you call him or I will."

"Okay, okay. It's a deal." Elizabeth pulled Frank's card from her purse and walked over to the phone and punched in Frank's cell phone number.

"What did he say?" Carol asked when Elizabeth hung up the phone.

"To say he's angry would be an understatement. He wants to come down but you heard what I told him. I need time to think. I promised to call him when I get back home."

Early Sunday afternoon, Carol followed Elizabeth as they drove out of Laguna and north on the 405 Freeway. Carol had decided to stay in Long Beach with Elizabeth for a few days rather than go home to an empty house in Manhattan Beach. They left the films to be developed at a one-hour stand, picked up a few groceries and a steak to barbeque, and sat at Starbucks and had coffee while they waited for the pictures.

"I hope your plan worked," Carol said as she idly stirred her coffee.

"If nothing else, we'll have a lot of pictures of each other."

"You'd better call Frank and tell him we're back," Carol suggested.

"Good idea. He was pretty upset when I talked to him yesterday. Do you mind if I ask him to join us for dinner?"

"Of course not. I'd like to get to know him. It sounds like he might be in your life for a while."

"We can all look at the pictures together," Elizabeth said, ignoring Carol's comment about Frank. The truth was, she hoped he would be in her life for a long while too.

By the time Frank arrived, Elizabeth had uncorked the wine, turned on CDs for music, and started a fire in the fireplace. Even in November the days were warm but, when the sun went down, a fire took the coolness out of the air.

Sipping a mellow Beaujolais wine, the three of them compared picture after picture, trying to find a familiar face or someone who showed up in more than one shot. Four rolls of film, over a hundred pictures, were strewn over the floor of the den.

"I don't see anyone I know," Carol sighed.

"How about someone showing up in more than one location?" Frank asked.

"Sure: Liz," Carol said.

"Very funny," Frank said. "How about you, Elizabeth. See any familiar faces?"

"Oh yes: Carol." Enjoying the banter, Elizabeth was glad to see her friends were getting along.

The ringing of the phone interrupted their laughter. Elizabeth crawled over the pictures, reached up, and pushed the button on the speakerphone.

"Dr. Wing, this is Maggie at the answering service. I have a call I think you need to take."

"Do you know who it is?"

"He won't give his name but he's talking really crazy. He's saying you're destroying him."

"Go ahead and put him through." Elizabeth stood up and started to lift the receiver and take the phone off speaker mode, but Frank shook his head.

"This is Dr. Wing."

"What kind of a doctor are you? You're supposed to be helping people not playing in Laguna."

"Are you a patient? Is there something you need?"

"Yeah, bitch. But you won't get it for me."

Frank was on his cell phone trying to get the call traced. "Keep him on the line," he whispered.

Carol sat staring at the phone in disbelief. Elizabeth had told her about the calls and now she was actually hearing one.

Keeping her voice calm, Elizabeth continued talking. "What is it that you want me to get for you?"

"You know," the caller yelled into the phone. Lowering his voice he went on. "Listen, bitch. You took my picture. You can't do that. That's my soul. You've got to give it back."

Trying to stall, Elizabeth continued to ask questions. "What picture? When did I take it?"

"In Laguna…Stop doing this to me…Give me back my soul…I don't have a Mommy. Go away, bitch." The sounds of the caller sobbing filled the room.

"Come and see me tomorrow morning at my office. I'll give the picture back to you," Elizabeth said softly.

The only reply, a click, and then, a dial tone.

Frank was the first to speak. "We've got him. They couldn't trace the call but somewhere in this mess," he gestured to the pictures covering the floor, "we've got him."

Carol caught Frank's excitement and began looking through the pictures. Elizabeth stood staring at the phone, a puzzled expression on her face.

"What is it, Elizabeth?" Frank asked.

"You know who it is," Carol said.

"I…don't know. But something he said. I've heard it before but I can't remember when or who said it."

"Come on, look at the pictures again. Maybe a face will trigger a memory." Frank passed her a stack of photos. "By the way, that was fast thinking telling him to come to the office and get the picture. I'll make sure there are detectives at your office in the morning."

CHAPTER THIRTY-TWO

Elizabeth and Carol sat outside on the patio drinking ice tea and talking. They'd planned a barbeque and were waiting for Andrew and Frank to finish their golf game at the country club. When the phone rang, Elizabeth almost let it ring but remembered she was on call this weekend.

"That might be my answering service," Elizabeth said as she picked up the cordless phone by her side. It wasn't. It was the call she'd been expecting for days. The call she'd hoped wouldn't come until the stalker was safely behind bars.

"Elizabeth," David Worthington's voice boomed into the phone. "Your mother and I are leaving Madrid on November fifteenth."

"I can't wait to see you," she replied and she meant it. Even though she hadn't told her parents about the attack in August, she was anxious to see them again.

"We're flying to Washington, D.C. I've got to spend a few days at the firm's head office," he continued.

"When will you be arriving in Los Angeles?"

"The day before Thanksgiving. We're going to Cape Cod for our anniversary and then flying from Boston to L.A."

"Is William going to pick you up?"

"No. He'll send a car. No need for him to hassle the holiday traffic. Come early for dinner on Thursday, your mother and I have some things to discuss with you."

Thanksgiving dinner at Grandfather's estate in Pasadena was a tradition. Elizabeth was expected to join the family but this year she didn't feel much like attending.

"Dad, I won't be at the family dinner this year. Can we go out Friday night? There's someone I'd like you to meet," Elizabeth stated, determined not to give in.

"Of course you'll be there. The whole family is expecting you, and your mother would be heartbroken if you didn't come."

Elizabeth racked her brain to come up with a reason for missing the dreaded dinner but her father's guilt trip was working. "Dad," she lied, unable to come up with a plausible excuse. "I have a date."

"Great. Bring him along. Glad you finally have someone in your life. I can't wait to meet him. Your mother sends her love. See you on Thanksgiving." He hung up the phone without giving her a chance to object. Her father would not hear of her missing the annual event. Her mother, on the other hand, would understand. Her mother had received the brunt of Aunt Nancy's rude behavior ever since Elizabeth could remember.

"Why do I feel like I'm nine years old when I try to disagree with my father?" Elizabeth said, putting down the phone.

"So who are you taking to the family dinner?" Carol asked, laughing at her friend.

"I'm not going. It's the same thing every year, Aunt Nancy and my cousins drink too much, insult me and my mother, and leave as soon as they find out how much more money they're going to get. I'm sick of it."

"You know you're going. Every year you say you're not, and every year you give in and go," Carol said, still laughing.

Andrew and Frank walked out onto the patio. "What's so funny?" Andrew asked.

"My father just called to invite me to Thanksgiving dinner," Elizabeth said.

"It's not an invitation, it's a command performance! Remember the year I went with you? It made me grateful for my screwed-up family," Carol said.

They all laughed, but Elizabeth was still thinking about how she could avoid the holiday dinner. She had hoped this whole ordeal would be behind her when her parents arrived, but they would be here in less than two weeks and there were no new leads in the case. In fact, both Frank and Elizabeth felt they might never catch the person responsible. Her parents would see through her attempts to pretend everything was fine.

Andrew busied himself lighting the barbeque, and Frank went in to open the wine.

"So, who are you taking to the famous Thanksgiving Day dinner?" Carol asked again.

"I'm not going. My father will just have to understand."

"You're going. And I think you should ask Frank."

"Ask Frank what?" he said, bringing the wine and glasses out on a tray.

Elizabeth glared at Carol.

"I have a dilemma," Elizabeth began. "I don't want to go to the family Thanksgiving dinner so I told my father I had a date. It sort of backfired on me and he told me to bring my date along!"

"And you don't really have a date?" Frank asked, smiling.

"It's a lot to ask on a holiday, but would you consider escorting me to dinner? If you don't have any plans, that is?"

"There's no one I'd rather spend it with." Frank leaned down and gave Elizabeth a gentle kiss on the lips. "It's a date."

The light pressure of Frank's kiss lingered on her lips and Elizabeth smelled a trace of his cologne even though he'd been golfing all afternoon. It had happened so quickly and naturally that she hadn't responded. She saw the look of approval that passed between Carol and Andrew.

"The family might be a little weird but the food will be terrific and there'll be an endless supply of wine," Carol said.

"Two out of three ain't bad," Frank teased. He poured the wine and gave a toast. "To meeting the family."

"Talking about weird," Carol began. "What was dinner like with Daniel?"

"I never should have gone. I don't know what possessed me to accept his invitation."

"So he took you to your favorite restaurant in Malibu, ordered your favorite wine, then what?" Carol asked.

"How do you know that?"

"He was at our place when he made the reservations and he asked me what kind of wine you liked. You don't really think he remembered, do you?"

"Well, the restaurant was a bad choice on his part. You know how they bring a side of beef to the table and carve it? Well, Daniel is now vegetarian. No, let me correct myself, a vegan. Nothing animal. I thought he was going to pass out when they started carving the meat."

"Poor Daniel. He never could manage to get anything straight," Carol said.

"But that's not all," Elizabeth continued. "I think he's become obsessive-compulsive. He separated all of the vegetables and nuts in his salad by color. He arranged them in some kind of special order and then ate one bite from each section. He did this with the main course as well, some kind of vegetable dish he ordered. It was really strange."

"He wouldn't eat anything at our house," Andrew said. "He had his own bottled water and that's all he drank."

"Even *your* family's not that weird," Carol said.

"Well, I can't wait to meet your family. And after dinner, I'll take your dad aside and tell him what's going on," Frank said.

"Frank, I can't let them know how bad it is."

"Just let me talk to your father. I'll explain it to him and tell him what precautions we're taking."

"It will spoil the holidays for them."

"They have a right to know. I have a daughter, and I'd want to know if she were in danger."

All of their ideas to find the man responsible for turning her life upside down had failed. The profile they had compiled didn't lead to any new suspects. None of the pictures she and Carol had taken in Laguna revealed anyone they recognized. Even the phone call from the perpetrator stating they had taken his picture didn't lead anywhere, and he never showed up at her office. It was all very frustrating.

"We'll see," Elizabeth said.

The obscene phone calls continued sporadically. Recent pictures taken of her with Frank were left at her office. Notes were left on the windshield of her car. But the identity of the stalker remained a mystery. It had been four months, and the only thing that had changed was that Frank no longer considered Tim Henderson a suspect. Frank had convinced her not to purchase a gun, at least for now, but lately she thought more and more about purchasing a dog.

"Time to put the steaks on," Andrew called from the barbeque.

"Coming right up," Elizabeth said as she carried a platter of filet mignon out to him. "I think it's too chilly to eat outside; let's eat in the kitchen."

Carol and Elizabeth set the table and brought out the green salad they had prepared. Frank kept the wine glasses filled and the banter between friends continued. The main topic: whose family had the most unusual characters. Frank said little about his family. They all voted that Andrew's family was by far the most normal, all-American of any of theirs. Carol didn't much like her own sister but agreed that they really weren't all that strange.

"Here's the steaks," Andrew called out, carrying in a sizzling platter.

"Sautéed mushrooms coming up," Frank added as he brought them to the table.

They all started eating, and the discussion about Elizabeth's cousins continued. The oldest, Phillip, had gone to Stanford. Obviously he was no dummy but he had never held a job and lived well using his inheritance. He and his wife had no children and spent their time traveling or at the country club.

"What a waste," Frank said. "All that money on a great education, and not doing anything with it."

Then there was Tiffany. She had gone to Bryn Mawr College but dropped out to get married. At forty-five she had been married and divorced three times and each time had ended up paying a hefty settlement to her spouse.

"I wish I were one of her exes," Andrew added. "Babe, we could be rich," he teased Carol.

The youngest, Eric, got kicked out of every boarding school and college he attended. He worked as a realtor but sold very few houses and had been in and out of several rehab programs for his drug use.

"Let's take a vote," Carol said laughing. "Who thinks the cousins are the most dysfunctional of all?"

They all agreed that Elizabeth's family won as the weirdest, and the subject of families changed to other holiday plans.

Andrew declined an after-dinner drink since he'd be driving, and he and Carol left soon after dinner.

"I can't wait to meet your family," Frank said later as he helped Elizabeth load the dishwasher after dinner. "After the discussion about your cousins, it should be quite a dinner."

"I wish it was just my parents for Thanksgiving."

The friendship between Elizabeth and Frank had become comfortable, yet until the kiss earlier this evening, Elizabeth had wondered if it would grow into something more. Two weeks ago, when the stalker had tried to break into her house and Frank had spent the night on her couch, she had longed to have him beside her in her bed. Tonight those same feelings were present, and this time it wasn't because of fear. Seated in the den, the flames from the fireplace the only light, Frank and Elizabeth sipped their brandy.

"It doesn't matter who's at dinner as long as you're there," Frank said. He put down his glass and turned to her. With his finger he traced the outline of her face; stopping at her chin, he tipped her head up and kissed her again. She could feel his excitement and she responded. Their lips parted, and with a hunger that surprised her he pulled her close to him.

"I'm sorry, I shouldn't have done that," Frank said. "It's unprofession…" but his words stopped as Elizabeth pressed her mouth against his. There was no stopping the passion that flowed between them. This time when the kiss ended Elizabeth whispered, "Not here," and took Frank's hand and led him upstairs to her room.

CHAPTER THIRTY-THREE

"Everything's changed," Elizabeth told Carol the next morning on the phone. "Frank spent the night."

"It's about time. The glances between the two of you when you didn't think anyone else was looking made it very plain it was just a matter of time before it happened."

"What looks?" Elizabeth asked.

"You know, desire, yearning, longing, passion. The looks that say, 'When are you going to ravage my body?' Those looks."

"Carol! We did no such thing."

"Well, was it good?"

"Wonderful. I don't mean the sex, that was good. I mean being together. Knowing that he wanted me. I thought I was reading the signs right but…"

"Liz, we all read the signs."

"All right. Anyway, we're having dinner tonight so we can talk. He had to leave early this morning for work."

The two friends talked a bit longer then hung up. Elizabeth had a busy day ahead of her.

Joanne entered Elizabeth's office just before noon carrying a square, silver colored box, tied with a red bow. "A messenger left this for you while you were with your last patient," she said, passing the box to her boss.

"Thank you, Joanne," Elizabeth said, placing the box on the corner of her desk.

"Aren't you going to open it? There's a card under the ribbon," Joanne said, obviously curious to see what the box contained and who had sent it.

"In a few minutes; I want to finish writing this report," Elizabeth said, dismissing Joanne.

She didn't need to read the card to know who had sent the gift; it had to be from Frank and she wanted to be alone when she opened it. Once Joanne left the office and closed the door, Elizabeth slipped the card out from under the ribbon. It read, "Until tonight." No signature, it wasn't necessary. She opened the box and pulled out the white tissue paper surrounding a glass ball. As she lifted it out of the box, she could see a snow globe holding a replica of a pair of gray-blue dolphins jumping out of the water. As Elizabeth turned the globe, silver flakes danced through the liquid. On the bottom, a key indicated that the base held a music box. Carefully Elizabeth wound the key and the delicate sounds of "Que Sera, Sera" filled her office. *How apropos, leave it to Frank to come up with just the right gift.*

Waiting for Frank to pick her up at home after work, Elizabeth felt a bit nervous, and it surprised her. Up until now their dates had been casual, but last night that all changed. The gift had been a subtle acknowledgment of their relationship moving on. Everything would be different now.

"Sorry I'm late," Frank said when Elizabeth opened the door. "I stopped at the market."

"The market?" Elizabeth asked.

"I'm cooking tonight and I needed a few things. Are you ready?"

"Yes, but where are you cooking?"

"At my house. Don't worry, I know my way around the kitchen."

An hour latter, sitting on a barstool on one side of the island, Elizabeth watched as Frank prepared their dinner.

"How do you like my kitchen?" he asked.

"Very nice," Elizabeth said. She was surprised to see that it was neat and well stocked with pots, pans, and cooking utensils hanging from hooks over the center island. Spices were lined up on the counter, and a wine rack held a dozen or more bottles.

"I love to cook. It helps me unwind. Have ever since I was a kid. I'm Italian; good food and good wine; what more can you ask for?"

He poured them each a glass of Chianti and put the pasta on to cook. He took a bag of frozen sauce out of the freezer and dropped it, bag and all, into boiling water.

"When I make spaghetti sauce, I always prepare a big batch and freeze half of it for later. My mother taught me lots of cooking tips."

He continued to prepare the garlic bread, make a salad, set the table, and keep their glasses filled, all the while refusing any help from Elizabeth.

"I hope you don't mind, but we're eating in the living room at the coffee table. My ex-wife took most of the furniture and I haven't bothered to replace the dining room set."

"No problem," Elizabeth said as she helped carry in their dinner.

Frank lit the candles and, using a TV tray as a serving table, dished out their dinner. His living room had only a TV set, a recliner, a stereo, and a couch and coffee table. The conversation during dinner consisted mainly of their work day; there was no mention of the prior evening. After dinner Frank, cleared the dishes and brought back two glasses of brandy. He sat down next to Elizabeth again and slipped his arm around her shoulder.

"I've wanted to be with you for months," he began. "I only held back because I didn't feel comfortable pursuing a relationship with the case still open. The last couple of weeks we've been seeing a lot of each other, and I broke my own rules letting it happen."

Elizabeth stared at him. *Is he trying to break up with me before we've even given it a chance?*

"Elizabeth, we may never catch the man who attacked you. I don't want to wait any longer to have a real relationship with you. After last night I think you feel the same way." Frank pulled Elizabeth closer to him and pressed his lips against hers.

"I don't want to wait either," Elizabeth whispered. *Finally, after all this time.*

Frank cleared his throat. "Here's to our future," he said, tapping his glass against hers.

"Yes, to our future," Elizabeth whispered.

As they sipped the brandy their eyes met. Putting down the glasses, they were in each other's arms within seconds.

"Let me show you around," Frank said.

Without another word, Frank guided Elizabeth into his bedroom. His arms wrapped around her as they kissed again in the darkness. Their bodies pressed against one another, and they both knew that there was no stopping the avalanche of emotions that had been unleashed. Frank's fingers found the zipper of Elizabeth's dress, unzipped it, and slipped the dress from her shoulders. It fell to the floor and she stepped out of her dress and shoes. Within seconds they were naked on Frank's bed.

Hours later, lying beside Frank, Elizabeth listened to the rhythm of his breathing. Even as he slept, she could feel his strength as he held her close.

He must have felt her watching him and his eyes opened. "You okay?"

"Yes. For the first time in a very long time, I feel safe."

CHAPTER THIRTY-FOUR

Elizabeth wanted answers. Disjointed memories, nightmares, an unknown stalker, what had happened to her orderly life? She wanted to put the attack, and everything associated with it, behind her. Everything but Frank, that is. Meeting Frank had stirred emotions long buried. Emotions she no longer feared. *I just want to get on with my life.*

"I'd like to talk about what you've told me in prior sessions," Tim began as she sat down in his office.

"No. I want to see if I can remember who talked about losing their soul if someone took their picture and I want to try to bring up the face that keeps haunting my dreams."

"Okay," Tim agreed, "but we need to talk about the previous sessions as well."

"We will, later. Remember, I'm the patient. It's my agenda, not yours. Let's get started," Elizabeth said as she sat back in the chair, closed her eyes, and took a deep cleansing breath. She was ready for the induction process.

"You're right, you're the patient. Listen to my voice," Tim began. "Continue to breathe as I count backwards. Allow me to guide you into your subconscious. You are relaxed. You will describe the memories as they surface. Ten...nine...eight...deeper and deeper into your subconscious. Seven...six...five...you can hear the words. Four...three...Who is telling you about photographs?"

After a long pause Elizabeth began to speak slowly. "A...little boy."

"Who is the little boy?"

"I don't know. He has his back to me."

"What is he saying to you?"

"No pictures. He tells me not to let anyone take my picture. He says they will steal my soul and I will go to hell."

Another long pause.

"What's happening now?" Tim asks.

"I ask him what hell is. He says in hell there's fire and you burn up and die. I tell him I don't want to die and he laughs and runs away yelling, 'Jamie's going to burn in hell, Jamie's going to burn in hell.'"

"Who's the little boy, Elizabeth?" Tim asks again.

"He doesn't look at me. He just runs away."

Elizabeth's breathing is shallow and irregular.

"Take a cleansing breath," Tim instructs. "Now breathe slowly. Good. As you breathe you will go deeper and deeper into your subconscious. Deeper, deeper. You are safe. Are you alone now?"

"No. A tall man is there. He's dressed in black."

"Do you know who he is?"

"No. My mother is there too. She calls him 'Father.'"

"Do you know where you are?"

"We're in a church."

"You and your mother are in church with a priest?"

"Yes. He's talking about my soul and hell and being baptized."

"What else is happening?"

"My mother takes my hand and we leave. She tells me not to worry, I'm not going to hell. She tells me I've been baptized and God will keep my soul safe. She tells me the little boy doesn't know what he's talking about."

"Do you know who the little boy is?"

"No."

"Can you tell me what he looks like?"

"He's got curly hair like me, but his hair is yellow not red."

"What else can you tell me about him?"

"He's bigger than me."

"Anything else?"

"William is driving us home."

"Does anyone else talk about the little boy?"

"No. We just go home."

"I'd like you to move forward in years. You are older. Let me guide you. Take a deep breath. You are a teenager. Breathe again. You are an adult. Breathe slowly. You will remember the dreams you had last night. They will not frighten you. You will watch them as if you were watching a movie. Then you will repeat what is happening in the movie."

Elizabeth's breathing continued slowly and evenly. Her eyelids flutter. She begins to speak. "Phones are ringing; muffled voices are yelling, 'Bitch, Bitch.' Faces are swimming around me."

"Describe the faces."

"I can't see them. Clouds are covering them. Then the features start to emerge and then they're gone again. Pieces of my hair are floating across the faces. He laughs. The faces swirl faster and faster and become one. It gets bigger and bigger, and then all I can see is the mouth, wide open. I hear him scream 'Bitch' and then he's gone."

"Elizabeth, take a deep cleansing breath. Now tell me where you are."

"I'm on the beach."

"Can you see a face?"

"Behind clouds, the face is behind clouds." Elizabeth's breathing becomes rapid and irregular.

"Don't be frightened. You are safe. I will count backwards from five to one. When I reach one you will open your eyes. You will feel rested and relaxed." Tim started counting. He didn't give Elizabeth the usual posthypnotic suggestion not to remember the session. These memories might be helpful.

Elizabeth opened her eyes and took another deep breath.

"Liz, it was a little boy who told you about pictures stealing your soul," Tim said.

"I don't know any little boys."

"Think about it. Something may come up. Do you remember how old you were when you started having nightmares as a child?"

"I was thirteen. They started while I was visiting my grandparents. It had been my first visit alone. They told me it was some kind of separation anxiety."

"What do you think now, were you anxious about being away from your parents?"

"It doesn't seem logical. I'd been separated from them before. They'd taken vacations without me. I'd gone on trips with my friends from school and I'd never had a problem."

"I think there's more to it. Let's explore more about your childhood."

"There really isn't anything to tell."

"Don't fight me on this, Liz. You're the patient, remember? Sit back, take a deep breath, and relax. I want conscious memories."

Elizabeth sat back and tried to relax.

"I remember once, Mother let me wear play clothes, jeans and a sweatshirt, and we went on the bus to the university she attended. It must have been daycare or a nursery school for the children of college students. I loved it. When we came home, my grandparents were furious. I didn't hear much of what they said but I never went back. I never got to ride on the bus again either. From then on, if I went anywhere, William drove me."

"Sounds like your grandparents controlled your mother. Do you know why?"

"My mother was very young when she married my father. He was away at law school and then working in Spain and I think they felt they needed to protect her."

"What else can you tell me about your childhood?"

For almost two hours Tim questioned Elizabeth about her childhood. Most of her memories were happy.

"Time to call it quits, Liz. We've been at it quite a while."

"I told you, Tim. There was nothing traumatic in my childhood."

"We've got to talk about what you revealed under hypnosis. It doesn't tell me a lot but it may make sense to you."

"Okay, Tim. At my next session we'll talk about it."

When Elizabeth left Tim's office, she felt emotionally drained. She'd forgotten just how exhausting dredging through the past could be. As an intern, she had gone through the mandatory personal counseling but she had tried to keep it as light as possible, talking mostly about the breakup of her marriage. Now, suddenly she had a flash, a memory, of sitting in another counseling office, and then it was gone. Had she been in therapy before and not remembered it? Trying to pull back the image, she could only recall feelings of fear.

Driving home through traffic she knew tonight would be another sleepless night.

CHAPTER THIRTY-FIVE

Cash couldn't stand it. The craving for cocaine filled his every thought. How could he get it? Who could he trust? He needed the drugs. He thought going cold turkey would be easier this time. He'd taken himself off coke before. But this time, he knew how much worse it was going to get. He took time off from work, telling his boss there was a family emergency.

Why the hell couldn't he find Squirrel? Word on the street had it that he was still in jail. That had never happened before. Squirrel's father had always hired an attorney and he'd been released after a day or two. Something was wrong.

Cash phoned his mother several times to ask about Thanksgiving. Her answer was always the same, "It will be just like every other year."

He had to know if she would be there. He'd waited so long to see her again. He could make it a few more days if he just had a little coke. His obsessions were taking over. Every morning he would look at her picture and remember how close they had been before. He would dust the frame, admiring her beautiful face, always putting the picture in exactly the same spot on his nightstand. Each night he washed and ironed the shirt he had worn that day. He counted his shirts and suits, hanging them in the closet according to color, making sure none of them were missing. Each morning he carefully arranged his shoes, placing them under the suit that they matched.

Paranoia about his journal persisted. Although he lived alone he hid the journal, fearful that someone might find it. In it he had recorded every contact with Elizabeth, each phone call and note written. Every time he had followed her, taken pictures of her, or gone to her house, he recorded it in his journal.

But even more unsettling, he had recorded how he felt, the thrill, the fear, the adrenaline rush that went along with harassing and stalking Elizabeth.

Lately, that cop seemed to be spending a lot of time with her. Early in the morning they jogged; they went to dinner several times a week; weekends he was always there. Sometimes he spent the night. Cash didn't want to take any chances getting caught, so his contact with her was only a few phone calls. The rush he had gotten from Elizabeth was now limited to reading and rereading his journal, remembering the thrill of scaring her.

He needed more coke. He had no choice but to make the buy himself. Out on the street, the clichés swam in his head. "Just say no." "One day at a time."

"It's all crap! I need a fix."

Chapter Thirty-Six

"Are you sure your parents won't mind a stranger coming for Thanksgiving dinner?" Frank asked, giving Elizabeth a friendly kiss and a hug when he arrived to pick her up Thanksgiving morning.

"I think they'd prefer a stranger to the family."

"But this is a holiday," Frank continued. "And they just arrived yesterday."

"William takes care of everything. Besides, my parents love to entertain and you were invited," Elizabeth said.

"William. Ah yes, caretaker, butler, etc.?"

"A permanent fixture. He's worked for the Worthington family since before my father was born. He did a little of everything when he worked for my grandparents. Now, he supervises the family parties, fundraisers, and charitable events that are held at the estate."

"The estate?" Frank questioned. "Just how big is this place?"

"It's big. As a little girl I would stand at the foot of the front stairs and call up to my grandmother so I could listen to the echo," Elizabeth joked.

"Sounds like you grew up in a mansion. Do you know if the whole family is coming to dinner?" Frank asked, trying to prepare himself.

"I'm afraid so. No one wants to miss the big announcement."

"Announcement?"

"Years ago, Grandfather started the tradition of announcing the profit and loss figures for Worthington & Associates to the family after dinner on Thanksgiving Day. He thought they should know in advance what their income would be for the following year. The annual report is released to the public on December first."

"Does everyone in the family work for the company?" Frank asked.

"No. My father is on retainer as a consultant and Duncan was a VP before he retired. As part of our inheritance, we all get a portion of the company profits each year."

"So who specifically will be there?" Frank asked again.

"My parents, of course, Aunt Nancy, my father's sister, and her husband Duncan. The cousins, Phillip and his wife Susie, Tiffany and whoever she's married to or dating at the time, and Eric. There may be someone from the company too, but I doubt it."

At exactly one o'clock Frank drove through the wrought-iron gates, up the tree-lined drive, and parked his car in front of the big house. Out of the corner of her eye, Elizabeth watched the expression on Frank's face.

"This is it," she said, trying to act casual. She knew she hadn't prepared him for the sight of the old mansion in the foothills overlooking Pasadena. Acres of citrus and avocado groves still surrounded the old, three-story, ivy-covered brick house.

"Looks like a hotel," Frank said. "Should I have worn a tux?"

"I think William will let you in the front door without one. If not, we'll just go out back to the cottage. That's my favorite place anyway."

Elizabeth loved the casual banter between them. She enjoyed their time together, and now that the relationship had progressed to a more intimate stage, she hoped they could get the stalker out of the way.

William opened the double doors with a flourish before Elizabeth could ring the bell. He swept her into his arms, giving her a big hug.

"You must be my competition," William said to Frank as he released Elizabeth.

"William, this is my friend, Frank Gualdoni. Don't you tell him any secrets about me," she added.

"Pleased to meet you, William," Frank said, and with a wink he added, "I want to know *every* secret there is."

William ushered Elizabeth and Frank into the foyer and took their coats. Then he led them down the hall and into the library, poured each of them a glass of chilled champagne, and left them to wait for her parents.

"Wow," Frank said.

"I guess I should have prepared you, but how do you explain all this?" Elizabeth said, gesturing to the massive library.

Frank gazed around the room. Built-in bookcases along two of the interior walls; three sets of French doors along one wall showing a beautiful rose garden outside; a baby grand piano in one corner of the room; a massive mahogany desk and high-back leather chair; matching leather couches and chairs facing the enormous fireplace that filled one end of the room; but what dominated the room was a life-size portrait of Edward Worthington looking down at them from its place of honor over the fireplace.

It was obvious to Elizabeth that Frank was impressed and a bit ill at ease.

"That's my grandfather," Elizabeth stated, motioning to the painting. "Don't be surprised when you see my father; they look just alike."

"You've got your grandfather's eyes," Frank said.

"Wait until you meet the rest of the family. We've all got the Worthington eyes."

When David Worthington walked into the room, it was as if the painting had come alive. Every feature; the blond hair graying at the temples, cut short to keep the curls under control; the even tan from hours out of doors; the blue pinstriped suit and maroon tie; and the unmistakable, piercing blue eyes. His wife, Kathleen, stood by his side, his arm resting lightly around her waist. Except for the eyes, Elizabeth was a taller version of her mother. Kathleen's once flaming red hair now softened by strands of gray, the beautiful, pale alabaster skin with barely a wrinkle, and sparkling emerald green eyes.

Elizabeth rushed to hug her parents; tears filled her eyes. She had missed them so much. She wanted to tell them everything that had happened; to be a child again and let Daddy make everything all right. But she held back her emotions, knowing that they could read her well, and introduced Frank to them.

Within minutes, Frank and David were chatting like old friends, Frank's plans to enter law school giving them a mutual interest.

"I like your young man," Kathleen whispered to Elizabeth. "I'm surprised you never mentioned him when we talked on the phone. How did you meet him?"

"We'll tell you and Dad after dinner," Elizabeth said, stalling for time.

"Sir, if you could find the time, I'd like to speak with you alone after dinner," Elizabeth heard Frank quietly ask her father.

"Of course," David replied with a smile.

No, Daddy, he is not going to ask you for my hand! I wish it were that simple.

The rest of the family arrived promptly at 2:30. William poured the perfunctory glass of champagne for the arriving guests. As they all walked into the large, formal dining room, the lights in the crystal chandelier sparkled like sunlight on the ocean. Elizabeth remembered how she loved that room as a child. She would play hide and seek with William and her favorite hiding place was under the table. Today, on the table, the wine and water goblets glistened in the light. Sterling silver chargers beneath the china dishes matched the silver flatware. A low bouquet of flowers graced the middle of the table, and candles had been lit. As the family gathered around the table for dinner, none of them had much to say to each other. They hadn't come for conversation, only information.

William carried in the perfectly roasted turkey, placed it on the sideboard, and began to carve. The staff brought in hot rolls, bowls of mashed potatoes, carrots, peas with baby onions, cranberry sauce, stuffing, and gravy. The plates were filled and placed in front of each person. William managed to remember just what each family member liked, and didn't like, as the plates were filled. He asked Frank for his preferences of white or dark turkey meat, vegetables, etc.

The wine flowed with dinner and the personalities of each person became more apparent as the alcohol loosened their tongues.

"The safari to Africa this fall was marvelous," Susie gushed, trying to impress everyone. No one bothered to respond.

"They're building a new tennis court at the country club," Phillip said with such pride the listener would have thought it was his own personal court. They droned on about the latest gossip at the club, next year's planned vacation, and the next charity function they planned to attend.

Tiffany came alone this year. She lamented over the breakup of her last marriage and complained about how much the divorce had cost her.

"You look so pretty, Kathleen," Eric said as he sat down next to his aunt instead of his usual seat next to his brother.

Elizabeth watched Eric's behavior as he interrupted anyone trying to talk with Kathleen. He insisted on monopolizing her attention. His eyes had bags under them and were dilated and red; she wondered if he had started using cocaine again. He wasn't eating much and seemed thinner than she remembered, another sign that he may be back on drugs.

Nancy and Duncan asked for refills of their wine glasses before the staff had a chance to fill them and ignored their adult children's rude behavior.

After dinner, the staff brought in several desserts: pumpkin, mince, and apple pies, and spice and chocolate cake. Hot coffee was available in a silver serving set on the sideboard but it was apparent that those who needed it the most weren't going to drink any.

When dessert was served, it became obvious that David could not stand his sister and her family for one more moment. He reached for the sealed folder that had been lying beside him on the table during dinner. Conversation stopped.

Frank stood to leave. "Since this is a private matter, I'll wait in the library."

Elizabeth put her hand on Frank's arm but before she had a chance to ask him to stay, David intervened.

"No need. This is all going to be public knowledge on the first. You're a guest, and Elizabeth wouldn't have brought you today if she wanted to keep this a secret."

Frank sat back down and David continued to open the envelope and began to read the figures. The company had done exceptionally well during the past year and the dividends reflected it. Smiles were visible on most of the faces around the table, and one could imagine the wheels turning in their minds, contemplating just how the new windfall would be spent.

"Uncle David," Eric slurred. "Considering the amount of money Elizabeth has, don't you think dating a cop is beneath her?"

Elizabeth and Frank exchanged questioning glances. *How could he know?* Her parents were the only ones present who knew Frank was a police detective. Elizabeth started to tremble. Not wanting to alarm her father, who would easily pick up any unusual behavior, she concentrated on her breathing and the pumpkin pie sitting before her on the table.

"Elizabeth is free to date whomever she pleases. It is none of your business or anyone else's in this family." Teeth clenched, David stood up. "Since you now have all the information you came for, I'm going to have my coffee in the library. Nancy, please join me when you've finished your dessert; we have business to discuss."

Nancy looked surprised. She stood up, left her pie sitting on the table, picked up her wine glass, and followed her brother out of the room. They heard the library door close and the murmur of voices.

"Shut up about your divorce," Phillip yelled at Tiffany.

"Well, he broke my heart," Tiffany sniffled.

"Right, and you had another man beside you in bed before the sheets had cooled off."

"You're mean," Tiffany said.

"And you're stupid. If you don't want to pay spousal support, don't run off to Vegas and get married without a prenuptial agreement."

"I'm leaving," Tiffany said. "Daddy, will you call me a taxi?" she said, turning to Duncan.

As if he were used to being told what to do, Duncan left the table and went to make the call.

With Tiffany gone, Phillip turned his attention to Eric. "Are you still working at that dumb real estate agency, little brother?"

"Shut up, Phillip. I'm talking to Kathleen," Eric replied.

"Like Aunt Kathleen wants to talk to you."

"You want to talk to me, don't you, Kathleen?" Eric said putting his arm around the back of Kathleen's chair. His voice continued to get louder and he laughed as he slurred out the words.

Elizabeth could see her mother's discomfort but knew she would never say anything to cause a scene with the family.

"Remember, Kathleen, when you used to take me to the beach house in Laguna?" Eric asked, sniffing and rubbing his nose.

"You were just a little boy then, Eric," she replied.

"But it was my very favorite place, and Grandfather left it to Elizabeth. That wasn't fair, was it, Kathleen?"

"It was your grandfather's decision, Eric."

Frank gave Elizabeth a puzzled look and they stood up to leave the table. Suddenly, David's angry voice could be heard though the library door. As they walked past the door on their way to the back yard, Elizabeth wondered what had caused her father to have such a volatile outburst. But she was more interested in discussing Eric's comments with Frank. A walk in the rose garden out back would ensure their privacy.

"Eric's on drugs, isn't he?" Frank asked.

"It certainly looks like it, and how did he know you were a cop?" Elizabeth asked.

"Maybe your mother told him?"

"No. Mother wouldn't tell Eric anything about me. I have no idea how he knows."

"Did you know about your mother taking Eric to Laguna?"

"No. It must have been before I was born."

"Has he always been that obsessed with your mother?"

"Well, he always wanted lots of attention from her, but never like this."

"Remember the note the police found at your house? The comment about you dating a cop?" Frank asked.

"Oh, my God!"

"Elizabeth, is it possible that Eric is the stalker?"

"Yes, it's very possible. We've never gotten along, but I...I don't understand why he would want to hurt me." Her voice quivered and Frank saw the fear in her eyes.

"Forget the why. Let's look at the facts. That bastard knows where you work and live, the kind of car you drive, the location of the beach house. Why, he even knows what gym you belong to; anything Eric doesn't know, he could easily find out."

Frank was angry at himself for not doing a more thorough check on Elizabeth's family.

"He's also addicted to drugs." Elizabeth added. "Cocaine was his drug of choice and he's relapsed after every drug treatment program. I should have thought of him but I never imagined anyone in my family hated me so much."

"Give me his full name," Frank said, taking out his cell phone and pushing the automatic dial number for his precinct. "I'm going to run a check on him and any of his drug buddies."

"Eric Stanley Nelson," Elizabeth said and added his date of birth.

Frank gave the information to the desk sergeant along with his cell number and hung up. He knew in his gut that he had found the stalker. Now he had to prove it.

Walking through the rose garden, they waited for the sergeant to call back. Hand in hand they looked like carefree lovers, but the tight grasp Elizabeth had on Frank's hand was one of fear.

"Mother!" Elizabeth almost shouted. "All those comments about mother during the phone calls. It's *my* mother that he wanted, not his. Come on, Eric's in there with my mother right now."

Together, hurrying back to the house, they found Eric and Kathleen in the sunroom. He kept touching her arm as he talked to her. Smiling and asking questions as if she had all the answers to the problems of the world.

"Tell me more about Spain, Kathleen. Why do you like it so much?"

He hadn't called her *aunt* in several years. Now he seemed obsessed with being near Kathleen. His actions were becoming more and more obvious.

She tried to move away from him but he kept edging closer. Her look of discomfort was easy for Elizabeth and Frank to see.

David's voice bellowed from the library. "You really messed up this time, Nancy. The company doesn't belong to you."

"You win, David." Nancy shouted back as she opened the door and walked down the hall. "As always, you win."

In the dining room, Duncan, Phillip, and Susie sat finishing off the last of the wine. "Get the car," Nancy ordered. "We're leaving."

Without saying a word, her husband stood up from the table and walked into the foyer, pausing briefly to grab his overcoat and the car keys.

"Nancy," David called as he stood watching her slide her arms into her full-length mink coat, "I'll see you at the office at three o'clock on Wednesday. We'll sign the preliminary papers then."

Without a word she walked out the front door. Phillip, puzzled by his mother's sudden exit, stared after her. Susie and Phillip stayed for a few minutes longer, but their attempts at small talk failed and they soon followed Nancy and Duncan. Eric hung around watching Kathleen's every move and continuing to try and engage her in conversation.

Frank's cell phone rang and he quickly answered it. Walking away from the others, his words were inaudible. After a brief conversation, he hung up.

"Elizabeth, I'm going to talk with your father now," Frank said and then whispered to her, "I think we've got him."

"I want to be with you when you tell him everything that's happened."

"No, I'll send William in. The two of you keep an eye on Eric and your mother."

Frank walked into the library with David and closed the door. Elizabeth could hear the muffled voices of the two men. A few minutes later, they reappeared. She'd seen her father angry many times but the look of rage she now saw on his face surpassed it all. With a controlled calmness, he walked directly into the sunroom, pushed Eric aside, and sat down between him and Kathleen, and put his arm around his wife.

Frank came to Elizabeth's side and put his arm around her shoulder. The faint scream of sirens in the distance grew louder. "Brace yourself, the roof's about to fall in."

CHAPTER THIRTY-SEVEN

The ringing telephone echoed through the empty rooms. The calls had come at fifteen-minute intervals all afternoon. Each time, the answering machine responded with the cheery voice of Elizabeth Wing, and each time, the machine recorded the harsh sound of the caller banging down the receiver.

Returning after a late-afternoon run with Frank, Elizabeth saw the red light on the machine flashing. She pushed the replay button and went to the refrigerator for ice tea and the plate of fruit and cheese she had prepared earlier. Placing them on a tray, she listened to the series of calls.

"Damn it," she whispered to herself. "I thought this was over."

Elizabeth took a deep breath and carried the tray out onto the patio where Frank sat looking at the front page of the *L.A. Times*.

"Anything I can do to help?" Frank asked.

"It's under control," Elizabeth answered.

Their afternoon together had been fun. She didn't want to spoil the mood. For the first time since her divorce, she'd met someone who she could really care about. Frank was secure and not intimidated by her profession, her family, or her money. They knew Eric was the stalker. When the police had arrived to take him in on an old warrant, he had confessed everything. Now, he sat in jail waiting for the hearing on Monday morning.

"Frank, there are several hang-up calls on my machine," she said, trying to sound casual. She watched his expression change from relaxed to intense.

"No messages?" he asked.

"No."

"How many calls?"

"There were six," she replied, feeling safe knowing that Frank would handle it.

He started to get up but Elizabeth put her hand on his arm. "Let's have our tea first. Then we can check it out."

The phone rang twice while they ate. Each time the caller left no message, only slammed down the receiver as they hung up. But on the third call, a woman's shrill voice filled the air.

"You little bastard. Why are you trying to ruin Eric's life? Haven't you and your mother done enough to our family?" Then, sobs, followed by the phone being returned to its cradle.

Frank looked at Elizabeth. "Do you know who that is?"

"It's Aunt Nancy."

The color had drained from Elizabeth's face and Frank, once again all cop, took charge. "I'm going to call your father and see if he's had any calls. You stay here and try to relax."

Cell phone in hand, Frank went into the house. Elizabeth could hear his voice from time to time, but couldn't tell what he was saying. She only knew that he talked to her father for a long time. When he finally walked back out to the patio, the look of concern surprised her.

"Your father has had several threatening calls from Nancy as well." He was choosing his words carefully. "Sometime tonight, Nancy and Duncan are going to bail Eric out of jail. They're arranging for him to go back into treatment."

"He won't stay. Don't they know he's dangerous?" she asked, her voice quivering.

"Elizabeth," Frank said in a firm voice, "go upstairs and pack. Your father and I have decided that you may not be safe here. We're going to relocate you."

"What do you mean 'relocate' me? I'm not going anywhere!"

"Elizabeth," Frank sounded impatient, then his voice softened. "We know where Eric is right now. We may only have a few hours before he's on the streets again. Pack everything you'll need for a...for a month, maybe longer. We want you in hiding until the trial."

Astonished, Elizabeth looked at Frank. "What else did my father say? There's something you're not telling me."

"Go and pack. We'll talk later."

"I want to know now!" she said firmly.

"Yesterday when the police arrested Eric, he said some pretty bizarre things about your mother. Then, early this morning he called her from jail. Your father is worried that he will try to...kidnap your mother. Eric thinks that your mother loves him and that you are the one keeping them apart."

"Oh, God," Elizabeth said, "he's delusional. He's gone over the edge."

"Diagnose him later. Go and pack. Your father is making arrangements for you and your mother to disappear for a while."

Elizabeth and her parents spent the weekend in seclusion at a hotel in downtown Los Angeles. Their meals were room service and their only visitor was Frank. Much of the time, her father tried to convince her that she and her mother would be safer if they went back to Spain. Both women were against it. Next he suggested they go to Mexico and stay with friends until the trial, but Elizabeth adamantly refused.

"Monday morning, I'm going to work as usual," Elizabeth said. "My patients have had enough interruptions in their therapy. Besides, now that I know who the stalker is, I don't feel as vulnerable."

Sunday evening Frank joined Elizabeth and her parents for dinner. He answered all of their questions regarding the stalking but Elizabeth had a few questions of her own for her parents. Fortified by the alcohol, Elizabeth did something that, even as adult, she had rarely done. She confronted her parents. Looking directly at them, she asked the question that had been haunting her since the information had surfaced during a counseling session with Tim.

"I've been in therapy with Tim for a couple of weeks," she began. "Nightmares similar to what I had as a kid have returned."

She saw a look pass between her parents, and she was certain Frank noticed it, too.

"Under hypnosis, memories of prior psychotherapy emerged. I have no conscious memory of any trauma or the therapy. But, when I was fourteen, someone tried to rape me. Who was it?"

The shocked look on her mother's face made Elizabeth wonder if she had known about it. Her parents looked at one another and then her mother walked over, put her arm around her daughter's shoulder, and spoke in a soft voice.

"You were visiting your grandparents the summer it happened. The psychiatrist told them you had no memory of the attack. He told them there was no need for you to ever know. That it had been erased from your mind."

"It doesn't work like that," Elizabeth said. "Everything remains in the subconscious. Was I raped?"

David spoke up. "No, you were not raped. Someone tried to…he… tried to force himself on you but your grandfather stopped him."

"Who was it? Did they catch him?" Elizabeth fired questions about the incident at her parents. "Was there a trial? Why didn't you tell me about it?"

"It was complicated," her father began. "It happened at the country club. Your grandfather stopped the boy and thought it best not to press charges. He was the son of a prominent member and…a friend of Eric's."

"Eric again. Why does Eric hate me so much? I thought it was because Grandfather left me more money than the others, but this happened years before that."

Kathleen answered her daughter's question. "It's not that Eric hates you; it's that he believes he's in love with me. If you are hurt, or in danger, he knows I'll come to be with you. If I'm here, then he can see me. Be near me. This has been going on for a very long time. It's one of the reasons we decided to continue living in Spain."

"You moved to Spain to be away from Eric?" Elizabeth couldn't believe what she was hearing.

"Not entirely," David said. "I worked in Spain because I wanted to practice international law and not work at Grandfather's law firm. I liked Spain, and after your mother and I married, it seemed like a good place to live."

Kathleen looked at David. "It's time she knew it all."

"You're right. The secrets have been kept for too long. She needs to know why the family behaves as they do," David agreed.

Elizabeth looked from her mother to her father. *What were they talking about?*

"Elizabeth," her father said, clearing his throat. "Can we speak freely in front of Frank?"

"Of course," Elizabeth said.

"Let me tell her," Kathleen said. "Elizabeth, you know I grew up in Boston and came to California after my mother died. What we've never told you is that my job was working for your grandparents. I was hired as their housekeeper." Kathleen sat down next to her daughter and let the information register before she continued.

"I had just graduated from U.S.C.," David added. "I'd been accepted at Harvard. Your mother had just arrived from Boston; we started to talk. I fell in love, madly, passionately in love, with a beautiful young redhead with an Irish brogue. She wasn't like anyone I had ever known."

"I discovered I was pregnant after your father left for law school," Kathleen continued. "Your grandparents were furious. They talked to me about abortion and adoption but I wouldn't hear any of it. They did everything they could to keep your father and me apart. Even though your grandparents eventually forgave us, Nancy never did. She just couldn't bare the humiliation of people knowing that her brother had married the family maid."

"Well, that explains why Aunt Nancy has always been so aloof with you, but what about Eric? He was only a kid when all that happened."

"Eric was a lonely child," Kathleen began. "He craved attention. I read to him, played games with him, and in some ways became a surrogate mother. After you were born, he resented the time I spent with you. We had to watch Eric because he would do things to make you cry. I would respond, and he got my attention, even if it were to punish him for hurting you."

"This is bizarre. I feel like I'm reading about a case study," Elizabeth replied.

Kathleen continued. "When I moved to Spain with your father, Eric was about twelve. He started experimenting with drugs and he's been using them ever since. Your grandparents had no use for his excuses but Nancy blamed every problem Eric ever had on me."

Elizabeth let what her parents had just told her sink in.

"That's about it," David said. "But the fact that we live in Spain seems to have led Eric to use extreme methods to get Kathleen to come back. The attempted rape was orchestrated by Eric. Eric's drug addiction, the fact that he has money and doesn't need to concentrate on a career, and that we only come to visit once a year, seem to have triggered more acting-out behavior."

"Why didn't you tell me all this?" Elizabeth asked.

"For the same reason you didn't tell us about the stalker; you wanted to protect us," David responded.

"If we'd told you about the stalker, you'd have known it was Eric," Frank said.

"Family secrets hurt us all," Kathleen said almost to herself.

"Are there more?" Elizabeth asked.

"Yes," Kathleen said fingering the plain gold band on her finger.

Elizabeth had wondered in the past why her parents had chosen such plain wedding bands when it was obvious to her that they could afford much more.

"No matter what my father said, I intended to marry your mother." David smiled at his wife. "I sent her a ticket and she flew to Boston. We tried to get married but she was too young. We drove down to Cape Cod hoping to find someone to marry us but had no luck, so we had our own private ceremony. It wasn't legal or binding but we stood together in a deserted church and pledged our love. That's why we go back to the Cape every year on our anniversary, to visit that church and renew our vows. That ceremony means more to us that the one performed by the priest before we left for Spain." David came over and kissed his wife, and the love they shared seemed to fill the room.

"I need some time to let this sink in," Elizabeth said. "I think I'd like to go home tonight."

"That's not a good idea," David said.

"It will be all right, sir," Frank said. It was obvious Elizabeth needed some space from her parents. "I'll stay with her tonight."

"Call us when you get home from work tomorrow?" David said as Elizabeth and Frank left the hotel suite.

As promised, Elizabeth called her parents when she arrived home from work on Monday evening. Her voice rose as she spoke to her father on the phone. "What do you mean, they're not going to prosecute? Eric confessed."

"Princess, I've spent the whole day with Eric's lawyers, the district attorney, and a judge. Believe me, I tried my best to get them to prosecute but the judge recommended we all accept the deal being offered."

"It's not fair," Elizabeth cried. She wanted to smash something, but years of self-control create a habit hard to break. Instead, she sat doodling on a pad by the phone and listened to her father.

"Sometimes the law works in strange ways," her father tried to explain. "The confession made at the time of the arrest was without benefit of legal counsel. It can't be used in court."

Elizabeth was not satisfied with her father's attempts to defend the court's decision.

"But you heard him. Frank heard him. Can't you testify as to what he said?" Elizabeth's frustration kept building.

"Frank is a cop. Eric's lawyers would never let it happen," David said in a calm voice. "Without the confession, we only have circumstantial evidence. Besides, Eric says he had nothing to do with the attack. He's blaming a guy with the street name of Squirrel. The police know him from several drug busts; his real name is Jason Jenkins. He's in custody but he isn't talking."

Elizabeth started to cry. "Isn't there something we can do?"

"I'm sorry, Princess. Please don't cry. There's not much more we can do. There are no fingerprints, witnesses, or any other evidence to prove whether Jason or Eric was responsible for the phone calls, the break-in at your house, or the attack. I'm sorry, but this case isn't going to court."

"So that's it. They'll just walk away. One of them almost killed me and there's not even going to be a trial?" Anger had replaced Elizabeth's frustration.

"There will be a permanent restraining order placed on both of them. They are not to contact either you or your mother."

"A lot of good that will do; it's only a piece of paper," she all but yelled into the phone.

"I know it's frustrating," David said, "but the deal we're working on sounds pretty good."

"Deal? What kind of deal?"

"I've been negotiating with Eric's lawyers. If we don't push the DA to proceed with the case, Eric will be committed to a one-year rehabilitation program. Nancy and Duncan agree that Eric needs help. The judge will appoint them as guardians because of his longtime drug history. This time, he will not be able to sign himself out of the hospital."

"What about Jason? What's going to happen to him?"

"He'll be evaluated by a court-appointed psychiatrist tomorrow. His addiction is contributing to his criminal actions; I'm not sure of his ability to understand right from wrong."

"What you're saying is that Jason may not be capable of standing trial, right?"

"That's right. It seems he and Eric did drugs together. Eric would tell him about harassing you on the phone. Jason got caught up in Eric's fantasy about being in love with your mother and that if you were in trouble, she would come to help. He wanted to please Eric to get more drugs, so he started to harass you as well. This is where things get cloudy. While Eric thought he was in love with your mother, Jason became infatuated with you. Eric won't say who did what except that he didn't attack you. If we can believe him, that means Jason did."

"They both belong in jail, not a country club rehab center!" Elizabeth shouted and the pencil she had been doodling with snapped in her hand.

"Jason won't be in rehab. His criminal record shows years of arrests for drugs, robberies, and violence. If he's found guilty, it will be his third violent offence. If he's incapable of standing trial, he'll be in a hospital for the criminally insane. Probably Atascadero State Hospital," David stated.

"Can we continue with a civil case if the courts won't prosecute?"

"All deals are off if we do that. Besides, it will be expensive and there will be a lot of publicity. None of us need or want that. I know this is difficult for you, but believe me, this will be the best for all concerned. Give yourself some time to think about what I've told you. Talk it over with Frank. The two of you come for dinner tomorrow night; there's more I want to discuss with both of you."

Elizabeth slammed down the phone. *Damn it. Everything is about money. What ever happened to justice or whether or not something is fair?*

She was furious at the deal her father had agreed to. *Why won't he continue with the case? Doesn't anyone care about what I've been through? My whole life has been turned upside-down and no one cares.* But in her heart she knew that Frank cared.

CHAPTER THIRTY-EIGHT

Elizabeth had never been one to avoid a difficult situation but this time she had no control over the outcome. *What do I do now?* She dialed Frank's number but his voice mail answered. She tried to sound cheery, "We're invited for dinner at my parents. Can you pick me up about six-thirty?"

During dinner, neither Elizabeth nor her father brought up the subject of Eric and the deal the attorneys had made. After dessert and coffee, David asked to speak to Frank privately in the library.

"What's that about?" Elizabeth asked her mother.

"Don't worry about it," Kathleen said. But Elizabeth worried. *I'm tired of secrets!*

"Frank," David said, after William had poured the brandy and left the room, "I know you plan on entering law school in January. Are you aware of the scholarship program U.S.C. has for police officers?"

"No, sir," Frank replied. "I've been accepted at Western Law. It's much less expensive. Even with a scholarship, I doubt if I could afford U.S.C. on a retired cop's income."

"Anything is possible when you know the right people. Let me give you the name of a friend of mine," David said, passing Frank a business card. "He's the head of the Law School and can give you all the details. As I understand it, all you need to do is keep your grades up and the tuition is paid in full."

"Thank you, sir," Frank replied, taking the card. "I'm surprised I didn't come across that information when I researched available scholarships."

"It must be a well-guarded secret," David said. He surmised Frank would never accept money directly for helping Elizabeth and felt the best way to express his gratitude would be to secretly assist with his education. This man had saved their daughter's life; no amount of money could repay that.

They talked for a while longer before Kathleen knocked on the door. "Enough lawyer talk," she said as she and Elizabeth joined them for brandy.

"Dad," Elizabeth said. "We've got to talk about Eric. I doubt if he will change, even if he does spend a year in the best rehab center they can find."

"They hope that once Eric kicks the cocaine habit, he'll be able to undergo intensive psychotherapy and come to terms with his fantasies about your mother," David said.

"I see that as highly unlikely," Elizabeth said. "What about the decision not to continue with the case against Eric? Don't you think he should take responsibility for his actions?"

"Yes, of course I do. I know you're disappointed, Elizabeth, but let me explain the legal issues. First, we don't have any hard evidence against Eric. Everything is circumstantial and Eric can blame everything on Jason and vice versa. According to the psychiatrist, Jason's not capable of standing trial. Frank can explain it to you; there's not enough hard evidence to win a conviction."

"But..." Elizabeth interrupted.

David went on. "Second, it will be expensive. The state doesn't want to take on a case that they don't think they can win, especially when the defendant has the money to fight them for a very long time. Third, there will be a lot of publicity. The press would love to smear the personal problems of prominent families across the front pages of the newspaper. Think what a negative effect this will have on your practice.

"Lastly, and perhaps this is the most important," David continued. "It would be a long time before the case ever came to trial. There will be postponements, delays, and the defense would drag this out as long as possible. During all this time, Eric, and possibly Jason, would be free.

Free to continue threatening you, harassing you, and possibly finding a way to hurt you again. We will all be better off if this matter is settled quickly and quietly."

Frank walked over and sat down next to Elizabeth. "He's right, sweetheart, getting Eric off the streets and into a serious rehabilitation program will be in everyone's best interest. As far as Jason goes, I hope he'll be hospitalized for a long time."

"Is that really the best you can do?" Elizabeth asked.

"I did manage to convince the judge to give me control of Eric's trust fund. Any breach in the treatment, the restraining order, and the agreement we've made, and I will cut off his money."

"Hitting him where it hurts?" Frank asked.

"Absolutely," David replied.

Elizabeth knew intellectually that her father and Frank were right, but emotionally she wanted an outcome that would punish these men for their actions. Jason was an unknown entity, but she had no expectations that rehab would ever change Eric.

David, Kathleen, and Frank sat and watched Elizabeth take a sip of her brandy. She sighed and sat back on the couch, overwhelmed by all of the information that she had been given over the last two days. Frank put his arm around her shoulders. "It will be okay, Babe."

Elizabeth looked from her parents to Frank and back to her father. "What do I do now, sit around and wait for them to get out and start all over again?"

Unexpectedly, it was Frank who spoke. "Elizabeth, I will keep you safe. Please believe me. I will do whatever it takes to keep you safe."

CHAPTER THIRTY-NINE

On the drive back from her parents, Elizabeth was quiet for a long time. Her parents had given her a lot to think about.

"I can't believe my parents kept so many secrets from me."

"They were only trying to protect you. That's what parents do," Frank replied.

"Not telling me that they met because my mother worked for my grandparents, that they didn't get married until after I was born, is an important part of my family history. Not telling me that my grandfather wanted to put me up for adoption and that they lived all these years in Spain because of the turmoil my birth caused would have explained why the family treated me and my mother with such disdain."

"How could they have told you that? When would they have told you? It's not a bedtime story you tell your child."

"Well, at some point I should have been told," Elizabeth lamented.

"Take a step back and look at your parents. It is so obvious, even with all the family uproar about their marriage, that they are still deeply in love. That's all they wanted you to know, that they love each other and you. Accept it; that's your real family history, loving parents who would do anything to protect their only child."

Elizabeth knew Frank was right. Her parents loved her. They would do anything to protect her, but the secrets, so many secrets.

"And the attempted rape when I was fourteen? Why didn't they ever discuss that with me?" Elizabeth continued.

"You're the therapist. You know the answer to that question. You couldn't remember any of it and they didn't want to further traumatize you," Frank said.

"But that's when the nightmares started."

"They aren't professionals. They didn't understand the connection. Elizabeth, don't be so hard on them. Parents make mistakes sometimes. God knows I've made plenty of mistakes with my kids."

Elizabeth sat looking out the car window. "What was the secret meeting with you and my dad all about?"

"Your father suggested I go to U. S. C. I told him I couldn't afford it on a retired cop's income and that I had been accepted at Western Law. He said he'd been talking to the Dean of the Law School and that there was a little-known scholarship for police officers. From what he said, all I need to do is keep my grades up and the tuition is paid in full. He told me who to call for all the details."

"That's great, Frank, but he could have told you that in front of me. What else did he have to say?" *There's more. I know there's more. What is my father scheming now?*

"He told me that he and your mother will be leaving to go back to Spain soon."

"That's no secret; they always go back after Thanksgiving."

"I think they want to surprise you with the news," Frank hedged.

"What news? I don't want anymore surprises," she demanded.

"Okay, but will you try to act surprised when they tell you?"

"Frank!"

"I'm getting to it. Your parents are going to stop in Washington, D.C., on their way back to Spain. Your father has decided to resign his job and move back to California. They'll only be in Spain long enough to make arrangements for the villa and to finish up some work your father has in Europe."

"But they love Spain. Why would they do that?"

"I don't know for sure, but I think they have decided it's time for him to take his place heading up Worthington & Associates. And I think they want to be closer to you. He also asked me about our relationship. I think they want grandchildren."

"He said what?"

"Relax. He didn't say it in those words, but I got the feeling he would like to see you married. He asked me to keep an eye on you while they're gone and I promised him I would."

Frank took Elizabeth's hand in his. "The bad guys have been caught. That means the case is closed."

Three months later.

Frank had left the police force and been accepted at U. S. C. School of Law. As David had predicted, the scholarship was available and paid his tuition in full. Elizabeth had taken a sabbatical from teaching and spent more hours at the rape center. The couple had not made any long-terms plans, but the relationship was on a collision course with wedding vows.

This morning Frank sat reading the paper before he tackled the stack of law books spread out on the table in front of him. Hidden on page nine of the *L.A. Times*, a brief article caught his eye.

Atascadero Inmate to Be Released All charges of assault have been dropped against inmate who was wrongfully charged with crime while under the influence of drugs. Psychiatrist who initially interviewed suspect may have been bribed. Family spokesperson states Jason Jenkins, son of a wealthy import/export tycoon, will be released early next week.

Frank couldn't believe his eyes. This monster who was obsessed with Elizabeth would be out of jail. He'd soon be walking the streets again. He had to do something. David and Kathleen Worthington were still in Spain. He had promised them he would take care of Elizabeth and he intended to keep his word. He had to do something. He wasn't going to let Jason Jenkins get to her again. He hoped she hadn't seen the article.

Frank couldn't keep his mind on his studies. The hours dragged by. He could only think of one way to protect Elizabeth. Three times he picked up the phone, and three times he hung it up without completing the call. He had cut himself off from his family and their illegal activities years ago. He had moved 3000 miles away. Now, all he could think of was asking his brother for help.

He picked up the phone again, punched in the numbers, and listened as the call connected.

"Speak to me," the voice with the Jersey accent ordered.

"Get Johnny," Frank snapped.

"Who are you?" the voice on the line grumbled.

"Tell him it's Frankie."

"Frankie who? He knows lots a guys named Frankie."

"Just tell him, he'll know."

Frank listened as the voice gave Johnny the message.

"Gimme the phone," Frank could hear in the background.

"Frankie, what do ya need?"

"The legal system failed me, Johnny. I need some help." Frank explained about Elizabeth and his need to protect her.

"She special, this Elizabeth?"

"Yeah, Johnny, she's very special."

"You want I should persuade this guy to stay away from her, right?"

"That's right, Johnny. Whatever it takes."

"It's a done deal. Anything for you, Frankie."

Frank hung up the phone and wiped away the sweat pouring down his face. He'd never asked his brother for a favor before and he hoped he'd never have to again.

Two days later.

L.A. Times

Atascadero Inmate Found Dead in Cell Hospital spokesperson stated patient was depressed and fearful of adjusting to life on the outside. His death, an apparent drug overdose, occurred just one day before his scheduled release. The family of Jason Jenkins blames hospital staff for not putting their son on suicide watch.

It's over, Frank thought. God forgive me, but it's finally over. Elizabeth is safe.

ABOUT THE AUTHOR

Dr. Bevans is a psychotherapist and has maintained a private practice for over twenty years in Orange County, California specializing in both victims and perpetrators of domestic violence, child abuse, and rape. She has been the Program Director at two battered women's shelters and Family Advocacy Program Manager, Clinical Supervisor, and Family Service Center Director at a United States Marine Corps base.

Whatever It Takes is her first novel changing her focus to the written word. Her writing credits include several published short stories and a research paper on violence in the lives of women.

Born and raised on Cape Cod, Massachusetts, she currently lives with her husband in Orange County, California. You can contact the author at donnabevans@comline.com or through her webpage at www.donnabevans.net.

Printed in the USA
CPSIA information can be obtained
at www.ICGtesting.com
JSHW021720081024
71085JS00003B/33